# DARKNESS CALLS

# DARKNESS CALLS

THE LINE BETWEEN LIGHT AND DARK IS THINNER THAN YOU THINK.

## JOE CHIANAKAS

An Imprint of Roan & Weatherford Publishing Associates, LLC
Bentonville, Arkansas
www.roanweatherford.com



**Library of Congress Cataloging-in-Publication Data**
Names: Chianakas, Joe, author
Title: Darkness Calls | The Pit of Darkness #1
Description: First Edition. | Bentonville: Rogue River, 2025.
Identifiers: LCCN: 2024946536 | ISBN: 978-1-63373-952-9(hardcover) |
ISBN: 978-1-63373-953-6 (trade paperback) | ISBN: 978-1-63373-954-3 (eBook)
Subjects: | BISAC: FICTION/Horror | FICTION/Thrillers/Supernatural |
FICTION/Coming of Age
LC record available at: https://lccn.loc.gov/2024946536

Rogue River trade paperback edition June, 2025

Cover Design by Casey W. Cowan
Interior Layout by Michele Jones
Editing by George "Clay" Mitchell & Don Money

*For Mom. Without her, I have no love for horror. Without her, horror is meaningless. But with her, even a horror story can inspire and change the world.*

*Writing this book—and fighting my own darkness—was how I grieved through the hardest death I have ever experienced.*

*We all have darkness inside, but Mom always had a way of seeing the best in others. I wish I could have saved you. The best I could do is write this book. Readers—when you get to Teddy's part—I hope you'll remember my dedication and smile with me.*

# PART ONE

CHRISTINA

## CHRISTINA

"What would an ocean be without a monster lurking in the dark? It would be like sleep without dreams."

—Werner Herzog

# CHAPTER ONE

"It wants us to kill again."

The voice rips a chill up my spine. Images of smeared dirt and the coppery smell of blood flood my senses.

"They're remembering."

It's early morning, and I'm sitting in bed, the covers pulled tight to my chest, running my daily Google search. For years, I've searched for their names, starting with Asher, the boy who went missing that no one remembers. But as usual, there's no new information.

At the sound of the voice in my room, my mouth turns dry. A silhouette against my bedroom window prompts me to kick the covers off my bed, as a memory wraps its hands around my throat. I scurry to the mirror in my room, fearing what I will see in my reflection.

I flinch at the flickering flame in my hazel eyes. Part of the Darkness is already in me.

Goosebumps tear across my arms, and my eyes search for an uninvited visitor. Although I don't see anything now, it doesn't mean she isn't here. Fiara has a way of being present without being seen—it's one of her many tricks.

"Fiara, are you here?"

I scan my room for her bright blue eyes and pale skin.

"They're remembering, Christina," the voice repeats, a faint hiss that drifts to me in the air. My breath rushes out of me.

I duck down under my bed and dig through a bunch of books scattered everywhere. Next to my copy of *The Complete Arthurian Legends* sits my shoebox of missing posters of children that no one remembers anymore. I didn't want to forget the victims, as much as I'd like to forget the victimizer.

No one remembers the children anymore. Except for me.

And Fiara.

A foot pounds on the floor above me making a *thunk* sound. "Christina," Mom calls from the kitchen, her voice muffled by the floorboards. "I'm hungry. Can you make me breakfast?" Her voice is scratchy and hollow. She hasn't been fully here since... since the Darkness hurt her, too, all those years ago. But I take care of her, in an ironic mother-daughter role reversal.

"Who's remembering?" I ask. I rub my arms and legs, trying to warm up. I'm scared, but I know all too well what this evil can do. If I'm going to fight it this time, I need to know who to protect. I guard that thought, hoping it's not reading my mind.

I will have to fight this time, unless I want to watch everyone around me die before it takes my life, too.

A cold hand presses against my shoulder, and I jump. I don't have to turn around to know who it is. When Fiara touches me, the room turns icy. I see my breath in front of me. She has something to show me, but it can only be seen with the mind. I close my eyes and embrace for Fiara's warning.

Visions of my classmates and friends—Elle, Lawson, Teddy, Angelica, and others—rush through my mind.

Opening my eyes, I grab Fiara's hand. It's colder than the chill that rips through my flesh.

"Not again," I say, holding back hot tears. "I can't do this again." I choke on the words, like there's a hand squeezing my already dry throat.

Fiara presses my hands against her face. "Look into my eyes, Christina. Look what it did to me."

Her pale face looks doll-like and leathery, the skin not human. Her hair is long and braided, but it doesn't feel like hair. She's never let any classmate touch it except for me. Her hair feels slimy and wiggles like it's alive.

"This is what it did to me," Fiara exclaims, her voice hardening. "It will do worse this time if you don't bring the Darkness the people it wants. Worse things to you. To your mother. I've seen it in my dreams. And we knew this day would come again. We always knew." She turns away, and her hair dances when she walks.

My knees wobble, and I sit back down on my bed. "Every day, I pray that I can forget. Forget like everyone else. You know?" When I look up at her, she wipes at her eyes. "Why can't we just forget and have normal lives? And now you're telling me I have to go through it all again. Why?"

I slam my fists against the mattress. I'd scream, but I don't want to disturb my mother. Tears threaten my eyes, but I wipe them away quickly. Whatever Fiara sees, the Darkness can also see. I don't know how everything works, but it's a part of her, ever since it did this to her, when we were only little girls.

If I don't do what it wants, it will become a part of me, too.

"Why does it want them?" I ask, steadying my breath.

Fiara walks to the one window in my basement bedroom, pulling the already closed curtains tighter, extinguishing even the tiniest rays of light. She returns to me and speaks in a low voice.

"They're remembering the Secret," Fiara says. "The one Mister Lee told your class. The Darkness doesn't want them to remember the Secret, but that's not the only reason it needs them. One of them is the Seer. I do not know which one." Fiara sits next to me, digs her fingers into my shoulder, and I wince. I'm scared to ask about the other reasons.

"We can help them," I say to Fiara, drawing back and rubbing my shoulder, "and we can help you. Maybe if we fight the evil, then it can turn you back... you know, back to, how you were."

*Charlamae can help.* It's a different voice in my head, softer and feminine.

A fire glows in Fiara's blue eyes. I have a glimmer of that inside me, but not like Fiara. She grabs my wrists and squeezes hard.

"Shut up!" she yells. "It hears you!"

"We're not kids anymore," I say. "Not like last time. We can do something."

Fiara slaps me. My face stings, and my jaw drops in shock. Then she lowers her head and cries.

"I'm sorry," she mumbles. Her hands fidget with her clothes. She dresses in a way that's formal and old for her age—a gray blouse over dark slacks.

I put an arm around her bony shoulders.

"I want to help," I tell her, but it's so much more than *want.* I've been carrying the weight of this evil and its memories for years. Feeling worthless. Worthless to do anything about it. Now I can do something by resisting. Rage washes over me, a deep hunger for justice for all the kids who have lost their lives in this town.

So, one of these kids is a seer. *The* Seer. I heard the same stories eight years ago. It was a riddle, something that I thought was a child's playful chant.

> And one of them can see,
> Webs but not a spider's
> If only they believe
> And bathe in the light.

"It will kill your mother right in front of you," Fiara says in a cold, hard voice. "You must do what it wants."

My phone buzzes, and we both jump. It's an alarm, but one I certainly didn't set. I try to silence it, but a message screams at both of us.

AMBER ALERT: A CHILD ABDUCTION EMERGENCY HAS BEEN ISSUED. LAST SEEN IN BLACK JEEP CHEROKEE. ELIANA, BLONDE HAIR, BLUE EYES, 12-YEARS-OLD.

"Oh my God," I whimper. "It's happening already."

"I don't know if it ever stopped." Fiara's eyes turn icy blue. "Not really."

"What does it need us for, if it's already taking children again?"

Fiara rests her head on my shoulder. "Don't you understand?" she whispers. "Real evil isn't only about hurting others. Real evil is getting good people to hurt others."

I won't be a pawn this time. The guilt, the sleepless nights, the pills I sneak from Mom's prescriptions to numb myself—I can't do what it wants.

"Christina," Mom calls again from upstairs. "I'm thirsty."

"I need to help Mom," I tell Fiara. "I can't believe this is happening again." With my arm still around her shoulders, I give her a little hug. "I know it... it did all these things to you, and I understand your fear. But I will fight it." I think of the shoebox full of missing children posters. "I won't let it use me. Not again. I will fight it, with or without you."

When I remove my arm, Fiara wipes away her tears. She doesn't answer, and I don't like the empty look on her face. She's someone I need on my side. Standing, I move to the window and snap the drapes open. Fiara covers her face, the sunlight assaulting her.

"There's more to life than the Darkness," I tell her.

"It will take all the light," she whispers, slowly lowering her hands. Her gaze locks with mine, and she blinks slowly. "All the *light* will soon be gone." The way she emphasizes light makes my entire body tremble. "There's nothing we can do about it. It will happen with or without your help. But if you don't help it, it will kill everything you love." Fiara's lips tighten, her eyes turn from blue to red, and then she vanishes.

Gone. Air explodes from my lungs. I've seen her disappear before, but I haven't seen those full red eyes since—since the first time the Darkness took control of us years ago.

Rushing, I change into jeans that are a bit too tight and throw on a sky-blue Worthlapp High T-shirt, taking my athletic clothes with me so I can change for cross-country practice if I don't skip it.

Gripping the banister, I walk upstairs. My legs shake, and I don't know if I can trust them. Mom sits at the kitchen table reading an old magazine. She hasn't washed her hair or taken a shower in who knows how long. She's killing herself with a toxic mix of prescription drugs, and I try not to think about the day I will find her dead in bed. My father left us a long time ago, right after—

There's enough to think about today. If I can get to Mr. Lee, maybe he can help. He knows about the Secret, obviously, from what he's told our class. Someone must help me. I'm done feeling worthless.

Grabbing some bread, I put two slices in the toaster. Then I go into the pantry and take out the peanut butter. When the bread is toasted, I spread the peanut butter over it, pour a glass of orange juice, and hand the drink and toast to Mom. She looks up at me and smiles.

"What would I do without you, my baby girl?" Her eyes look vacant, like no one's home. I love her so much it hurts. The pain I see on her face and hear in her voice every day—the Darkness tortured her in front of me when I didn't want to bring it any more children.

And now it's all starting over.

I kiss Mom on the cheek. "I love you. Eat both pieces now. You need more protein. I grilled chicken last night. It's in the fridge. Eat that for lunch. Promise me? Before you take any more pills?"

Mom nods. “You’re the sweetest daughter.”

Wheels crackle against the driveway outside, and that must be Rob. I take a pitcher of water from the fridge and pour it into a cold glass. Drinking it all in a few quick gulps, I set the glass down and head outside.

“Wait a minute,” Mom calls after me, slowly, like she took a double dose of narcotics this morning. “I had the strangest dream I wanted to tell you about.”

I pause, and a choking sensation returns. I rub my throat.

“It was about snakes,” she says. “The longest, most frightening ones I’ve ever seen.”

My body twitches from a cold chill.

Mom’s eyes roll to the back of her head. Her tongue flops out of her mouth, and I shudder. It transforms into the tongue of a monster, hissing and dancing. My feet root to the floor in fear. Then she coughs, shakes her head, and looks at me once more. She blinks and picks up a piece of toast like nothing happened.

Rob honks from outside.

Taking a hesitant step forward, I study Mom. Is she okay? I take several deep breaths, and then I swallow my fear. “Bye, Mom,” I whisper. She doesn’t look up. The evil leaves her alone, for now. It’s a threat—warning me what will happen if I don’t do what it wants.

Rob flashes a smile of perfectly white teeth and waves at me from his brown Pontiac Aztec, a used car he’s so proud of because of some old TV show. I keep my head down, wishing we could talk about movies or stupid pop culture things. I don’t know what to say to him. We’ve been dating for over a year, ever since we were freshmen. Part of me thought I could have a normal life.

There are only two things that allow me to escape the pain of my past. Rob is one. When he comes over, streams some stupid show, and puts his arm around me, I let everything go, even if only for a few minutes. Years of pain and guilt wash away when he touches me.

The second thing that allows me to escape is running. I’m on the cross-country team and not because I enjoy it. I'm on the team because slamming my feet on hard pavement for as many miles as it takes for me to throw up from the pain of cramps is my self-punishment.

My hand grips the handle of the passenger side door. I hesitate. Something tells me I should run now. Just run far away from this town and everyone I care about. The smile on Rob's face lingers, and I open the door. I could use his comfort now. He knows all about Fiara, too. He was one of the few who treated her like she wanted to be treated—not as a freak, but as a friend.

I climb into the passenger side of the Aztec and turn to Rob. Cherry red hair nearly covers his warm, caring eyes.

"Is something wrong?" he asks. Freckles crinkle on his lightly sunburned nose. He could spend five minutes in the sun and turn a pink shade of lobster.

I take a deep breath and look at him. I want to tell him everything. All he knows is that I had a traumatic childhood "event" and that Fiara had a terrible "accident." But Rob doesn't know half of it. He's never pushed me to talk about my past, but he's made it clear he'll always listen. I don't want him to think I'm losing it. I'm also worried that if I ever told him the truth, I'd risk his life. Now these fears explode into reality.

"I'm fine," I say curtly, but Rob doesn't notice. "How are you?"

He just nods, his messy red hair bouncing. He leans in and kisses me gently on the lips. "I like your hair," he says. "A beautiful brown that always turns my frown upside down." He kisses me again, and tears well in my eyes. He's so sweet. Cheesy, yes. But still sweet. "Did you do something different to it?"

Shaking my head, I pull down the passenger-side visor and look in the mirror. I forgot to brush it, most likely. Messy brunette hair falls below my ears. I adjust my blue Worthlapp T-shirt. Then my reflection makes me gasp. The hazel in my eyes is gone! A flame dances instead, and I shut the visor hard.

Out of nowhere, Fiara's hand squeezes my shoulder. I jump and cover my mouth. The car turns cold.

"It wants Rob," she whispers, and she releases a sob. "It demands a sacrifice to show your loyalty. You shouldn't have said those things this morning. Now it demands Rob's blood. I told you it would come after those you love! This is not a joke, Christina."

*No!* I close my eyes and shout with my mind. *He doesn't know anything!* She sits in the backseat like a ghost, but Rob hasn't noticed her. *I won't do it! I won't be its monster again!*

Fiara cries in my ear and then vanishes before Rob sees her.

That's when Mom screams. I open the car door, hop out, and run inside, just as Rob had started to back out of the driveway.

Rays of morning light fill the messy kitchen. Dishes with crusted pasta sit in the sink, and unopened mail covers the counters. I search for an intruder or a creature.

"Mom, are you okay?" I ask, not seeing anything unusual.

She looks at me like she's seen a demon. "Baby, I felt... I felt like someone was choking me." She looks around the room in a panic. "It wasn't the pills, I promise. Someone was choking me!" She cries and slams her arms on the table, knocking over half a dozen plastic prescription bottles and spilling the orange juice I gave her.

Fiara appears in the corner, and her eyes turn a blazing red, a sign that the Darkness has complete control of her.

Her lips turn up slowly, and she lifts her right hand and makes a throat-slitting gesture. Then she stares at my mother and laughs.

The red in her eyes turns blue, and Fiara cries again. "I'm sorry," she whimpers.

Taking a moment to rub Mom's back, I tell her, "It'll be okay." I will do what I must. I put my arms around her and hug her. *Oh, Mom. It hurt you so much already. I won't let it hurt you anymore. I can't.*

I run back down to my bedroom, and I pull out the shoebox again. Under the missing children posters and my notes are yearbooks that I collected throughout grade school. Inside the yearbooks, I wrote the names of the children the monster killed. Their images have vanished, along with the town's memories of them.

There's something else in the box, too—a knife with a black handle and a long silver blade. I grip it hard, and—no, that's impossible. I see something I've never seen. The blade curves, transforming in my hands. My stomach sinks, and I drop the blade. I don't want to touch it. I can smell the blood the knife has tasted, and my mouth turns dry again. I need it, though. This knife came from the Darkness, and I hope my instinct is right—that maybe this blade can help me.

I touch the knife again, ever so carefully. Nothing changes this time. Was it my imagination all along? Trauma can do terrible things to the mind. I put the knife in my backpack and go upstairs. Mom sleeps face down on the table.

I kiss her on the cheek again. She looks so much older than she should. I let the image sink in, trying to muster the courage for what must be done next.

Rob stands in the doorway, a look of confusion spread across his face. "Is everything okay?"

I shake my head. I don't want to say the words, but something takes control of my voice. "Will you skip school and take me somewhere? It's important."

I hate it when I feel worthless. I hate it when it feels like I have no control.

It's time to change that.

# CHAPTER TWO

He puts his arms around me, hugging me tightly. He kisses me on the cheek. Taking my hand, he turns, and we walk back to his car. No questions asked. He'd do anything for me.

Why is this all happening again? The Darkness must have something to lose. It was afraid of Fiara once, thinking she may have had the gift of sight, and look what happened to her.

Rob doesn't question my intentions. "Where to?" he asks, holding the passenger door open as I hesitantly enter.

"Head out of town, by the closed-off old park district road, and I'll show you from there."

"What's going on, hun?" he asks, his voice calm and sympathetic.

"I'll tell you everything when we get there." I rub my eyes. "Tell me a story. Distract me, will ya?"

I rest my head against the back of the seat and close my eyes, and he hops in behind the wheel.

"Do you remember the first day I told you that I loved you?" he asks. A warmth fills my chest. He's the sweetest boy. The tires spin on the pavement, and the vibration relaxes me. "I walked into your bedroom, and you had all those old yearbooks and posters spread out over your bed. I had loved you for, I dunno, a long time by then. So, I said it to you right there."

"I remember," I say. I had put my head against his chest and cried until I had no more tears left that day. Looking at all the posters of so many missing children, most of whom *I* had taken to the Darkness, filled me with great sorrow. It made me do such awful things. Things I cannot do again.

"Where to now?" Rob asks as we approach the end of town near the abandoned park district road.

I direct him where to go, and he plays with the radio and starts singing along to a fun Taylor Swift song. He's adorable, and I wish I felt some kind of joy so I could sing along, too.

Instead, I know what I must do to keep my poor mother safe. She's gone through hell, and she never quite made it back. It will torture her and hurt others until I do what it wants. It's not fair. The more I think about it, the harder it is for me to breathe.

Fiara is right about evil. Getting others to do the worst things imaginable is its greatest joy.

We drive beyond the small-town streets of Worthlapp. It doesn't take long. Rob parks his car at the edge of a barely visible dirt path that leads to the Darkness. It's not something an average person would even notice, but its location is unfortunately embedded in my permanent memory. We step out, and he adjusts a pink button-up shirt that looks mismatched here by the woods. Walking slowly, he follows my lead. Tangled underbrush blocks part of the trail. Thorny bushes cut at our ankles while we walk. I step over small, fallen trees that lead to a trail carpeted with pine needles and dead leaves. I move quickly, glancing back at Rob as he struggles to keep up. My eyes focus hard on the path, and I call to the Darkness with my mind. Cool air whips my hair over my shoulders. Our feet hit the ground with a thud that echoes throughout the woods.

*I can't go through this again. I won't.*

The Darkness doesn't respond. I breathe in the brisk air. It smells of dead leaves. I catch a whiff of burning wood and smoke in the distance. The temperature drops, chilling the terrain.

Rob catches up to me. "What is this place? And why is it so important?"

I reach for his hand. I have a plan, and I'm certainly not here to kill my boyfriend. The Darkness thinks it can use me again?

Smiling, I picture the knife. If I can hurt it or take some of its power, then I can fight back.

The adrenaline in my veins and the wind against my back push me forward.

The trees open willingly to our left, and I lead Rob deeper into the woods. We walk ahead on a small dirt path, where the sunlight is almost entirely blacked out over us due to the thick trees. The path bends in between trees older than the two of us combined. The temperature continues to cool, easily ten degrees less than the air outside the trail. Although mostly dry, a few parts of the path feel soupy, and it muddies our shoes. It hasn't rained in weeks, though, which makes it even stranger. Something makes a rattling sound, startling us. Rob looks over his shoulder.

"What's that? What is this place?"

His fear is palpable and justified. Anything that needs the coverage of darkness to grow and survive is the stuff of nightmares.

I grab his hand and pull him closer to me. Rob's heart races, and beads of sweat form on his face.

Darkness consumes us, and electrifying energy buzzes throughout these woods. "Just hold me. Please."

Rob hugs me. I hold onto my bag with one hand, and I swallow, trying to ease the dryness in my mouth.

"What's wrong, Christina? What's going on?" He starts to let go, but I press him tighter against me.

"I love you. What happened in my childhood—I have always wanted to tell you, but I figured you'd think I was losing it. Literally . You have to help me."

"Anything. You know that." He puts my hand over his beating heart.

"There's a monster here," I say. "Evil. I must fight."

He cocks his head to the side.

"Not far ahead, there's a pit. I have to go inside. But I may never return."

His eyes narrow. "Is this some kind of joke?" When I shake my head, he says, "I don't understand."

"I know. It's all happening so fast. Just remember me. That's all I ask."

"This is weird talk." He grips my shoulders. "Christina, what *are* you talking about?"

Something grabs my throat, and I can't speak. I look around, but I don't see Fiara. A shadow appears, the monster within the darkness. It runs right into me! I'd gasp if I could breathe.

My hands move on their own. I can't control them. One hand pulls Rob close, and the other reaches into my bag to grab the knife.

My fingers wrap around the handle. The ground spins while my mind floods with images of blood and death. Even the blade morphs into various styles, from a dagger to a scythe. I try to scream but nothing comes out of my mouth.

With all my strength, I push Rob away. "Get away! Go! You have to get as far away from me as possible. Right now! GO!" I shout. He stares at me with confusion. A rattle in the underbrush buzzes loudly, vibrating the ground.

*No! Stop it! Stop it right now!* I push and shake with all my might, but my arms move on their own, and my feet won't budge no matter how hard I try to run away.

Rob's eyes grow wide, as do mine. "What's happening?" His face turns as white as a ghost. He reaches for me.

"Run! *Ohmygodfuckingrun!* Now!"

"You're scaring me!" Rob shouts.

My mouth releases a primal scream, and finally Rob turns to run.

But it's too late. I grab Rob and hold him with abnormal strength.

My hand, controlled by the evil here, rises in front of his face. A tiny sliver of light perfectly hits the blade of the knife. Fear the color of the pale moonlight flashes across Rob's face.

I try to speak, but I am not in control.

My hand grips the knife harder, so much so that pain shoots through me.

And then—*No!*

My arm lashes out, like a rattlesnake striking a mouse.

The knife slashes Rob's throat.

Blood sprays out, and the trees shake. Rob gurgles and blood spurts from his neck and his mouth. It hits my face, and the blood is hot. The ground shakes, and my stomach drops. The woods darken even more, except for that sliver of light reflecting off the blade. Now the light finds its way onto Rob's face.

I regain control of my body and lower Rob to the ground. I sob, louder than I've ever cried before, my tears now mixing with his blood.

The evil here can take many forms. It's a monster in the woods, but it's so much more, too. This time, hands reach out from under the ground, but they aren't exactly hands. They are finger-like shadows, each finger as long as a broomstick. They run over my face and through my hair, patting me on the head like a child who has done a good deed.

Then the fingers surround Rob's body and pull him through the ground, claiming another victim.

I close my eyes, scream, and punch the ground beneath me, repeatedly, until my knuckles bleed.

---

I MUST HAVE blacked out. I don't know how much time has passed, but I'm back outside the woods on my knees, beyond the path that leads to the Darkness. I know what's happened, but it feels distant, like it happened years ago. Everything feels numb.

"Rob!" I bury my face in my hands, and the tears pour out. My stomach turns, and I vomit everything that's inside me. The water I drank earlier comes out hot and acidic, followed by dry heaves. My abdomen hurts, and my throat feels like it has been slashed by a—

I cry again, thinking about how ignorant I am. How worthless! How did I ever think I could stop this evil? And look what it made me do!

How could I have been so foolish? I am its pawn, and I always have been. I'm not strong enough to stop it.

Then another memory hits me—I shouldn't have driven here! No, there's another trick, one I had forgotten, a different way to approach the Darkness. I don't know if it would have made a difference, but I shouldn't have driven here.

And I shouldn't have tried to fight it by myself. I clench my fists and rise. I need to get help. The Darkness wants me to bring my classmates to it? It wants more!

*I'll get them. But I won't be so stupid this time. I'll stop you. Somehow, I'll stop you.*

I scratch at the dry blood on my hands and clothes. Splashes of encrusted copper stain my blue Worthlapp shirt and jeans. It all seems unreal. I hop into Rob's Aztec, and the keys are still in the ignition. I glance in the mirror, and the flames in my eyes grow bigger. I can't let it consume me. If it takes control of me—I shake the terrible thought away.

I need to go to school so I can talk to Mr. Lee and my classmates.

I race to school, certainly the fastest I've ever gone to get to that hell hole. I park in an old, small parking lot behind the school that gets little use. There's an athletic storage shed nearby, and out from it runs Elle. Is it a coincidence that I see her now? Can I trust my mind? She sprints into school.

Walking toward the school, I turn and look back at the shed from which Elle came. It's not the shed that captures my attention. Rob's Aztec completely disappears in front of me, and I gasp. That's not something you can ever unsee. Terrible fear forces tears out of my eyes again, and I pray that the evil won't take away my memories of Rob.

I pause for a minute to bring focus to my body. From the athletic shed where I just saw Elle, Coach Nathan—our cross-country coach—emerges. He wears a blue Worthlapp baseball hat, but it's on backward. When he walks out, he turns it around and adjusts his shirt.

An uneasy, ill feeling pulses through me.

First, I run into one of the girls' locker rooms, making sure to pick one I knew would be empty. I shower, throw away the clothes I had been wearing, and change into the practice clothes I had with me in my bag. With all my willpower, I try to block out the image of Rob's throat spraying blood all over me and those broomstick-like fingers coming out of the ground.

*You did what you had to do, just like you always have,* I tell myself. *It would have killed Mom, it would have killed you, and you tried to fight it. YOU didn't kill Rob. The Darkness used you.*

The thoughts provide enough comfort to keep me from going completely out of sorts, but something in my mind feels off. This time I don't look into any mirror. I don't want to know how much of it is inside me.

After showering, I quickly slip into Miss Hurst's biology classroom, and I take a seat right next to Lawson's desk.

He comes in but doesn't pay me any attention. Why did I see him in my vision when Fiara touched me? I study him, his chestnut hair styled neatly. What's so special about this boy that the Darkness wants? I take a deep breath and focus on him. Lawson looks terribly sad.

Lawson realizes I'm staring at him, and he gives me a puzzled look. *What's her deal?*

I force a half-smile. I need to talk to Lawson, and I don't want to creep him out. "Hey. I don't mean to stare."

"Huh? Oh, okay," he mutters.

"I want to talk to you about something," I say and lean closer. "About Mister Lee's... um, project."

"What about it?"

"I know you and Elle... well, I know what you discovered as kids. I did, too."

*Holy shit. Really?* I hear his thoughts. This happens sometimes after interacting with the Darkness, and once again, I can't imagine this is a coincidence.

I open my mouth to say more, but the words don't come. Instead, I turn away, my eyes inexplicably drawn to the classroom windows. Something's there—I can feel it. Goosebumps pop up on my legs and arms. Suddenly, blue eyes appear.

Fiara stares at me from outside the window, and her eyes change from blue to red.

"Anyway," I continue and shift back to Lawson. "Can we go there together? I need someone I can talk to about it. Maybe after school today?"

*What am I doing? That's not what I meant to say. I meant to tell him about the evil and ask him to help me fight it, not take him into the heart of evil where he'll die, just like Rob!*

Lawson stares at me, and my lips curl into an innocent smile, but I don't feel happy.

"Uh, okay," he says. "But I don't remember where it is."

I nod, and I reach over and put a hand on his knee. "I do. After school, then?" The smile continues to grow on my face, and it's the strangest feeling because I'm not the one smiling. I'm a puppet, as if those dark fingers from the woods have control.

"Um, okay." He's confused but not suspicious. "Sure, I guess."

Inside my head, Fiara cries and the Darkness laughs—the laughter resembles nothing like a human's. It's the rumble of the sea before a hurricane, the crackling of snow before an avalanche. It's the excitement, fear, and anticipation of nature preparing for its next victim.

My consciousness swims in silent screams.

# CHAPTER THREE

The Darkness closes my eyes.

I see a deep yellow. It's not bright—not like the sun. Closer to a sunset, but not orange, either.

What is this light, and why do I see it?

My eyes pop open. Quick, shallow breaths try to fill my lungs with oxygen. Is that panic? Something slipped from the Darkness to me, something I wasn't supposed to see.

*Light.*

My mind searches for an answer or a memory. Some understanding as to what the light could indicate.

Did the Darkness tell me anything about light when I was a child? Maybe Fiara discovered something before she—well, before the evil changed her.

Our teacher reminds us that we should be working on our assignment. My mind shifts from the classroom to what feels like water. A nothingness.

*You want to remember something, Christina?* It shows me my eight-year-old self.

*Let this remind you that you work for me.* It forces me to revisit a memory.

My family was having a picnic in a park not far from the wooded entrance to the Darkness. There were at least five families there, including my cousins and some friends of my parents. It was a beautiful fall afternoon, but it wouldn't be beautiful for long.

Although I was the oldest, I enjoyed playing with the other little girls. My cousin Amber, just a year younger, said, "I wanna play dress up."

"I don't wanna play that," I had told her. "We're outside. Let's do something else."

"But I wanna dress up!"

*I watched you play that day,* the Darkness tells me now. *I whispered in your ear, and you did as I told you. Do you remember?*

My chest aches. I can't shake away the memory, but I don't want to see this!

My eight-year-old self rubbed her temples. When she opened her eyes, they flickered with blood orange.

*But what about the yellow light? What does that mean?* I ask now.

*Forget the light!* It shouts. *Observe the memory.*

"I've got a game for you," I told the little girls and motioned for them to come. "It's called Jack Rabbit. It's like Hide-and-Seek but the opposite. One hides. The rest try to find her. When you do, you scream Jack Rabbit and run back to base. I'll be 'it' first. What do you say?"

They looked around at one another, and no one spoke up.

"Don't be scared," I said. "It's a fun game." I didn't wait for a response. It looked as if—my heart races watching the memory—as if something possessed me. "Now, you all close your eyes, count to twenty, and then come find me. Close your eyes!"

I ran without looking to see if anyone was peeking. My feet raced along the edge of the field, bordered by the woods, and took a sharp left at the first trail. I ran hard, too—as fast as my little legs would allow. I discovered a gravel path off to the side and took that, which led to the entrance of the Darkness.

Like a shadow, night covered these woods even if it was still the afternoon. Immediately, I was drawn to it, and as I walked closer, the woods opened up, welcoming me.

My heart was already beating fast from running, but I felt a new adrenaline rush.

When I entered, the air cooled and the blackness intensified, like I'd been swallowed by a void. I walked slowly, following gray, swirling mists that danced in the darkness. It was as if this wooded area was its own ecosystem. Everything felt new, and even though it was dark, I could somehow still see. Then a voice spoke to me.

*Christina.*

I craned my neck. "Who's calling?"

*I've been waiting for you.*

Fear dried my mouth.

"Who are you?" I croaked.

A rustling noise from behind startled me, and I turned. A shadow danced around me. At first, it was long and slender, and it stood over me. Then it shifted and became wide and fat, more like a creature than a man.

*I am everything. I am you. You are me. My Christina.* It kept its voice soothing, like a lullaby. *You've already brought me my first gift. Thank you.*

"Huh?"

Footsteps crackled the fallen leaves, and when I saw who approached, I gasped. My cousin Amber had found me, and her pale face glowed in the dark woods. "Ja... Ja... Jack Rabbit!"

The shadow spun around Amber, and she released a scream that made me cover my ears. Its shadow twirled around Amber like a tornado. Stunned, I simply watched, and then it was over.

Amber was gone. A gray mist swirled where she once stood and floated away in the blink of an eye.

*Bring me more.*

"What?"

*You are special, and I have fantastic plans for you.*

I gulped. I didn't understand what was happening. "Is Amber really gone?"

Then it slapped me. I fell backward, and I saw my parents. They were sitting at a picnic bench, and a snake dropped from a tree. The snake wrapped around my father's throat and squeezed. My mother tried to help him, but the snake hissed and snapped at her.

"What are you doing?" I asked.

*You will bring me whatever I ask for, or I will hurt those you love. Do you understand?*

"No!" I cried.

I raced back to the field, and the other girls were playing with each other. They looked up at me and waved.

A snake slithered through the grass. It stared at me and hissed a warning, and I couldn't help but cry. My eyes rained tears, and the snake did a lap around my feet before it moved on.

Then I ran to my parents. They were talking with Amber's mom and dad, and now Amber was gone.

"Mom!" I cried. "Daddy!" I looked down at the ground and kicked at the grass. "Something happened."

"What is it, honey?" Mom asked.

"It's Amber. I think... she's dead." I looked up and saw the strangest reaction. Amber's parents looked confused but not concerned.

"Sweetie," Daddy asked, "who's Amber?"

I blinked and examined their faces. "My... my cousin." I pointed at Amber's parents. "Your daughter."

They broke out into laughter.

"We don't have any children, Christina." Amber's mom smiled. "Not yet anyway."

"That's enough stories for now," Daddy said. "Such an imagination! You go play with the other kids." I stared at him, my mouth hanging open. "Go on. Now."

I turned around and walked away, and the monster chuckled at me. But apparently, I was the only one who could hear it. Everyone continued talking and eating like nothing had happened. But something did. A little girl was gone! It took her, that thing in the woods. It took all memories of her, too. But why? Why would something be so purely evil?

Then the Darkness whispered one last thought for the day. *This is just the beginning, my dear. We will do so much more together.*

---

THE BELL SIGNALS the Worthless High lunch, but I have no desire for food. I jump out of my seat, the bell waking me up. Somewhat in control of myself, I run to the girls' restroom and hurl instead. Once it comes out, I can't stop, and on my third projection, I cry-vomit, which is one of the worst things ever. Rob should be here, holding my hair. Instead, all I picture is my knife curled within my fists slashing at Rob's throat. His expression of pure shock and incredulity, his beautiful, pale face, his eyes, eyes that will never look at me again—I continue to cry-vomit, snot mixing with the acid of my empty stomach.

And then the memory of Amber. And all those in between her and Rob.

I've been worthless my entire damn life.

I rest my head against the cool toilet seat, not worrying about germs. I'm infected by something far worse than any flu. When my tears dry and my stomach settles, I walk to a sink, wash my face, and look in the mirror.

Pushing my leafy-brown hair to the side, I see the fiery glow in my hazel eyes. Yeah, this is no flu. This is—

Fiara appears behind me, and I jump.

She has tears in her eyes, and her pale, doll-like face is wet from crying. "Christina, I'm so sorry. I wish there were something I could do."

I place my hands on the sink and squeeze it so hard I might rip it right from the wall.

"There is." I wipe my nose and turn to face her. "You could fight it. Help me fight it."

She appears to shrink in front of me. “It would be like a fly trying to kill a dinosaur.”

“Do you know what it did to Rob? What it made me do?” My temples throb a terrible burning pain, and my heart races.

Fiara nods, and the tears that roll down her face elicit no sympathy from me. I grab her wrists.

“We have to fight it!” A girl walks into the restroom, sees us, and freezes. “What are you staring at?”

The girl runs away, and I face Fiara.

“You can help me. You have to.”

Fiara’s eyes roll back, and a burning red consumes them. It’s the Darkness, and I try to let go of Fiara. My arms are stuck, though. I can’t move. Invisible hands choke me. The pain is unbearable, and I can’t even find the breath to scream.

After a minute, Fiara’s eyes turn blue, and I let go.

“Did it... is it in you?” she asks.

My hands drop to my side, and my stomach feels sick again. Before I can answer, I puke in the sink.

Something is inside me.

And I’m afraid it’s going to kill me.

I’m in the bathroom for several more minutes, and I just stare in the mirror. It’s hypnotic, the way the flames leap in my eyes. I take a deep breath and exit the bathroom without saying anything else to Fiara.

---

To kill someone is the absolute worst thing I’ve ever had to do, even if it wasn’t really me doing it. I don’t know how people can watch horror movies and laugh at them. One moment you feel a person’s heart beating rapidly because of the adrenaline rushing through his or her body. The next you feel that heart abruptly stop. I’ve pressed blades into someone’s neck and have seen skin rip open and blood pour out. Blood doesn’t drip—it rains. It shoots outward in all directions if you cut deep enough, and I have.

It's not something I ever wanted to do, but I know what real evil can do.

The thoughts bounce through my mind as I walk toward the cafeteria. My body moves, but I'm not exactly in the driver's seat. My thoughts are my own, but something else moves my body.

Has anyone else in this Worthless High School killed someone? Maybe Ronnie the Rattler? Ronnie is the school bully, and he likes to hurt people, but would he go that far? I've asked the Darkness to use someone else, but it insists upon using me. What makes me so unfortunately special? I'm not the Seer. I'm a messenger, a delivery girl, running errands for evil.

The cafeteria is a beehive of noise and activity. A lunch lady scoops food and drops it methodically on students' trays. She smiles, but something's not quite right about her. Her arm moves like a robot. Maybe she's just done this ten thousand times. My eyes scan for other adults. Some staff monitor the Worthless High Commons. They walk without purpose. They look around the room, but they don't appear to see anything.

Maybe they don't care, or they're tired of watching teenagers, burned out on the daily drama of high school life. My gut rumbles, fear lining my stomach.

Are other things happening here that I don't understand?

I watch the sycophantic cross-country team pamper Elle. She's one of the girls everyone else wants to be. She's also one of the classmates from my vision, one that the Darkness wants. Keeping my eyes on her, I grab a yogurt for lunch. I don't want to eat, but this thing inside me knows my physical body needs strength. Besides, a little something to coat my stomach may help. Every teammate except for Angelica and I surround Elle, which makes my skin crawl—it's like they're cocooning her.

Do they want to be like her, or do they have the power to change her into who they want her to be?

It's a strange thought, and I look for Angelica, the only other teammate not cocooning Elle Bloom. This other presence in me minimizes my emotions so that it has more physical control, and my mind wanders to thoughts as strange as this sensation.

Angelica sits with her friend Pauline. There's an energy in the room I haven't noticed before. I walk over to Angelica and Pauline, thinking about the noise and why, apparently, no one else heard it. "What's up?" *Bring me these two as well. One of them will...* laughter replaces the inner voice of evil, and I try not to think about what will happen to one or both of them.

Pauline gives me an inquisitive look, but Angelica shrugs and scoots over on the bench. I sit next to her. Like Elle, she's another classmate I saw in my vision.

I focus on Angelica, wondering what the Darkness wants from her. She has beautiful, black skin. Round black-frame glasses give her a sleek, smart look. Long, straight hair sits above her shoulders.

"Why you lookin' at me like that?" Angelica asks, sitting up straighter.

I sense something strange about her, but I don't know what it is. I don't know Angelica well, but she has always seemed like a good person—someone real, who speaks her mind, who won't stab you in the back.

"No reason," I lie.

I scan the room for others from my vision. A cacophony of voices sounds like waves hitting the ocean shore. There's something different about the voices here. People talk to distract themselves. Laughter sounds higher than normal, like it's forced or fake. It's the sound of hundreds of teens living in a town where children go missing.

A Worthless High staff member walks by and cracks a fake smile. He doesn't make eye contact with anyone. His eyes look stoned and remind me of my mother.

Looking away from him, I search for Lawson. He's sitting with Teddy, another boy from my vision. They're playing some kind of hand-held video game. My heart beats faster at the sight of them. *I need to consume them. Stop wasting time and bring them to me!*

That's certainly not my thought—that inner voice strengthens, and I feel light-headed.

"What's new with you two?" The voice speaking isn't mine, either. A sharp pain hits me from the inside, like I've swallowed razor blades. Am I taking a backseat to my own existence?

"Pauline was just telling me about Ronnie," Angelica says, adjusting her purple T-shirt.

"The Rattler?" I ask. *Why can't you use him instead? Ronnie likes hurting other people.*

"Yeah," Pauline says. She has a bright smile and smooth brown skin. She wears her hair pulled back tightly in a perfectly shaped bun. She looks around and leans closer to us. "Did you know Ronnie's adopted? He just found out, too. Isn't that interesting?"

"So?" I say.

"Well," Pauline continues. "He's been all depressed lately. I know he's a jerk, but someone should talk to him. There's usually a reason why someone's a bully, you know. I wonder if he had a bad childhood."

Angelica eats a chip and nods. I wish I could be closer to Pauline. There's something special about someone who sympathizes with a bully.

"I do rather enjoy seeing him pick on these losers," I say. Pauline gasps. *What did I just say? Why are you doing this?*

Angelica gives me side-eye through her glasses but doesn't comment. Pauline looks at me like I said that babies are ugly.

"Ronnie's a real jerk," Pauline says. "Just because you think a kid is a loser doesn't mean they should get picked on. Who are they bothering?" She folds her arms and sets them on the table.

I shrug and look away. "I actually think that Lawson is kinda cute. What do you think?"

Pauline's eyes light up, and she looks at Angelica. "Tell her," Pauline says.

Angelica almost smiles. She's tall, athletic, and absolutely gorgeous, but come to think of it, she looks miserable most of the time. The more I listen to Angelica and Pauline, the more I like them.

*Leave them alone! Leave all of us alone!*

"Yeah, I think he's cute," Angelica says, but her eyes move from Lawson to his friend, Teddy.

So, Angelica has a crush on Lawson, perhaps. Doesn't she know he likes boys? Come to think of it, I don't think Lawson has ever come out. I've seen the way he looks at Teddy, though. Maybe I'm wrong, but that's a look of more than friendship. When you know what love feels like, you can see it in other people's eyes, too. It's the same way I look at Rob.

*Looked.* Past tense. Another pain hits my gut. How is it even possible that my boyfriend is gone, killed by my own hand, and I'm sitting here talking about other cute boys? This Darkness is a powerful drug.

This isn't real. I must be trapped in an alternate reality, and I need to find my way back to the one where Rob is alive and kids don't die or go missing. I want to cry and scream, but something else controls my voice.

"I agree," I say. "I was thinking of asking him out." *What are you doing?*

This time, Angelica's eyes widen, and the half-smile vanishes. That's the look I'm used to seeing—not exactly sadness, but anger.

"What do you think?" I say. "Do you think we'd make a cute couple?"

"No," Pauline says without hesitation. "No, I don't."

I laugh. "Well, we're hanging out after school today."

"You are not," Pauline says.

I nod. "We are. We're gonna go for a walk in the woods. Maybe we'll be naughty. Who knows?" *Oh my God!* I want to run away and shut the hell up. I hear the words, but I have no power to stop them.

I take a chip from Pauline's tray. Then I stand, smile, and head over to Lawson's table.

Pauline and Angelica's eyes burn into the back of my skull, and I want to run out of the cafeteria far away from this place. But my legs, like my words, do what the Darkness wants.

Striding across the cafeteria, I pretend to drop a spoon right in front of Lawson. I manage to catch Elle's attention, too. The Darkness sends me a thought. *Let's start with these two. These are our first two victims, staring right at us. The Seer is in this room—I feel something I haven't felt in years!*

I hate this. Why me? What the hell is all this—a throbbing pain hits my temples. *If you care about your mother, you'll stop questioning me. You will do as I say, or we will kill her.*

I turn toward Lawson. His chestnut hair forms an old-school boxed haircut. He's very well groomed. He wears a *Monty Python and the Holy Grail* T-shirt, or rather the shirt wears him. He has a skinny frame and sharp cheekbones—he kind of looks like a skeleton.

I hope he can help me.

There's another Secret, one Lawson knows about, beyond the Darkness. It has power too—enough power that it could stop the monster in the woods, perhaps. *Take me to it,* I want to shout at Lawson. But there's another part that is getting stronger by the minute that wants to kill him.

*It's him or your mother. Don't fight me, Christina. You know I will do it.* Images of Rob's bloody throat flood my mind. I press hard on my temples, forcing away the thoughts and the tears to the best of my ability.

I march over to where Lawson is sitting, trying to shake that terrible vision from my mind. I squeeze right in next to him and put my arm around him.

Feeling the stares of Angelica, Pauline, and Elle, the Darkness flashes my most flirtatious smile.

I *am* the monster, and not for the first time.

"Hi," Teddy says from across the table. He has messy, curly

hair that bounces on his head. White teeth shine even brighter in his smile, contrasting with his light brown skin. I've managed to catch his attention as well.

"Hi back," I say. "I don't think I've met you. I'm Christina."

"Tuh... Tuh...Teddy," he manages to say. Teddy starts to extend his hand for a greeting but gets nervous and weird. He pulls it back and wipes it down a yellow *Cobra Kai* T-shirt.

"Whatcha boys playing?"

"The new Mario," Lawson says. He runs a hand along the sides of his nicely styled brown hair.

"Cool," I lie. "Maybe I can play a game with you after school?" They have no idea what I'm really asking them, and my smile reaches my ears. I feel like the Joker, a permanent grin scarred on my face that I can't control. The real me screams on the inside.

"Sure," Teddy says. "Wanna hang out today?" he asks Lawson.

Lawson looks up at Teddy, then over to me. "I thought you wanted to go... on a walk?"

"Oh, yeah. You were—" I pause and lean in but say it loud enough for Teddy to hear. "You were gonna show me something special, right? A, um, secret?"

Lawson's face turns as bright as a tomato, and Teddy's eyes narrow.

"Are you... taking her to... you know?"

Still blushing, Lawson says, "I dunno." He shifts toward me.

"You told her about *the* Secret?" Teddy asks. "You said you didn't know how to get to it, or even what it really was!"

"No," Lawson says and sets down the game system. "I mean, yeah, but—"

"Boys," I interrupt. "Let's all three go. Today. It will be magical. And after we can play more Mario. Okay?"

I grin and reach across the table to touch Teddy's hand. His eyes shift from Lawson to me, and I know that I've planted the seed I need. Nothing can get between two teenage boys like a girl, even if one of them likes boys more.

"Okay," Teddy says and Lawson nods.

"What about Rob?" Lawson asks. "Will your boyfriend be joining us?"

The question breaks my heart. Lawson remembers Rob!

"There is no Rob," I answer, and if there was anything left of my heart, it would break again.

*How does Lawson remember?* Rob's car vanished in the parking lot. The victims the Darkness takes—I thought I was the only one who could remember them.

With all my inner willpower, I try to move my hand. It feels like I'm lifting a car, but I move it, inch by inch. I'm close enough, and I touch Lawson. I yell a thought that I hope he can hear.

*Help me, Lawson!*

He flinches. His eyes narrow, and my heart races. *Oh, please! Tell me you hear me. Don't trust the words that I say. Just listen to my thoughts!*

His gaze turns back to Teddy, and his eyes soften with affection. Did he hear anything?

Another voice pounds inside my head, but certainly not the one I want to hear.

*It will be a shame what's going to happen to your poor mother. She's screaming right now. She's having a nightmare, and it's showing her exactly how she's going to die.*

It's a knock-out punch to what's left of my inner consciousness.

The bell rings, signaling it's time for fifth hour. Lawson and Teddy go in separate directions, but I remain seated and watch everyone move. I catch Elle's eyes for a second, and I flash a smile. Elle's beautiful. Thick blonde hair bounces just below her jaw line, and I can't help but stare at her chest. It's the desire of every boy in this school and certainly some girls, too.

Oh, I've got big plans for you, the monster thinks.

My bladder needs to be released, and the monster walks my body to the bathroom.

The men's faculty restroom is the closest one. As soon as I enter, I open a stall and throw up again. There goes the yogurt and that potato chip.

Not just once, but over and over, even though it seems impossible. There's nothing left inside me. My abdomen feels like it's been to war.

Once I'm finished, I flush and sit on the toilet. Then I reach into my bag and take out a permanent marker. On the bathroom stall, I write.

*Worthless High Biggest Slut:*

*ELLE*

*She'll screw you for extra credit.*

I watch my hand moving, but it's not me who is really writing it, of course. This evil continues to consume me.

My face smiles at the artwork, and my real mind slips deeper into my subconscious. I can still see, but I am paralyzed, a ghost in my body.

Someone's here.

It's Ronnie the Rattler, the school bully. He unzips a bright blue track jacket. And... no, really? Ronnie the big bad boy appears to be crying. I sit in the stall and listen to a few sobs, smiling—not the real me, the real me is still screaming for help—and soaking it in. Boy cries are the worst kind of cries, but this evil finds pleasure in Ronnie's.

"Pussy," I whisper. I hate myself for not being able to control my own words.

He immediately stops crying and wipes his eyes. "Who's there?"

I giggle teasingly.

"Who the hell is in there?" Ronnie shouts. He's a big kid, built like a truck and full of muscle.

"Pussy boy," I say in my deepest voice. The Darkness takes

pleasure in torturing not just Ronnie but also me. I mentally squirm and struggle to stop the words. It just laughs at me.

"I will kick your loser ass. Get out of there right now. I'll kill you!" The anger in Ronnie's voice excites the evil in me.

"Come in here and show me how tough you are," I say.

Through the crack of the door, I spy on his confusion, nearly laughing again. He must think it's a girl who taunts him, certainly not a monster. He peers through the corner of the door.

I open it and grin.

"What the hell, bitch?"

"What the hell yourself? Why are you crying?"

"None of your business." He pauses and looks hard at me. "If you tell anyone, I'll kill you."

His anger and pain attract the Darkness even more.

"Why don't you try?" I ask. His jaw drops and he stares at me incredulously. "Or are you too much of a pussy?"

"What the hell are you on?" Ronnie asks, his face twisting back to anger.

I thrust my hand forward and grab him by his crotch. When I try to pull him toward me, he pushes me against the toilet. That's more like it.

"Is that all you got? Pussy!" I slap him across the face.

"Am not!" Then he slaps me back, and I smile.

I don't know who the real me is anymore. The Darkness is in me—that much is certain. My brain feels like soup. My mind mixes with the monster, until I become it. Or it becomes me. I'm not sure which, but all I know is that I want Ronnie.

I want Ronnie right now.

I want to taste his blood.

"Harder," I say, and he hits me again. My own blood fills my mouth. I lick my lips and grin.

"You hit like a girl," I tell him. Then he makes a fist and his knuckles connect with my jaw. Yeah, baby, that's what I need.

He hits me repeatedly, but I don't cry.

After a few slugs, he looks at me in total shock. "What's wrong with you?" He whimpers, and for a second I think he's going to burst into tears again.

"Oh, Ronnie." I reach for him, but he flinches. "Look in my eyes!" He does as I demand, and I lock contact with him. I reach for him again, and this time he returns the gesture. I hold his hand and pull him forward.

I gently kiss him on the neck, and I move to his lips. My tongue enters his mouth, and while he doesn't return the kiss, he doesn't pull away either.

When I let him go, the dumb returns to his face. He leaves the bathroom, having no clue what I've really done to him. I wait to hear the door shut. Then I study myself in the mirror.

Bloody and bruised, fire consumes me. I'm beautiful. Absolutely gorgeous.

When I leave, Fiara appears in the hallway and wipes at the tears running down her cheeks. "Stop crying," I tell her. "You're tougher than that. Stay close. I'll need you soon."

Fiara doesn't speak. She nods, and she vanishes. I don't know where. Let her haunt someone in the bathroom.

I continue walking until I reach the principal's office.

The principal's assistant speaks on the phone and doesn't look up. "Another one of our students? Oh, Lord. How many have gone missing now?"

I smile. That's my work she's talking about.

"Any trace of them at all? Lord help us. Kidnapped you think? Oh, God!" The assistant looks up at me and gasps. "I'll call you back." She hangs up the phone. "Honey, are you okay?"

I force some tears out and manage to sound upset. "I need to see Principal Walper, please."

The assistant picks up the phone and calls into her office. Walper opens the door and motions for me to come inside.

"What's happened?" Walper asks.

I sit down, look the principal right in her eye, and say this. I've got a new plan, one that should expedite things. I need Lawson and Elle, and this should do the trick.

"Coach Nathan. He hit me!"

# CHAPTER FOUR

The administration calls the police and my mother. I sit here in Principal Walper's office, crossing my legs and folding my arms. The Darkness pushes tears into my eyes. It feels ironic—that's one thing it wouldn't need to force if I had any control over my body.

This can't be real. I must be losing my mind. Perhaps something has infected my brain. Could it be a neurological disease? That would make more sense. I'm certainly not possessed by an evil force. There's no way my boyfriend was murdered, and certainly not by my own hand. And there is no such thing as—

My arms raise on their own. Principal Walper fishes for something in her desk. My middle fingers extend, and I am unable to stop them. Gasping, I don't know if the gesture is for the principal or for some retaliation to my own thoughts.

I cry, and it's easy to fit the narrative that the Darkness wants. It's the only thing that feels real right now. Sobbing, I hurt for what's happening to me, what's happened to Rob, and what else this thing inside me will make me do.

Its desires pump toxicity in my veins. Surrounded by a school full of children, the Darkness wants them all. We could snag a few on the way out, take them to the woods, and hide them until—

*Until what?*

What does it do with these children? Where are the missing kids? If they were dead, the others wouldn't remember them. Chills rip through my flesh. My skin crawls like worms move underneath. The Darkness kills some children, yes. But the Darkness also saves some of the missing children for something very special.

That's why we remember them, for now anyway, and why we get the Amber alerts, see their missing children posters on the walls, and watch the parents cry on the local news. If we can remember them, there's still a chance.

Panic spreads across Principal Walper's face. She has soft, caring eyes, and perhaps this is the first time she's had to deal with an accusation of assault between a faculty member and a student. She wastes no time getting the police here, and the empathy in her eyes turns to anger.

Using my words, the monster tells her what it wants her to hear, and my mind wanders back to Elle, Lawson, Teddy, Angelica, and Pauline. One of them is the Seer, the monster thinks. But which one?

I rub my legs, warmed by the sunlight that beams through the window.

Two officers stand next to Principal Walper. They ask me several questions, and I answer with one story. It's not the story I want to tell. I want to scream and ask for help, but the monster controls my words.

"I was late for practice yesterday. The punishment for being late is to mop the locker room floor, and I was supposed to do that over lunch today. I filled the mop bucket but accidentally knocked it over. It spilled on him, and Coach thought I did it on purpose. That's when he snapped and just hit me!"

Twisting and shaking, I fight for control of my mind. I hate this! I will break through. I have to!

Why did it choose me? Am I a random pawn in its plan, or do I serve a specific purpose? I'm not the Seer, or I'd be dead. But what is my meaning? Like a dream, I mentally toss and turn, but my body doesn't even flinch. The monster has planted roots in me, its hold deep and strong.

*I will never become evil! I will never willingly do what you want ever again!*

I've surprised the monster. I don't know how I know that, but something changes. I'm stronger than it expected.

*Anyone you care about I will hurt. Remember that, Christina. Remember Rob. Do you want to do the same thing to your mother when we get home? Think of all the blood you'll have to mop up.*

Rob's name stings me, sharp pain like stepping on a bee barefoot in the grass. Poor Rob. I should visit his family, but I can't even do that. Not that they'd remember him anyway.

Several hours of questioning go by, and it's dark outside. Finally, I'm allowed to go home.

If only I could ask Mom for help—but even if I could, would I? Mom's aged twenty years in the last ten. She looks more like a grandmother, thick streaks of gray burying any other color. This monster hurt her before. It drove away my father. No, even if I could ask for help, I'd leave Mom out of it.

I wish there was a way I could give Mom back all the years the evil took from her.

The Darkness has other plans, though. It's time to visit Elle. I search for inner strength, terrified that the monster within will use my body to kill her.

---

I GO INTO the garage and look around for a means of transportation to get to Elle's house. My body trembles at the sight of my bicycle. That's strange. Of all things, the Darkness avoids my bike.

Next to that sits my father's dusty motorcycle, unused in years, ever since the Darkness drove him away. Wiping dust from one of its mirrors, I watch flames dance in my eyes.

*There is something that could help*, I think. I turn sharply away from the mirror, guarding my thoughts carefully.

*Something beyond the woods. The Secret. Go there, and it could help.*

Yes. That's why it shuddered at the sight of my bicycle. I used to ride my bike to the Secret. My memories are fuzzy, but I think the Secret beyond the woods may have saved my life once before. Maybe it can save my life again.

Pain rushes in my head like a door slamming on a stormy night. I wince and cry out. Oh, the Darkness can hear me all right, and it's pissed.

My head turns back to the motorcycle's mirror. The image that looks back at me is enough to make me lose all control of bodily function, not that I was in control in the first place. A sinister smile, bloody lips, and flame-filled pupils stare back at me.

*You will stay away from that place, or I will kill you. You really don't care about your mother, do you? Help me, and I promise she will survive. Fight me, and I will make you kill her like you did Rob.*

*You don't have to hurt them!* I shout at the reflection.

"Oh, you stupid, stupid bitch." My own voice talks back to me. Is it possible this is all an illusion? Maybe the lunch ladies at school finally went nuts and drugged all the students. Yes, the one I saw who moved so mechanically, like she was a robot, drugged us all. She was stoned herself. That would explain the blank expression on her face.

It would also explain the emptiness in her eyes—that nothing that reminded me of—

Mom. Yes, she and the other staff members who walked around like zombies reminded me of my mother.

*What does that mean? What's going on here?*

"We have something very special planned for you, dear, if you choose to stop fighting me." Flames frame my image in the mirror. "If that magic gets out, if these kids really understood that Secret—"

*They could hurt you! They could stop you!*

"There's more to it than that," it snaps. "You think you can beat me if you understood the Secret? Or found some bonkers old lady to help you?" I cackle, a loud, delirious chuckle, my own voice laughing at me. Now I really feel out of sorts. "You should try. You think what you did before was bad? Wait until you hold your mother's beating heart in your hands."

Laughter pours out of me, but on the inside, I squirm. I will break free of this hold. And when I do—

Pain! I can't finish the thought. My head feels like it's been hit with a baseball, and my consciousness fades.

The next thing I know I'm parked in front of Elle's house, my body behind the driver's seat of Mom's car.

Apparently unfazed, the monster in me skips up to the front door like we're having a fun evening stroll down the yellow brick road, and I knock.

An ugly man answers, but I don't think it's her father. If I remember correctly, her parents are divorced. This must be her mother's hook-up.

"Can I help you?" His nose is crooked, and I stare at it instead of making eye contact.

"Is Elle home?" I ask.

"She's upstairs. Do I know you?"

The Darkness forces me to wear my good girl smile. "I'm on the team with Elle. We're friends. I've got a project due tomorrow that I put off, and I could use Elle's help."

"It's a little late, isn't it?"

*Keep it up, and I'll rip out your spine from the inside of your throat.*

"I'm sorry," I say. "It will just take a minute."

He nods but grunts, and my body runs upstairs to her bedroom.

"What are you doing here?" Elle asks. She wears an oversized T-shirt and sweatpants and brushes her thick, golden hair.

"I need to talk to you." I walk into her room without waiting for an invitation and sit on her bed. "Look," I start. I pound on the inside, an incessant knocking to drive it away. I want out, and I'm not giving up.

*Very well, bitch, let's speed things up.*

"What happened to your face?" Elle asks, referring to my bruises.

"That's what I want to tell you about," I say. "But first, I'm sorry I haven't been closer. This year on the team—I don't know where my head has been. You're doing great in *everything* it seems." I take a little breath and the Darkness adjusts my tone. "I've been jealous of you, but I also missed our friendship. I miss those slumber parties and staying up all night talking."

"Where's this coming from?" Elle asks, her eyebrows lifting suspiciously.

"There's something you need to know," I tell her, my voice hard and low. "And I don't think you're gonna like it."

She crosses her arms and leans back in her desk chair. "Okay?"

I bite my tongue, and it bleeds. I may not be able to stop the words from coming out of my mouth, but I'll be damned if I don't try. "It's about Coach." The Darkness swallows the blood in my mouth and flashes a humorless smile.

Elle's jaw drops.

"I wanted you to hear it from me first," I say. "It will be all over school tomorrow."

"*What* will be?"

It forces my eyes to tear up.

"Coach Nathan beat me up. He snapped and hit me. He gave me these bruises. He's crazy!"

"The *hell* he did," she says and doesn't even blink.

My heart sinks. Why is Elle so defensive of Coach Nathan? Not that I agree with what the Darkness is doing, but that's a grown man taking advantage of a teen girl. That's not cool.

"Yes, bitch, he did." I'd gasp at the words coming out of my mouth if I could. I try to bite my tongue again, but Elle has pissed it off. "I reported it. The cops will be arresting him any minute, if they haven't already."

Elle stands and gets right in my face. "You're lying! You're jealous all right. Jealous of a lot of things including him and me. So, you made this up. How could you?"

*What do you want with Elle? You've got me. Just take me back to your stupid woods and use me!*

Pain rushes into my head again. If this evil is powerful, why does it need us? There's something I haven't figured out yet, and in that something might be the secret to defeating it.

The Darkness yells back at me with its own thoughts. *What I tried to do with Fiara failed, but I'll try again with all your friends. I will be born—*

It stops abruptly. Of course! How could I be so stupid? The monster is looking for human flesh to take over. It can control people like it is doing with me, but only for short amounts of time. It must want to not only consume one of them—but to become one of them. Is that it?

*Close, Christina. You're so close to getting it, but that won't change what I need to do.* The Darkness turns its attention back to Elle.

"He hurt me, Elle. He's an abuser. Scum!"

Tears roll down my cheeks. The Darkness doesn't need to force them. They rush out easily. "I think I can help him. I mean, *we* can help him."

Her face flashes with confusion, and a nervous tremble rocks her hands. "What do you mean?" Elle asks.

"We take him to... to the Secret. I know you know about it," I say, as her face twists again, this time with surprise. "I know about it, too. It's the only thing that can wipe away evil." I take a deep breath and look away. "I think it can erase memories and even change time. Do you remember that?"

Elle bursts into tears. "I can't believe he would hurt you. I'm sorry," she says, rubbing her eyes. "If we take him there, will it keep him from getting in trouble?"

I nod slowly.

"What about my relationship? Will he still want me?"

"Of course," I say, only because it's what she wants to hear.

She breathes deeply, and I remain silent to let her calm down for a moment. Then I ask, "Do you remember where to go?"

"I think so. We have to go through... through something bad, though. Do you know? My memory is weird. There are woods, and... Darkness." She swallows hard, and her face reddens. I can tell that even saying the word brings back more of her memory.

"Yes, there is a monster in the woods that we must get through first in order to reach the Secret. We did it as children. We can do it again. Call Coach and tell him where to meet us. We'll walk through the Darkness together."

Inside, I fill with confusion. Beyond the woods is the Secret, the one that may give me the strength to break free! Surely, the Darkness knows that. Or—is it tricking me?

Fear rushes through me. I'd shake, scream, and run if I had any control over my body.

*What are you going to do?*

All I hear is laughter, and my body turns cold.

Elle reaches for her phone and calls Coach. "Leave a message if he doesn't answer," I say, wondering if the police have arrested him yet. "And hope for the best."

But Nathan does answer.

*Just wait and see what we do to them.* Internally, my head splits with pain at the high-shrieking laughter only I can hear. But even through the pain, I hold on to a shred of hope.

I don't know what the Darkness will do before we get to the Secret. But the Secret has power—just as much power as the evil that controls me. If we can get it to first, we have a chance, and I can at least regain control of myself, I hope.

It may be my only chance.

# CHAPTER FIVE

We drive in silence, but Elle fidgets. The drive makes me nervous. There's another trick, one I had forgotten when I drove down here with poor Rob. Not that I'm in control, but if I want to find the true power of the Secret, I'm not supposed to drive.

We're supposed to... I remember the Darkness trembling at the sight of my bicycle. Yes, we need that. Perhaps it takes us on a different path or something, but I can't do anything about that now.

Elle twirls her golden hair, bounces her knee, and stares out the window. We pull up near the field where I had that picnic with my cousin Amber years ago.

When I park, we exit the car without talking. It's a quiet walk, dark except for a sliver of moonlight. Up the gravel path we go and then we reach the entrance.

The trees open and welcome us. Elle doesn't flinch, but her eyes widen.

"When's the last time you were here?" I ask.

"I'm not sure," she whispers, barely audible. "I was gonna come with Lawson, but, well, he hasn't been talking to me much these days."

We walk through the opening, and she marches ahead.

"We're supposed to move quickly," she says. "I remember now."

"Are you sure?" The Darkness wants to toy with her. "I think it's the opposite. The slower the better."

"No," she says with certainty. "Fast, otherwise... oh, God! It's here."

The woods burst with palpable energy.

"Elle!" It's a man's voice, and it's calling from way up ahead, from the other side of the woods.

"Hey!" Elle shouts back and she takes off running. She's fast —she's the best on the cross-country team after all, but surely, she'll trip on one of the many tree roots popping out from the ground.

There's more energy here than I've felt before. There's obviously something special about Elle. Just her presence here electrifies something in the woods. It hungers for her. The Darkness forces my body to race after her, and I trip over a tree root from the ground.

*Shit, shit, shit.* The monster swears. It's afraid. Now, if only I could find a way to get it out of me.

"Hurry or it will catch us!" Elle yells.

The Darkness cackles. *Oh, yes, I will catch Elle and Nathan and everyone I want. Christina,* the voice within me warns, *if you fight me now, I'll eat your body. I will annihilate you. I'll leave your dead heart on the ground for the worms to ingest, and I'll go to your house and eat your mother, too.*

*Do you understand me?!?*

My stomach turns, and bile rises in my throat. I scream internally, hoping to distract the Darkness with my cries.

It calls to its shadow that slumbers in the pit, and the shadow bursts through me. The evil here—it is one monster and one-hundred monsters all at once. It can become so many things. I yelp in pain.

The Darkness isn't lying. It's going to kill me. No—worse, if that's possible—it's going to eat me.

The shadow spins and faces me. Long, sharp teeth threaten me from a hungry mouth. Filled with panic and adrenaline, I find whatever strength I have left, and in control of my own voice for just a second, I have enough power to shout two words.

"ELLE! RUN!"

The shadow turns. Back in control, the Darkness searches the woods through my eyes.

Elle is gone. Did she hear me?

"NO!" The Darkness yells and runs toward the top of the woods.

This is the path that leads to the Secret.

I walk forward and stumble out. Ahead, Elle positions herself by Coach Nathan.

Elle stands on railroad tracks at the top of a rise, but when I approach the top, I tumble again. My body is exhausted. It doesn't matter who is in control right now. I barely have the energy to stand.

I place my hands on the railroad tracks to push up, and a rejuvenating electricity pulses from them.

"What is that bitch doing here?" Coach Nathan asks.

I freeze. He steps out from behind Elle and moves toward me.

"Why would you call me that?"

"Funny story," he says, adjusting his Worthlapp baseball cap. "Some bitch accused me of something I didn't do."

"Is that true?" Elle asks, her blue eyes wide with shock. "I knew he wouldn't do something like that!" She steps closer to Coach. "Why are we here, Christina?"

I take a deep breath. "Of course what I told you is true. Remember, we're here to help him. The magic is just up ahead. It can help us—him, I mean."

Coach Nathan shakes his head, and he scratches stubble on his chin. Shadows under his eyes make him look ten years older. "You should be in an insane asylum for your lies! Do you know what could happen to me?" His body shakes, and he looks like he's going to attack.

Coach reaches for Elle's arm. He looks at her, ignoring me for a second. I push all my mental energy into Elle. *"Elle, it's a trick! Help me!"*

Elle looks around in a panic. Did she hear me?!? Did I get through, even a little? The Darkness ignores me, and we move closer to them.

"We can help you," Elle tells Coach, and I wonder if the Darkness has slipped inside her, pushing her toward what it wants, slowly taking control of her like it did to me.

"That's why I wanted you to meet me here," she continues. "The Secret will help." Her gaze looks up to these giant Y-shaped wires that follow the direction of the railroad tracks. "We walk down the tracks, and off to the side, we'll find the entrance. If we can get to it, well, uh, there's, well, um, magic. Magic that can erase what you did to Christina."

"I didn't touch her," he says, drawing back quickly and folding his arms. "Principal Walper called me right away, and I didn't know what to do. At first, I thought she had found out about our relationship. But hitting Christina? I don't understand the accusation. It didn't happen."

He glares at me, and slowly Elle turns.

"What's going on here?" she asks. Her arms shake, and her chest rises.

*Elle, we have to get out of here! Don't let it in you! Can you hear me?*

"He's a horrible person, Elle. Look what he's done to you!" Was that my voice or the Darkness? Its grip is slipping, especially when it tries to control Elle. Confusion covers her face, like she's hearing other voices. I'm getting through. I may be able to push the Darkness out of me.

But then what? What if it takes over Elle instead?

"You and your lies," Nathan snaps at me. "I'm not going to let your lies ruin my life!"

"Nathan, it can't hurt," Elle says. "Even if you didn't do it, there's something special here. Maybe it can protect you and me."

She reaches for his hand, and she pulls him ahead. He whispers something fast.

They run toward the Secret.

I look at my hands. Am I me? Is the Darkness gone?

Answering my questions, my arms move against my will. My hand reaches into my bag. It takes out my knife, the same one that slashed Rob's throat. At the touch of it, my mind fills with more visions—a brown-skinned woman holding this handle, the blade sharp but curved, the tip of the blade coming right at me.

My heart sinks, and my hand grips the knife firmly. Horror rushes through me at the thought of another person dying by my hand.

The vision vanishes, and my body races after Elle and Nathan.

In seconds, we'll see the Secret, a magical place, a place I haven't seen since—

It doesn't matter. What matters is that it may give me the strength to break free and save Elle.

# CHAPTER SIX

Cool, crisp air—very different from that within the woods—whips at my face. Coughing, I sprint ahead at full speed, but I haven't caught up with Elle or Nathan.

Thoughts not belonging to me race through my mind.

*Consume. Devour. Transform.*

I rub my forehead with one hand and clench the knife with my other while scanning for Elle and Nathan. The railroad tracks look infinite, an ocean of never-ending steel.

I've gone too far, I think, and turn around. The Darkness doesn't know where to go, not exactly. It avoids this side of the woods. Its home and its power are below, and here—well, something else controls this part.

The Secret can help me break free, so why is the Darkness taking a risk to be here?

Because we didn't travel here the correct way, I think, remembering how the Darkness trembled at the sight of my bicycle, and how I failed with Rob, perhaps—in part—because I had forgotten about that.

I step slowly, listening and scanning the nature that surrounds the tracks. The entrance must be somewhere. Dizziness hits me. Maybe it's the air or fatigue, or maybe something's here that's more powerful than the force that controls me.

I search for some sign of movement, and then I see it! Bushes dance in the wind. Green and thick with life, they look more like hands gesturing a welcome than bushes. Yes, that should be the entrance. But is it a trick?

*There's more to life than you have ever known*, I tell my possessor. *You don't have to do this. Life is beautiful. That's the real magic, up ahead. You, this, whatever you are—it's ugly. Don't you understand?*

"No, you don't understand." I catch my reflection in a puddle of water near the railroad tracks, flames consuming my eyes. Listening to my own voice, powerless to control it, sends another shiver through me. "There is one path to complete power, and I will show you soon what that looks like."

I sense frustration. The Darkness tries to quiet me, but I'm stronger—much more so—than it expected.

The welcoming bushes and the trees part, and the ground warms my feet even through my shoes. The air is thin and sharp here, like pure oxygen. I follow the path, and laughter echoes from up ahead.

My shoulders tense, and I clench the knife. That's Nathan's laughter. What are they even laughing about? This doesn't make sense to me—a grown man with a teenage girl.

*He shouldn't be here!* I yell. *If this is the Secret, then this is a place of innocence, of renewal. He's not a good guy, or he wouldn't be with a student. He doesn't belong here, and neither do you!*

"Shut up!"

Elle and Nathan come into view, but I can't see what's behind them. Are we at the Secret, or is this some other place? Suddenly, the air turns cold, and my lungs burn, like I'm breathing in sharp, winter air.

I walk toward them, feeling a shortness of breath, and everything brightens.

Elle and Nathan hold hands, and a look of confusion spreads across Elle's face. This isn't what she remembers either. The magic isn't here. I hide the knife behind my back. My grip loosens. I try to take control and make the Darkness drop the knife, but I fail. It shakes my head at Nathan and Elle. Behind them, scurrying animals hide in the dark. There's something terribly unsettling and frightening about what's out here—a nocturnal energy, a madness, palpable fear of things that need the dark to survive.

Where's the Secret? Where's the magic?

My head hurts. I picture mental claws, and I tear at the monster from the inside, doing everything I can to stop it. My hand squeezes the knife handle. The Darkness still controls that. Then it sits my body down, crossed-legged on the ground. Kicking off my shoes, I hide the knife behind my back. It's trying to make me look helpless and innocent.

"I want to be better," the Darkness says with my voice to all of us. "Help me be better. Take me into the Secret."

And then I get it, or at least I think I do. Perhaps it needs humans to enter the Secret. Or maybe someone innocent. It's certainly not going to let Coach Nathan or the Darkness enter, at least I sure hope not. And after everything I've done, it may not allow me, either. The Secret is hiding somewhere back there, covering its magic with the cloak of night.

Nathan and Elle come closer, and the monster pushes tears out my eyes. They each reach out an arm, slowly, as if unsure how to comfort me. Nathan takes another step toward me, and that's when my arm swings out from behind my back.

Elle and Nathan look at me with more confusion than fear, and then my knife swipes at Nathan's throat—hard, deep, and fast.

Blood shoots out like a water gun, and it sprays all along the dirt. Nathan's face twists from misunderstanding to shock, and his hands dart up to cover his throat. The Darkness laughs and makes me stand. Elle screams in terror.

She wraps her arms around him.

I shout from the inside, kicking and stomping. The Darkness walks me over to Elle, still in complete control.

Crying, Elle holds Nathan in her arms and screams.

Laughing, the Darkness turns my body around.

We run.

I don't know if we're running from something or toward something.

I fear it's a little of both.

I return to the woods below the railroad tracks.

Goosebumps spread across my body as my skin meets a cool breeze. I slide down the hill from the tracks into the woods.

The shadow of the Darkness stands in front of me, and I repeatedly punch at the evil from inside.

I don't know if it's me who screams, but there's an ear-splitting shriek.

A burst of light—yellow, the deep yellow the Darkness didn't want me to see—flashes in the woods. It's like lightning. Every tree brightens for a split second. The leaves shake as if battling a storm. The yellow light surges again.

I gasp at the sight in front of me.

Deep, black oval eyes and a ravenous mouth appear ever so briefly on the shadow monster. Yellow light floods the woods for another second, and a dark, terrifying scream erupts from the shadow monster's hungry mouth.

Then, somehow, I eject the Darkness from my body. Or it leaves, perhaps called to join its shadow.

I'm not sure, and right now I really don't care. I'm finally one hundred percent me.

I crack my knuckles. I take my own deep breaths. I glare at the evil in front of me, and I decide to kill it or die trying.

The Darkness becomes one with its shadow, and the monster laughs. I look down at my hand, staring at the knife as Nathan's blood drips from it like a slow faucet leak.

"I don't care what happens to me!" I yell. "I'm not a little girl anymore. I *will* find a way to stop you."

It laughs again, and then surrounds me in its shadow form, spinning like a tornado.

Extending an arm, it begins to choke me. It's a physical impossibility—one arm stationary and choking me while the rest of its essence spins around me, dirt flying into my eyes and mouth. My throat clenches. I gasp for air. I close my eyes, yell, and charge right at it. I strike it, releasing a surge of electricity, a blast of that mysterious yellow light.

The shadow shrieks and dives into the ground. But not before sending me one last thought. *Well played, my sweet girl. You're learning what makes you so special. Just wait until you see what I can do when it's time to consume you.*

---

ADRENALINE RACING THROUGH my veins, I charge toward the pit. I still have the knife that slashed Nathan's throat and Rob's, and I'm determined to do one more thing before I leave. I'm going to find the heart of the Darkness and plunge the knife directly into it.

I spring ahead, approaching the pit. It's a black hole in the woods.

I dive into it, not afraid of what will happen, only scared of what may happen if I don't try.

I kick my legs, and I'm floating. The more I kick, the more I float around, like I am swimming in air.

I'm surrounded by darkness. Not layers of dirt, but miles of nothing, an unknown realm, perhaps not hell exactly, but a kind of hell.

I search for a heart or something to stab. Why would I have thought I'd find it here? Something... something in my subconscious, or a memory I've forgotten.

I don't see anything, though, and I'm losing oxygen. I can't breathe! I scream, releasing the final bit of air in my lungs, and still I can't find anything.

I pass out, and the dreams come.

Lawson and Teddy play some kind of game outside. They're chasing one another and look happy. Teddy's brother Sam joins them, and the three run like puppies with endless energy and laughter. The dream shifts settings to inside school. Angelica sits with her friend Pauline at lunch. Pauline shows Angelica something on her phone, and they giggle. Outside, Coach Nathan calls Elle, and she sneaks back to the athletic storage shed. He pulls her close and kisses her hard. Elle arches her back and moans.

I'm back in my basement bedroom suddenly, looking into a mirror and feeling my chest. Mom stumbles around upstairs, and a car honks. Rob. Oh, Rob—I'm so sorry. I wish I could do something to bring you back.

Then Fiara appears, and her hair dances. Her eyes flash from blue to red. That pale, clay-like skin looks like it could break and fall off. She didn't always look like that—the Darkness did that to her. Or was it the Secret that did that? Maybe the Secret isn't good, and I just can't remember.

It all happened the day we protected Asher. Or tried to protect him. But what good did that do? The Darkness still found a way to get Asher, and our childhood friend went missing like so many others.

*Find Charlamae.* There's another voice within me, a sweeter, kinder voice. The voice of the Secret. Yes, Charlamae. That was Asher's grandmother, and besides me, she's the only person who remembers that Asher even existed. Charlamae is a part of this, and I will find her, too.

I float through my basement floor and pass by Fiara and Asher, where dozens of missing children cry.

*Why? Why do you do this?*

I keep floating and appear outside next to Rob. He turns to me and puts a gentle hand on my face. "There is no power in life, only in death," he whispers. Then he vanishes, and Ronnie the Rattler appears. I'm back in the faculty bathroom, and this time he doesn't just hit me. He removes his pants, and he forces my legs open. I cry and try to shove him away, but it does no good. He pins down my arms, and when he takes down his pants, his penis hisses at me.

It's a snake.

The snake attacks me and it hurts. I yell for help, and Ronnie's face changes. It's dark and long, and it's not a face at all. It forms into the shadow with dark oval eyes and that ravenous mouth, and it laughs at me.

Blood drips from the snake's head, having bitten me several times all over my body.

The night returns, and I'm back in the woods out of the pit. The tightness in my throat goes away, and I stare into the black nothing.

My body hurts like someone slashed me all over with a sword. I'm awake now, and I wonder what's worse, the nightmares or the infinite darkness that surrounds me? The Darkness punishes me for fighting back, for not cooperating. The pain becomes unbearable.

I look around, but I don't know where I am, just that I'm on solid ground.

Reality and my sanity become questionable, but I know some things for sure. My hand slashed both Rob and Nathan's throat. Dozens of children are missing, and I don't know where they are. And the Darkness has the power to kill me or use me to kill others.

Putting my face in my hands, I cry until I pass out. My body sprawls across the cold dirt, a premonition perhaps of what will become of me.

# CHAPTER SEVEN

Webs of sunlight break through my basement window, and I wake up slowly in my bedroom. Pushing blankets off my chest, I swing my legs out of bed and stand. That's when the pain hits me again, hard, like someone threw a bowling ball into my stomach.

*What happened?*

My memory is foggy. I walk to my nightstand, sit, and force a brush through my tangled hair. My hazel eyes blink back at me, and I'm grateful to not see any fire. Dirt lines my face, and my chest looks like I was someone's punching bag.

Then I remember the dream that I had. I sit down and close my eyes. Something about the dream is very important.

Who am I? That's the first question that bounces through my mind, and I'm so dizzy I have to hold onto the arms of the chair.

Am I me? The real me? Where did the Darkness go? I pinch myself to make sure I'm not dreaming. I look into my bedroom mirror. Still no hints of orange or red. Thank God. The dream fades away, and I try to remember yesterday.

Seriously, what the hell have I done?

I'll call Rob. He can help me, I hope. Help me remember and help me heal.

But first I need a long shower, and I don't even care if I'm late for school. I walk to my bathroom and let the water heat up.

"Fiara, are you here?" I ask softly and look around. She could help me, too, if she'd be willing. But she's terrified of the Darkness. It's hurt her more than it's ever hurt me, and that's saying something.

My body shakes with a cold chill.

Fiara's pain came with the ability to hide in plain sight and vanish whenever she wanted.

So, I look carefully. "Fiara, if you're here, please talk to me. I need your help."

No response. I sigh and get in the shower.

The hot water hits my skin. I lather up my loofa with about six times as much body wash as I need, but I want the soap to cover me completely. I scrub everywhere.

I rinse, towel off, and start to vomit. I can't hold it back.

Memory stings like a hornet. Rob is gone. I'll never see him again.

More tears, vomit, and snot run out of me, and when it finally ends, I step back in the shower. I let the water wash over me again, and I can't stop crying about what the evil has made me do.

I killed Rob, and it made me kill Coach, too. No, it wasn't me! But it was. It's all so confusing and painful, and I cry until my head hurts too much to continue.

I lay on the bathroom floor, my bare skin against the cold tiles. It feels calming, and I would prefer to stay here all day. But I can't. I have to be stronger than this. I have to find the others the Darkness wants and talk to them. I will not let it make me feel worthless again. There's no alternative but to fight or watch others die.

We have to understand the Secret, too. What exactly are its powers, and what does it do? Why couldn't we get to it—a layer of misty blackness had clouded it, blocked us from it? And, of course, what is the Darkness planning to do with all the missing children it has captured but not yet killed? Even though I didn't see them, they must be somewhere, or the people in this town wouldn't remember them.

The missing children—that means someone else has been helping. From what I understand, the monster can't leave its woods. But it can send its shadow to control someone. Only one person at a time, as far as I know, which is why it lost some power when bouncing between Elle and me in the woods.

And it loves to make people do terrible things.

I wish I understood why others forget about the people it ultimately kills, but that's another mystery I have yet to figure out.

"Hi, Christina," Mom mumbles when I enter the kitchen. Old makeup stains her face, and she pulls at a timeworn, raggedy green sweater. "How are you?"

I want to hold her hand and beg for help, but she's been through so much. I'm not sure if she can survive more. I reach for her arm and put my head on her shoulder.

"Did you sleep okay?" she asks.

I breathe in her smell. Mom is still here. Maybe she's buried under the effects of prescription cocktails, but I still have my mother. That's something. Maybe I can find a way to help her, too. Maybe she can return with me to the Secret.

Where is my father? If I called him and told him that the evil returned, would he help us?

Or would he hurt us? Those were bad days, and the Darkness did more than just kill. It tortured us in many ways, more things I wish I could forget and certainly don't want to think about now.

I pull Mom closer and hug her. This is all my fault. It's my fault she's been hurting all these years, that Dad left us, that Rob is gone.

It's my fault that Fiara is who she is, and that Asher and dozens of other kids have gone missing. For every ounce of confidence I muster, there's a ton of worthless thoughts threatening to paralyze me.

"What was that for?" Mom asks when I pull away.

"No reason." I open the fridge. I don't feel like eating, but I'm thirstier than I've ever been.

"Are you taking the bus today?"

I don't have a ride anymore now that Rob is gone.

"Yeah, the bus," I say and take a drink of juice.

Mom walks closer to me and puts a cold, frail hand on my shoulder. "It's back, isn't it? The Dark...?"

Mom is present. It won't last long, though, and I don't know if there's anything I can say that will help. So, I lie.

"No, no. Didn't sleep well is all."

Screechy breaks ring from the street, and that means the bus has arrived. I walk up to Mom and hug her again. "I love you." She smiles gently at me.

Then I take a deep breath and head for the bus. Crying will only get me so far. If I really want to help, I have to keep moving.

---

I SEARCH THE bus for the one I need to talk to, another who may understand what this evil is. Students stare at me and whisper to each other. I tilt my head to hide my bruises. My eyes find the boy I need, his overly styled chestnut hair impossible to miss. Taking a seat next to Lawson, I say, "Hey. We need to talk."

He sits up straight. "What's going on with you?"

How much I should tell him? Would he believe me or think I've gone off the wall? Looking around the bus, I search for anyone else who might be important. There's no sign of Elle, even though I thought she and Lawson took the same bus. I suppose that's lucky, as she and I need to have a very awkward conversation.

Fiara isn't here or hasn't made herself visible, which is both odd and comforting. I don't know what I'd do if I saw her eyes turn red.

I reach for Lawson's hand, and he gives it to me. "Can we just sit like this for a bit? I need to get a grip on my thoughts, and I'm gonna need your help."

The bus breaks suddenly, and we push against the seat in front of us to catch our balance, pushing Lawson and I closer together.

He lets go of my hand and moves away. I want to tell him that I know he's not into girls and that I just need a friend for a damn minute.

"My help for what? Is it bad?" he asks, his voice cracking.

"Worse than any nightmare you can imagine." Lawson stares at me with worry, but I don't have the energy to say anything else. It feels like the beginning of a very long day.

The bus pulls up at the front of Worthless High a few minutes later. "Let's talk after school, okay?" Lawson nods and heads to class, but he turns his head around several times to look at me, his lips pressed tightly together.

---

BEFORE FIRST HOUR, I go to the commons and look for something to eat. My stomach hurts, but I need something. I never did get anything at home.

Browsing the vending machines, I can't decide on anything. I sigh, step back, and bump into someone.

"Oh, sorry," I say, and turn around. My hands drop to my side, and my mouth dries up instantly.

It's Coach Nathan. He wiggles his blue Worthlapp hat and grins at me. He licks his lips, slowly, and his liquid-dark eyes swirl.

"Good morning, Christina." His voice is hard and cold.

"What? Oh my God! What? No!" Absolutely not. This is impossible. I'm not saying I wanted to kill him, but I know what happened.

Which means whoever is standing in front of me is not human.

He smiles wider, and there's a spark in his eyes. A fire!

My body trembles, and a sour taste crawls onto my tongue. He's not possessed like I was. It's not even the Darkness itself. I'd recognize that voice anywhere. It's as if the Darkness turned Coach into one of its monsters.

He's pure evil, a monster using his human flesh.

He touches me with an icy cold hand, sending shivers down my spine, and he laughs.

"You're so pretty," Coach says. "Why don't you come see me? Privately, outside, where we store the athletic equipment?" Saliva spills out of his mouth when he speaks. My stomach drops, and I cover my mouth, trying to keep myself from puking.

I turn around and run to my class. I don't look back. The bell already rang, and now I'm late. I don't know what's going on, but I can't face Coach—or the Darkness—like this. I can't do it alone. I've already messed up too much. I need help.

---

FIRST HOUR IS my mythology class with Mr. Lee. Elle and Lawson both sit up front. Elle's here! What happened after I left? She had held Coach's body and cried. Did she see him become the monster he is? I need to speak with her. I take a seat in the back next to Angelica, and Mr. Lee waves at me. He doesn't ask for a pass or reprimand me, and for that I'm grateful. I have to get control of the dozens of thoughts swimming in my head, and then I'll ask for help.

And therapy. Definitely therapy, please.

"I want to spend today talking about your project," he tells the class and scans the room. "Christina, why don't you tell us what you've discovered?"

Elle and Lawson turn around and look at me. Lawson gives me a weird look, and Elle glares. She has to know it wasn't really me who killed Coach, right? Her eyes say otherwise, though.

I sit up straighter and address the class. I can't do this alone. It's time to say at least some of what I know.

"Mister Lee, there is magic here. There's something... incredible here. But it's not easy to find."

"There's something else you know, isn't there, Christina?" Mr. Lee asks. Lips curl up on his chubby cheeks, and he adjusts his pants, which are strained at his waist. Dark eyes wait for a response through his brown-framed glasses.

"There's something evil," I say.

"Yes, there certainly is." Mr. Lee nods, adjusting the glasses on his thick nose. "Tell us about it."

"Before you can find the Secret, you have to go through... through *it*."

Mr. Lee smiles gently. "Yes, that's right. What can you tell us about it?"

I hesitate. Why are we even in a mythology class? First hour high school? And a lot of the people the Darkness wants are in this class?

Could there be a bigger force working against the Darkness right now? The voice that I heard near the Secret—the one who told me to find Charlamae. There's more going on than I understand, and I don't know what I should say.

Mr. Lee walks toward the window and looks out when I don't respond. "Look out at the world. Look up. It's infinite, isn't it? The universe is bigger than any of us can imagine. It's infinite, and it's growing bigger every day." He walks down one of the rows and looks at another student who has his phone out. "But we'd rather look at our technology than the wonders of the world."

"This project I created for you is about more than meets the eye. It's about understanding a piece of this universe and realizing the power that is in our own backyard. There's an evil that must be defeated," he says. "The Secret I've told you about is just the beginning. Something much deeper haunts this world. It's already taken lives. You just can't remember."

"Is that why so many kids have gone missing?" Angelica asks. She places her elbows on her desk,

"Yes, I'm afraid so. Kids, there's something I need to tell you,"

Mr. Lee says. He moves to the front of his teacher's desk and sits on it. His legs dangle on the side, and it makes him look like a child, but the expression on his face is very grim. "The police are doing their best, so please don't think I'm criticizing them. But I've been doing my own, um, investigation. The project I assigned you, to be honest, is my way of asking for your help. I can't sit on the sidelines. We must help find the missing children."

"How do we do that?" Lawson asks.

Mr. Lee looks back at me. "Christina, do you have something you want to say?"

"I know we can fight it. I want to fight it, but I need help."

"Excellent," Mr. Lee says. "We have a lot of work to do, and I hope you all are ready. I have a lot to tell you about the ways of the world and secrets you know little to nothing about."

# PART TWO

## LAWSON

"So, this is my life. And I want you to know that I am both happy and sad and I'm still trying to figure out how that could be."

—Stephen Chbosky, *The Perks of Being a Wallflower*

# CHAPTER EIGHT

What in the hell does Christina want with me? What's going on with her and everyone in Mr. Lee's class? So freakin' weird.

"Here, Gracie," I call my family's ten-year-old Australian Shepherd. She rolls over, and I crouch down and rub her belly, wondering what Christina is going to say to me when I see her next. Before school let out, she texted and asked if she could come over to my house this evening and talk.

I stand and look at myself in the long bedroom mirror on the back of my door. Ugh. I wish I could gain some weight. Mom tells me it's not cool to complain about being thin, but why not? I don't like it. I'm not saying I want to be fat, but I'm tired of being a bag of bones. I rub my shirtless chest, wishing for more. Sometimes I hate who I see in the mirror. I don't even know who that person is.

At least I have my hair. It's the only thing I like about my appearance, and Dad knows. I want to grow it out, and Dad likes to joke that one day I could go bald and lose it all. Why do parents have to be cruel?

Grabbing a fresh shirt, I get dressed and look out my window, which faces the street. The neighbors across the street are old—the kind of old where they mow the yard like every day because they have nothing else to do. Old Man Darius leans against his lawn mower. His mouth hangs wide, and his eyes turn toward me. His motionless head faces the mower, but the eyes roll, locking contact with me. His expression is blank, but hair rises on my arms. Old Man Darius gives me the creeps.

"Wanna go outside, Gracie?" She shakes her Aussie butt and waddles downstairs. I follow, eager to get out of the old man's view. Mom and Dad make dinner together in the kitchen.

"Lawson!" Mom screeches. Dad fries some bacon and wears his favorite apron over a shirt and tie. It has a Scoops Ahoy logo, and he never misses a chance to wear it. "Who's this girl that's coming over?"

I sigh and open the back door for Gracie.

"I remember the first girl I had in my bedroom," Dad says, not waiting for my response. "Your grandparents would always make me keep the door open a crack. I felt my first boob in that room with my parents outside." He tilts his head back and laughs. "Speaking of boobs, where's Elle been? Now she's got some nice—"

Mom slaps Dad on the arm, interrupting him. *Gross*. My father should not be talking about the boob size of my friends.

"Christina is coming over. She's just a friend," I say.

"Stop tormenting your son, and don't talk about girls like that," Mom tells him. It makes me want to hug her. "You don't have to keep your door open, either. You can shut it." She smiles at me, and that smile says something more. I know Mom knows more about me than I've ever told her. I know she'll be okay whenever I do—but I don't know how to talk about certain things, especially around my father who values boobs more than anyone I've ever known.

"Hey," Mom calls. "Um, isn't that Elle?"

"What?" I gaze out the front door. Old Man Darius hasn't moved. His eyes still focus up on my bedroom window, even though his head faces the mower. God, he's weird.

Sure enough, it's not Christina who approaches, but Elle.

Elle was my best friend when we were kids. We used to be neighbors years ago, but during junior high, her parents divorced. Her father moved out of state, so she spent her summers with him. Her mom got a smaller apartment in town. Elle only moved a few blocks away, but our relationship wasn't the same after that. Childhood friendships are made and broken simply due to geography, I guess.

"Two girls in your room, tonight?" Dad says with a cheesy grin. "What. A. Stud." He makes a fist for me to bump, but I leave him hanging.

"Hi, Mister and Missus Russo," Elle says when I let her in. I glance one more time at the house across the street. Old Man Darius turns his head. His eyes are closed now, but his mouth opens wide. He sticks his tongue out at me, and it dances like a—

"Law, can we talk?" Elle asks, and I shift my attention to her, quickly shutting the door.

Gracie barks at the back. I let her inside, and Elle and I run upstairs before my father can make any more inappropriate comments. Gracie barks enthusiastically at Elle. She hasn't seen her in some time.

We sit on my bed, and Gracie hops up with us. She rolls over, and Elle pets her belly. I'm about to tell her that Christina is coming over, but she speaks first. "I gotta tell you something." Her blonde hair bounces off her shoulders, and she sits up straighter. "It's been killing me. I haven't been able to tell anyone, but you have to promise you'll keep it a secret." She looks around my room, like she's making sure no one else is here. I follow her gaze, and something flashes in the corner. Gracie barks and puts her front legs across my lap.

A chill rips through me like I've seen a ghost. Is someone in my room?

Elle looks back at me. "Pinkie swear?" She leans in close and extends her right pinkie finger. I wrap my mine around it. Elle takes a deep breath and pushes her hair back. "Um, well, you know Coach Nathan?"

"Uh huh," I say. Coach Nathan is the kind of guy that every girl and a few of the guys have a crush on. He's hot. I'd never say that out loud to anyone else, but I may have thought about him on a few lonely nights.

"Now, you promise, right?"

Elle's never looked so serious. This is the girl who played tag with me, and the girl I went on endless bike rides with beyond our neighborhood to areas we weren't allowed to go. This is the girl to whom I told all my secrets. Well, almost all. She had told me hers, too, or so I think. But those deep blue eyes tell me something's different. Yeah, she has a secret, all right.

"I need to start at the beginning." She folds her arms over her chest. "We've been seeing each other."

I sit straight up, startling Gracie. "What?"

"We're together." She bites her lip. "It's serious. I didn't want anyone to know."

"No shit. It's illegal, for one. He's an adult. How could you?" My hands shake. I squeeze my fists so hard that my fingernails dig into my skin.

She reaches out and holds my hand. "Please don't be mad." She smiles, and her beauty is overwhelming. She's not the kid who used to ride bikes with me.

"But that's not the only reason I need to talk to you." She squeezes my hand and puts her head on my shoulder. "Law... I went back to... to *it*. With him." She looks away.

I take my hand away. Nausea rises in my throat. "Why would you take him?" My heart pounds against my chest, and sweat trickles down my forehead. Gracie licks me on the cheek.

"It's complicated. Christina came after us. You know what you heard about Coach supposedly hitting her? That was a lie." Her eyes glisten. Are those tears forming?

"I don't understand." I get off the bed and walk around my room. Shaking my head, I lean against the wall near my window. I don't mean to look out, but Old Man Darius is still there, standing in the center of the lawn. He's laughing. His eyes remain closed, but he's clearly chuckling. I shut my curtains.

"She killed him," she says. "Or tried to."

"What the—?" My jaw drops.

"It didn't work. The Secret—that's why I had to take him there. It healed him. He's fine. But I don't know what to do about Christina or any of this!"

She pulls at the bottom of her shirt, a light blue way-too-tight T-shirt that says *Angel* in cursive.

"You have to end it," I finally say. "With Coach. It never should have started."

Her eyes widen and sparkle. "Law, I'm in love."

I don't have any words for her. My stomach feels sick. I can't even look at her.

A soft knock sounds on my door.

Oh, shit.

"Lawson?" It's Christina, of course. Christina, who supposedly tried to kill the love of Elle's life. Talk about an exciting day in my bedroom. I open the door for her, catch my father grinning at me, and slam the door quickly.

Elle leaps out of bed. "What is she doing here?"

Gracie growls at Christina at first, but then her tail wags, and she nuzzles Christina's legs, welcoming her into the room.

"Oh, Elle!" Christina says as she enters, giving Gracie a quick pet. Flashes of green and yellow light spark in the corners of my eyes. "I'm glad you're here, too. Please. I need to talk with both of you."

Elle looks over at me for some kind of answer. Like I know what the hell is going on!

"You've seen Coach?" Christina asks.

Elle nods. "He's fine. No thanks to you." Elle looks like she's about to run away or call the police, which is what I'd do. But I suppose logical thoughts have long since been forgotten.

Christina takes a deep breath and wipes her red-rimmed hazel eyes. "First of all, I'm sorry. That wasn't me, but I'm still sorry. I was being controlled. Possessed." Her jaw tightens, and she puts a hand over her mouth. She holds it there for a moment, thinking. When she lowers her hand, her face looks uncertain. "I know how that sounds. But if anyone can understand, it's the two of you. I know you both remember the Secret. Right? That's why I'm here."

My throat burns with bile, and my stomach rolls. The room spins. Have I been drugged? I see things—ghosts, strange flashes of light, creepy neighbors—then this conversation? What the hell is in this town's water?

"I need your help to stop the Darkness," Christina adds. "It wants to kill you." She says it so causally that I pinch myself to make sure I'm not in a nightmare. What fresh hell is this? "But second of all, Coach is not fine. He's a monster now. Well, he always was, apparently," she says, rolling her eyes. That's the only thing she's said that I understand. "But he's a monster of the Darkness now. A monster's monster."

Elle groans, and the color washes away from her face. "You've got to be kidding me. Coach was fine last night when—"

"What are we supposed to do about it?" I interrupt. My body feels tense, and my eyes comb my room. The air feels cold. I don't see anything but my *Rick and Morty* posters hanging on the wall, and not even those can make me smile right now.

"We have to talk with Mister Lee," Christina says. "I need to be honest with him about what's happened." She looks sternly at Elle. "And so do you. We all do. We're in a lot of danger. I know you know stuff too, and what you know can help."

Elle shakes her head incredulously.

"Do you think he's still at school?" I ask, rubbing my cold arms.

"It can't hurt to check," Christina suggests. She shivers, too, and her eyes narrow. She inspects my room, and I hope I picked up all my dirty underwear. Even though I try to keep my room clean, Gracie takes great joy in dirty socks and day-old underwear, digging them out of the hamper.

Christina returns her attention to us and continues. "I wanted to talk to you guys before I said anything more to Mister Lee, especially in front of the entire class." Elle frowns, but I reach for her hand. Christina nods encouragingly, and we rush out of my bedroom. Gracie barks at the corner of my room, probably smelling but not finding my dirty socks, but then follows us downstairs. I hope Dad doesn't stop us and make some stupid joke. Elle's reluctant at first, and I pull her hand to get her to move. "Don't you wanna know what's going on? This is beyond nuts!"

"Just remember your promise," she whispers to me. My stomach turns again. What she's done and what she wants—ugh. Gross. Christina knows, though? I guess I'm just not supposed to tell anyone else.

Thankfully we avoid my parents, and Elle gives in. I say goodbye to Gracie, and we all run straight to Worthless High. Toothless Tonya, the wife of Old Man Darius, steps out her front door and waves at us as we leave. She flashes a smile that's all gums. She laughs at us too, and Darius continues to chuckle.

Christina and Elle either don't pay them any attention, or don't comment, which goes to show how much absurdity they've already experienced. We race to the high school. I struggle to keep up. Both girls are athletes and running a couple of miles to school is a walk in the park for them. I can barely breathe, but I force my legs to not give up, not wanting to seem weak. Not wanting to feel worthless like I have so many times before.

---

When we arrive at school that evening, the empty halls smell of cleaning solution, and our footsteps reverberate eerily throughout the corridors. My face is burning, and I'm soaked through my shirt. Christina and Elle don't look like they've even broken a sweat. I really need to start working out.

Finally catching my breath, I take in more of our surroundings. It's weird to be here when no one else is. A sea of dark lockers contrasts with the bright white floors. Take away the lockers, and this could be a hospital. Add some barbed wire, and it could be a prison.

All the classrooms are empty. Well, all except one, thankfully. In our mythology classroom, Mr. Lee sits at his desk, grading papers.

Christina clears her throat.

"Good evening, kids." Mr. Lee puts down his pen and adjusts his brown-framed glasses. "To what do I owe this surprise visit?" He smiles suspiciously, and although I know it's impossible, I can't help but wonder if he somehow expected us.

Mr. Lee is a short, heavy Chinese man. He is almost completely bald except for a few strands of thin hair, probably from spending so many years working with teenagers. He looks like he should be retiring any day now, yet he's here working later than anyone else.

Elle and Christina step forward, and Mr. Lee gestures toward the front row. We take a seat, and I wait to see who is going to speak first.

"You've been talking to us about the Secret," Christina says. "The mythology of our community."

"What exactly do you know?" Elle huffs. "I mean—what is going on in Worthlapp?"

I swallow hard, and my stomach rumbles.

"There's something magical here in Worthlapp," Mr. Lee says. "Something dangerous, too. But I have a feeling you kids already know that much."

"What do you know about the Darkness?" Christina asks. I want to know and don't want to know all at the same time. I could be home watching TV. Instead, it feels like I'm about to enter a war.

Mr. Lee folds his arms and looks at us like a parent who is about to tell us the family dog has to be put down. "Sadly, I have put you all in a terrible position. To remember the Secret puts you in the path of the Darkness. But to not remember—well, it could result in our destruction."

I place my shaky hands against my stomach. "What do you mean?" I ask.

He turns and moves behind his desk, turning his monitor so we can see. "These poor children. Look at them. These are the kids that have gone missing from Worthlapp." He removes his glasses so he can wipe his eyes. "It started with just a couple kids. But more and more have gone missing. I've been trying to find them, but I need help. I've talked with police and other adults. But it's your help I need."

I feel like I'm going to throw up. Why us? I'm too scared to ask the question because I'm afraid the answer will make it impossible for me to decline.

"How do you know that it's the Darkness that's taking them?" Elle asks.

"Because it's not the first time this has happened," he says. Christina shifts nervously in her desk. Elle looks about as confused as my stomach is sick. "What do you all remember about the Secret?"

Elle sighs and looks at me. "Lawson and I found the magic once. When we were kids. Don't you remember?"

"Yeah," I say. "I can't believe that I forgot."

"I will teach you what I know about Mofa and Kang Fu." He puts his hands on his hips and stands tall. "Mofa is what we call the Darkness in Mandarin and Kang Fu is the Secret."

Mofa. Kang Fu. What in the hell? Nope. I could go home now and throw Frisbee for Gracie.

"This isn't the first time children have gone missing in Worthlapp," Mr. Lee continues. "It happened when you were kids, but you may not remember it. It has happened many times. Sometimes the monster waits just a few years. Sometimes the monster sleeps for decades."

"What does the Darkness do to these kids? What could it do to us?" Elle asks.

"Mofa consumes humans for its energy. It turns some humans into monsters. Some it can control."

"You all also need to be careful of me," Christina says. "I'm not one of its monsters, but it took control of me once, and I can't promise that it won't again." She sighs and focuses on Elle. "And we have to avoid Coach Nathan. He is one of its monsters, and he won't hesitate to kill any one of us."

I gulp. Elle shakes her head. I can't tell if she's about to cry or scream. She's in love with a man who Christina tried to kill, a man who became a literal monster.

It's an awful lot to digest, and my temples pulse with pain. Then light appears again from both Elle and Christina.

Something also shimmers in the corner of the classroom, sending paralyzing horror and panic through me.

There's someone else in the room with us.

# CHAPTER NINE

"Fiara," Christina whispers, moving toward the apparition in the corner. "Let me see your eyes."

The flickering light in the corner reveals Fiara's body, and Christina grabs her. All at once, Fiara shifts from ghost-like to fully human. I know little about her. She takes classes here like the rest of us, but she's not like anyone I've ever seen. Her hair is slick, almost slimy, and her face looks more like clay than skin. Counselors and teachers have stressed the need for empathy over the years. Never providing specifics, they tell us about accidents and injuries. "How would you feel if something tragic happened to you and changed the way you look?"

Fiara has never given anyone a chance to get to know her, though, except perhaps for Christina.

"The Darkness has transformed another," Fiara says, her eyes wet.

"Who?" Mr. Lee asks, adjusting his glasses and closely examining Fiara. He walks toward her like he's approaching a scared creature on the street.

Fiara looks away, but Christina interjects. "Coach. I know." She holds Fiara's hand and asks, "How are you?" Fiara doesn't answer, and she looks warily over at Elle and me, carefully avoiding eye contact with Mr. Lee. "It's okay. They're a part of this, too."

*A part of what, exactly?*

Fiara's eyes are as blue as the spring sky, both beautiful and sad. What really happened to her to make her look this way?

"I haven't felt it inside me for some time now," Fiara mumbles.

"That's good," Christina replies, her eyes widening. She lifts her eyebrows, and I'm struck at the depths of despair and empathy inside the liquid-hazel. I've never seen anything like it.

"Not really. It means it's after someone else." Fiara sighs. The way she stares makes me uncomfortable—does she distrust us, or does she want to hurt us?

"Why are you here?" Elle asks. "What's going on?"

Christina continues to hold Fiara's hand, and she finally faces Mr. Lee.

"Can you help this time?" Fiara's voice strengthens. "For real?"

"Wait. What do you mean *this* time?" Christina asks.

"Let me explain," Mr. Lee says. "Please take a seat." He gestures to the front row, and Christina and Fiara sit next to Elle and me.

Mr. Lee looks out the classroom window. "I've been hunting Mofa a long time. I stumbled across Fiara years ago. I thought she may have been *Xianchi*, the Seer. But I was wrong."

"What's the Seer?" I ask.

"I failed once. I won't fail you again. I'm going to be very honest with all of you." Mr. Lee stands tall, his hands pressed hard against his wide waist. "I need your help your stop this. I have some colleagues across the country who have helped me research—"

"Whoa," Christina interrupts, her mouth wide. "Across the country? Is there more than one, um, Darkness?"

Mr. Lee's lips form a thin, straight line. He wipes his forehead, hesitating. "Evil can take many forms. What I know is that

Mofa won't hesitate to kill and consume anyone who tries to get to Kang Fu." A sympathetic smile lingers on his face, but he doesn't answer Christina's question. "And yet, you must go to Kang Fu. It is our only chance. We hope it's not strong enough yet."

Christina raises her hand but doesn't wait to be called on. "Fiara and I have a, um, a unique history. The Darkness has done terrible things to both of us. And now it wants us to fight for it. To bring it Lawson, Elle, and others."

"What the hell?" I mumble, blood rushing to my face.

He ignores me, though, his attention focused on Fiara. "Will you be able to resist? Will you fight with us?"

Fiara doesn't answer or return his gaze. Slowly, as if in pain, she puts her head on the desk and releases a soft moan.

Christina reaches for Fiara's hand again. "You all would understand her reluctance if you knew what hell she's been through."

"Wait a sec," Elle says. "Are you saying that you won't try to stop us but that Fiara will?"

My heart leaps into my dry throat.

Christina shakes her head. "No. But the Darkness can take her over. Like it did me. And then she might, well...." She pauses, biting her lip. Blinking hard, she finishes the sentence. "She might kill you."

*Jesus.* My stomach rumbles. I need to go to the bathroom. I stand and lean against the desk, trying to relax the twisted pain in my gut.

"Why doesn't the Darkness come for us directly?" Elle asks Mr. Lee.

"The thing about evil," Christina says, "is that it would rather make good people do terrible things."

Mr. Lee scratches his bald head, nodding. "Yes, that's true. Mofa is limited until it transforms. It needs to scare and even possess others into helping. For now. It won't always need help."

In other words, everything can get so much worse? Shit.

"The Secret, um, Kang Fu spoke to me, I think," Christina says. "It told me to find Charlamae."

"She was the weird grandmother, right?" I ask. "She's the one who insisted her grandson, Asher, went missing. But she never had a grandson." I pause, trying to search for memories. "I think she used to live by me, too. Like, right across the street." *Where Old Man Darius and Toothless Tonya reside.* I tremble at the thought of them, but I don't share this information with the group.

Mr. Lee's lips twitch. He knows a lot more than he's telling us. I get the feeling he doesn't want to tell us everything, at least not all today.

"Why does it do these things?" I ask.

"Why do you eat and breathe?" It's Fiara who speaks up, and her voice isn't the meek sound from before. It's stronger, full of fury, and it makes my legs feel weak enough that I sit back down. "You are human, and so you do human things. It is the Darkness, so it does what Darknesses do. It is pure evil, and there is no changing it."

"So, what do we do?" Elle asks after an awkward silence.

"We will train," Mr. Lee says. "We will learn how to fight it." A humorless smile spreads across his face.

"What is it?" I ask. "What are you thinking?"

"There are others who need to join us, I think. We don't have everyone yet," he says. "There will be others like you who are drawn to Kang Fu. Or to Mofa. We have to give them time, but..." Mr. Lee looks at the computer displaying the missing kids. He doesn't have to finish his sentence. The more time we take, the more kids we put in danger.

After a moment of silence, Mr. Lee continues. "I must meditate on the situation. Go home and stay away from... anyone strange, especially those older than you. If you have younger brothers and sisters, watch them extra carefully tonight. Then meet me here first thing before school tomorrow. Okay?"

We agree. Christina and Fiara leave first. I walk out with Elle, who fills me in on what happened with her, Coach, and Christina. She's guarded, picking up on the fact that I disapprove of her relationship, which seems to be the least important issue at the moment, considering Coach is a monster. After Christina, or rather the Darkness as Christina—it's still kind of confusing to me—slashed Coach's throat, Elle held him in her arms and cried. The Darkness returned in some kind of shadow form. It spun around Coach like a tornado, and it took him. He wasn't dead, not exactly, and he didn't vanish like the kids. Listening to her story, I realize one important fact—she didn't take Coach to the Secret after all. The Darkness did this to him, not the Secret, which explains a lot, but I don't say anything to Elle about this.

He came back as something worse. Something undead, and then he chased after Elle.

"I ran back through the woods and somehow got home without getting hurt," she says. Perhaps she managed to avoid physical pain, but the look in her eyes tells me that there's deep mental and emotional trauma here, for so many reasons. Her lover is a monster. "I was in such shock. I don't know how to explain it. I just couldn't stop thinking about it, and the only other thing I could think about was the Secret, how you and me found it as kids. How maybe it could help us now. So, I went to you today, to tell you this, but Christina showed up, and, well, you know." I nod. It's been a strange turn of events. We both absorb Christina's part of the story and everything Mr. Lee had just explained, trying to digest it all.

"So, you'll stay away from Coach, right?" I ask.

"No shit," she says, but her eyes flicker. It worries me.

"All right. See you tomorrow morning," I say, and we go our separate ways.

---

WHEN I RETURN home, I glance at the old couple's house across the street. Yes, Charlamae lived there once, I'm certain of it. I was too little to notice, but it wasn't always a scary house. No one's out in the yard. The house features a bay window with closed curtains. Suddenly, the curtains shift, and red eyes appear from the corner.

I gulp and run straight inside.

Avoiding my parents, I head straight to my room, followed only by Gracie. I stare at my video games. I'm almost finished with the new Final Fantasy I got. I would have finished tonight, probably. I don't even turn the game system on. I just get in bed. Gracie hops in next to me.

I double check that my windows are locked and my curtains shut completely. I don't sleep a wink that night. I get up several times to peek out the window. The first time, I don't see anything —no red eyes, no creepy neighbors.

Why did Mr. Lee warn us about strange older people?

I wrestle with my internal thoughts, unable to sleep. I check the locks and look out the window again. This time, I nearly lose control of my bladder.

Old Man Darius and Toothless Tonya are dancing in the middle of their yard. It's two in the morning. They wear night-gowns. They snap their heads to my window the second I look out, but they don't stop moving. They do a river dance, locking their arms together.

It should be a ludicrous sight, but terror pulses through me.

I jump under the covers and close my eyes. Maybe I'm hallucinating. Yes, that's it. My neighbors may be bizarre, but there's no way they are dancing in their front yard in the middle of the night. Reaching for my phone, I text Teddy.

*I know it's late. You up? Something weird is happening.*

I don't think sleep ever comes, not fully, but I don't get out from under my blankets until rays of sun break through the corners of the curtains. Teddy doesn't reply until morning.

*Hey man, I was sleeping. What's up?*

Mr. Lee told us we may not have everyone we need to fight the Darkness, and I can't help but think Teddy is a part of this, too.

*Can you get to school early and meet me? Now?*

I look out the window while I wait for his response. The street is calm. No dancing neighbors, and no red eyes peering behind curtains.

*Yeah, okay. What's going on?*

I get ready for school quickly, eager to be close to others who may understand my fears.

*Just meet me there. I'm on my way now.*

I hop on my bike and only look over my shoulder once.

---

IT'S STILL EARLY when I arrive at school. I lock up my bike, and I stumble through the halls groggily. I am one of the first ones here, and my footsteps echo in the empty corridors. We have a thousand students or so. There are thousands of high schools with thousands of students around the world, too. So, why am I part of this? Why is Worthlapp?

I think of *Ant-Man*. I love that movie. I'm small, like an ant. We all are. We're nothing, really. So, what does the Darkness want from me? What could I do to make a difference in the outcome of the world? I mean, won't evil always exist? And why would something so powerful need kids like Elle and me?

I walk to the commons, and a few kids groggily poke at bowls of biscuits and gravy. I take a seat at our usual lunch table and wait for Teddy.

It takes a few minutes, but he finally arrives. "You okay?" Teddy asks when he sits down, his curly hair extra messy like he rolled out of bed and raced straight here. Somehow it makes him look cuter than ever. "You look weird. You know, weirder than usual." He gives me this super goofy smile that gets the butterflies swirling in my stomach. Everything's making my stomach feel twitchy lately.

"Didn't sleep at all last night."

"Oh," Teddy's lips curl into a comforting smile. Ignorance is bliss, I've heard teachers say, and I question what I should tell him. He's peaceful, happy. If I could remain ignorant, would I choose to do so?

"So why did you want to meet?"

"I need to talk to you about the Secret."

"Oh," he says, his voice high, his dark eyes wide. He knows there is *a* secret, but he sure doesn't know all the details about *the* Secret. Not that I do, either, but I know more than him.

My stomach turns. If I tell him about this, won't I be putting his life in jeopardy? Is it selfish of me that I don't want to do this without him? I know I've got Elle and Christina, and now Mr. Lee and maybe Fiara. But Teddy's my... well, he's more than a friend to me. I want him by my side.

"So, what *is* the big secret?" Teddy asks.

No. Never mind. I can't tell Teddy. What was I thinking? I can't risk hurting him.

"Um, well he, Mister Lee, offered my class extra credit," I lie. "I think he's gonna offer it to yours today. We have to do a little group project. I just wanted to get it done, and I didn't want to do it with anyone else."

Teddy's shoulders deflate in disappointment. "Dude, you got me here early for a class project? That's super lame."

"I know. But will ya work with me? The library should be open now."

"Yeah, whatever," he says, shaking his head but smiling. Dammit, Teddy, why do you have to be so cute?

We walk to the library, and I brainstorm a fake project that we could work on. Then Teddy grins again, and it melts my heart. I forget what lie I'm telling. I'd like to tell Teddy that I brought him here to tell him I like him. Really like him. That he is the most handsome guy I've ever seen in my entire life. I haven't told him any of this. I haven't told anyone that I even like guys. When school started, I had hoped this would be the year I'd find the courage to be me. But now, it appears that there are monsters other than my closeted insecurities.

I search for the girls—we are supposed to be meeting Mr. Lee this morning, and I don't want them to ruin my story here with Teddy—but I don't see anyone. Maybe they will have to talk with Mr. Lee without me.

"Hey, whatever happened with Christina?" he asks.

"Oh, shit."

"What?" Teddy follows my gaze, and I don't have a chance to answer his question.

"Ronnie the Rattler," I tell him, when the doors to the study hall room by the library open.

"I hate that asshole. I thought he was suspended."

"No, he's probably here for morning detention." I sigh.

Ronnie slams the door shut and walks out to the hall. We're almost at the library. My arms shake. There's no one else in this hallway, and it's impossible to hide. His sharp blond hair spikes out in all directions. His body looks lean and strong, like all he does is throw big, heavy rocks. The teachers are well aware of the Rattler, as we call him.

We pick up our pace, but the Rattler sees us, of course. He twirls his keys in his hand and laughs as he walks. Hopefully, he will just want to tell us something stupid about his Jeep. He is always bragging about his stupid car because he is basically the only one in our grade with a license already. Although why he brags about it, I don't know. It's just a reminder that he was held back a year. It's not even a cool car. It's this old ass-black Jeep Cherokee, and I mean old. The engine barely runs, the tires look like they're twenty years old, and the black paint is more of a faded gray.

Ronnie looks right past us, though. He walks by us without so much as a nod, which is fine with me, until we turn around and see where he's going.

Elle stands at the other end of the hall.

"What do you want?" she asks. My stomach flips. What does the Rattler want with Elle?

"Elle and her lizard tongue. We know what Elle and her lizard tongue like to lick," Ronnie says and laughs. "That's what I hear. So, Elle the lizard, when you gonna lick mine?" Ronnie grabs his crotch and cackles again.

I run at him, and I shove him hard with all my strength. He stumbles a bit to the side.

"Get in line, kid. One at a time," Ronnie says. Then he turns back to Elle. "Unless you can handle two?"

I push at him again, but Ronnie sees me coming this time. He steps to the side, and I fall hard on the floor. He laughs at me, and the sound of his laughter hurts harder than the fall.

I get back up quickly and charge at him. "You leave her—"

Before I can finish the words, Ronnie's hard fist slugs my jaw. I'm falling again, and everything turns black.

---

I WAKE UP in the nurse's office. When I open my eyes, a wave of dizziness hits me. A few adults talk outside the office. I'm lying on a cot in the back. I close my eyes and wonder if I could get out of the rest of the school day.

What the hell happened?

I knew that Ronnie the Rattler was going to say something awful to Elle. I knew it would be sexual, too. But how did Ronnie know about Elle? Elle just told me about her and Coach yesterday.

I need to see Elle and see if she's okay.

"Easy, young man," the nurse says. "You hit your head on the floor. I've called your parents, and you're going to the hospital."

"What? I'm fine!" I try to stand.

"We need to check to make sure, and you need to stay put!" She frowns and pushes me back into the cot.

Can this day get any worse? I roll my eyes, and a splitting pain pulses in between my temples. Fine. Take me to the hospital. Let me stay there the rest of the week. Or year. Whatever. Now I've missed the meeting with Mr. Lee, and I have no idea what he shared with the girls. And did anyone talk to Teddy, or does he still think I just asked him to meet me here early for a project? Oh well. It's probably best that he doesn't know too much yet. Let him live in blissful ignorance. The same can go for me. Let Mr. Lee plan a battle with evil while I'm in a hospital eating Jell-O and ice chips. It's like everything I do makes me feel as worthless as this stupid school.

Mom runs into the nurse's office just as I close my eyes again. "Honey, are you okay?"

"I'm fine. It's proto... procedure or something."

She puts a hand on my arm and her other gently on my head. "What happened?"

"I got hit, and I fell on the floor."

"Why, honey?" Tears glisten in her eyes. It's strangely comforting to see her upset at my pain.

"I stood up for a girl."

She stares at me as if she's trying to figure out who I am. I understand, though. I've been trying to figure out who I am every single day.

"The nurse says we should take you to the hospital. Let them run some tests to make sure you don't have a concussion." She blinks away some tears and rubs my head.

I nod and slowly stand.

"We can get a wheelchair," the nurse offers.

"No, please. I'm fine to walk." Truth is I don't want anyone to see that. I think about the consequences of everything. If Ronnie were to see me wheeled out of here, he'd never forget that. One punch, and I'm in a wheelchair going to the hospital.

I'm tired of feeling fragile.

Mom walks a bit behind me in case I fall, I guess. I walk slowly out of here. Fortunately, school has now started, and everyone is in class. I don't want anyone to see me. I wish I were invisible.

I make it to the parking lot, and I don't think anyone has spotted me. Still, this sucks. Ronnie will surely tell everyone about this. I clench my hands into fists. I want to hurt Ronnie. I want to take a shovel and hit him in the back of the head as hard as I can, and I want to use the shovel to bury his dead body.

A chill rushes down my spine. My stomach turns. Those aren't thoughts I normally have.

I'm sitting in the passenger side of Mom's car, and we're driving to the hospital. I hope they admit me and never let me out. I rest my head on the window and look at all the houses and trees we pass by. They blur together, and it's mesmerizing. I relax a bit, shocked at my own anger. We hit the highway to get to the nearest hospital, and that's when I see it.

It's the way the trees come together in that particular spot. It's the railroad tracks on the hill behind the trees. There's a long-forgotten trail from the railroad tracks deep into the woods there. And beyond that? I remember it now. It's all starting to come together.

Beyond that is a lake with the great big Secret.

# CHAPTER TEN

I wake up at home the next day around ten with Gracie by my side. I've slept for twelve hours, and I still don't want to get out of bed. The doctor at the hospital told me I had a concussion, and that I was to rest, mentally and physically. No school, no activities, and for some reason, no video games or TV either. I have to rest my brain or something weird like that. Whatever. I could stay in bed all day and be content.

As long as the windows and doors are locked, that is. I peek through the corner of my curtain at the house across the street. Old Man Darius and Toothless Tonya sit outside on rocking chairs. I can't see any red in their eyes—I can't see their eyes at all. They're closed, but they both rock in the chairs with the exact same rhythm. What the hell are they on? Shivering, I shut the curtains and get back in bed.

Scary thoughts hijack my mind. What would happen if this street just blew up? Or if there was a huge disaster or war or something? Not bad enough to affect me, but bad enough to distract everyone from being normal. It's a strange thought, triggered by vague memories. I wasn't even born when September 11th happened. I don't remember anything about it. There are a few teachers who like to tell us how much they cried on that day, and some who still cry out of remembrance. That's weird to me, like they're trying to prove that they are human and empathetic.

I wonder what it would be like if you knew the world was going to end. Like climate change or nuclear war or something finally hit an end point and BAM. That's it. What if, one day, instead of an Amber Alert, we get a nuclear missile alert, telling us the world is about to end? Would people hide and cry? Would they hold hands and pray? Would they look up to a darkening sky and hope that there's more to it than this crappy little existence? Or would they scream "fake news" and hurl insults at each other?

Sometimes life is simply a pain in the ass, especially when I don't know how to talk to anyone about who I really am. I've pictured the day I come out to my parents, but even then I don't know what all I'd tell them. Mom would probably be fine. But Dad and all his boob jokes—I have no idea how he'd react. There's a beautiful moment every morning when I first wake up. For a few seconds, before reality hits, I feel perfectly happy. Once I realize that I'm living a lie, though, everything changes. The sadness creeps in. Teddy helps, though. Actually, Teddy hurts, too. I've never had such a crush on anyone in my life.

God, I hate my brain!

And now—well, maybe the world is ending. Something's going on. Something darker and more confusing than I can possibly understand.

I risk another glance outside the window. The old couple's eyes are still closed, but their mouths are open wide, and they're laughing again! I have a terrible feeling they're laughing at me, like they can read my mind and they're mocking me.

I shudder. I have to get away from this house.

Pulling the curtains tight, I head back to bed. I need someone to be more than a friend, someone to help me understand the thoughts that bounce inside my head. Teddy's curly hair and bright smile come to mind. What would happen if I tried to hold his hand? Probably another fist to my jaw.

I don't have anyone.

My eyes dart back to the window. Although the curtains are shut tight, a few webs of lights break through. Sometimes, I wonder, if it's best to not explore what's beyond the Darkness. Sometimes, I think, it may be best to not let the light in.

Pulling the blankets tight against my chest and closing my eyes again, I wonder if the Darkness is going to end the world, or if the Secret has what it takes to save us.

Right now, I'm not sure which one I prefer.

---

I WAKE UP screaming. Gracie barks at me, looking as startled as I feel. A dream lingers in my memory but fades as quickly as I wake.

I push the covers off, sit up in bed, and rub my eyes. Gracie whimpers and rubs her face against mine.

Pulling Gracie closer, I whisper, "It's all right, girl," as much to convince myself as her.

A vision returns, a memory from my dream. I saw something in my mind's eye, that's for sure.

I know why Elle and I stopped visiting our little hideaway.

I grab my phone to text Elle, but it's only two o'clock and she'll still be in class. I'm not supposed to be on my phone, anyway.

"Dammit," I mumble and toss the phone to the other side of my bed. No physical activity. No mental activity. All thanks to this damn concussion courtesy of the Rattler.

Did hitting my head that hard bring back these memories? I need to explore. I need to search for the lake, but I'm not supposed to do anything.

I can't sit here and not do something. It's doing nothing that brings all the worthless thoughts to my mind.

Grabbing my phone again, I do send someone a message, but not Elle. It's an impulse more than anything, but there's one person I still can't stop thinking about.

*Hey Teddy. Whatcha up to after school? I'm not supposed to do anything. Got a concussion. Yay. But I'm super bored. What's up?*

Then I refresh my messages one hundred times in a row. I keep refreshing the app, waiting for a response. It's ridiculous, but I've got nothing else to do.

Finally, an hour or so later, it shows that Teddy has read my message, but he doesn't reply. Ughhhh!

After a few minutes, little bubbles form. He's replying!

Finally!

*That sucks. Srry.*

That's it? I sigh. But then the bubbles appear again. I anxiously stare at my phone.

*Prbly just gonna play some VR with Sam. Wanna join us?*

"Yes!" I shout, although I know I'm not supposed to play video games. I need to get out of here, and neither of my parents will be home for a couple more hours. Besides, it's not video games that interest me. I need to get out to those woods, the woods I saw on the way to the hospital yesterday, and it would be best if I had someone with me in case I pass out.

I get dressed and write a note for my parents. I don't want to text them. They'd be able to text back. A handwritten note is better.

*Feeling better, just going to pick up my homework from a friend. Be back soon.*

They'll still be angry because I'm not supposed to be doing anything, but that's okay. I have to go to those woods, and I have to do it today.

I grab my bike—making a mental note to thank my parents for bringing it back here from where I left it at school. When I hop on it, Old Man Darius and Toothless Tonya stand at the same time.

Their eyes open, and they close their mouths. Their eyes look like the flames inside a lit pumpkin on Halloween. Old Man Darius raises his right arm and points at me. My heart skips a beat. Toothless Tonya raises her left arm and makes a throat-slitting gesture.

Nope. I'm getting the hell out of here.

---

I BIKE TO Teddy's house and don't look behind even once.

They're trying to scare me, that's all. Or the Darkness is trying to scare me through them or something. I won't let it. I'll get my best friend, and we'll defy the threats.

It's only about a fifteen-minute ride, and I feel okay. I'm not pushing too hard, though, just in case the doctors know what they're talking about. Teddy's house has this cool, open, wrap-around porch. It's not a super expensive home or anything, but it's really nice. I run up to the porch and knock on the screen door. It's mid-fall in Worthlapp, but it's still very warm. It's oppressive end-of-summer heat, and the hot air feels like it's about to explode.

Teddy opens the door. "Hey, Law. How ya doin'?"

"Concussion. I'm not supposed to be doing anything, but I'm really struggling."

Teddy smiles. He's wearing a *Beetlejuice* T-shirt, and I like him even more. His little brother Sam yells into a red headset in the living room.

"Aren't you supposed to rest if you have a concussion?" Teddy asks.

"That's all I've been doing! Mom took me to the hospital yesterday. I slept all day and all night and like all today. If that's not enough rest, I don't know what is."

Teddy nods. "Wanna play?"

"Actually, I was wondering if you wanted to get outside for a bit."

"Outside? You mean to the—"

"Yeah," I say, and his dark eyes grow wide. I haven't told Teddy much. When Christina sat at our table last week, Teddy got pissed. I didn't know then where the Secret was, just that it existed. Which made Teddy think that I had lied to him. Which also pissed me off.

I'm still trying to piece everything together, but right now I want to show my best friend the Secret. I think it will help.

"You do know where it is!" he says.

"Mom said you're supposed to watch me!" Sam yells at us.

We ignore him. "I think so. I didn't until yesterday, though. I swear!" I take a deep breath and brush hair out of my eyes. The usually styled top falls over my forehead. I was so anxious to get out of the house, I didn't even think about my hair. "Christina, um, hasn't been herself. There's a lot to tell you." But how much do I tell him? The more involved he gets, the more I put him at risk.

Maybe it was getting hit on the head, but I have a wild idea. I know involving Teddy is precarious. I don't want to put his life in jeopardy. But the Secret could help us. So, if I can get him there first, get through the woods without running into any trouble, then maybe we can get some of the magic from the Secret and we'll be safe!

At least I hope.

What's the best way to say it without sounding like a lunatic? *Hey man, I do know where the magic is, but there's also something there I just recently remembered. When we were kids, we called it the Pit of Darkness. It has monsters and all sorts of scary shit. The thing is, though, I need to see it. It's out to kill me and Elle, apparently, and maybe you, too. So what do you say? If we survive and make it to the Secret, we could be stronger than ever, and then we can decide if we want to save the world.*

"Where is it?" he asks.

"Mom said you have to stay! You know she's not feeling well!" Sam yells, staring at us now with his headset off.

Teddy turns to his brother and says gently, "I'll be back before anyone else gets home. Cover for me and, um, I'll let you control the drone the next time we take it out?"

"Deal!" Sam says with a cheesy grin.

I grinalso, hoping to tease him just a little. "You'll just have to come and see."

"Are we biking or walking?" Teddy asks me.

"Biking." Even though it feels like ninety degrees outside, a chill hits me. I'm going someplace that I had forgotten about long ago.

"Excellent. One sec." Teddy jumps off the front porch and runs behind the back of the house. A few moments later, he returns with a thick silver and black bicycle. It looks brand new, like he's never even used it. I glance down at my well-worn machine, a maroon bike caked with dirt that has more than a few scratches.

"So where to?" Teddy asks.

Scanning Teddy's street, I keep an eye out for anyone strange who may have followed me. Something catches my eye across the street from Teddy's, the last house on the left on this block. It's not a creepy old dude that sends a chill through me this time.

It's the tree in the front yard. It's a tall elm, its trunk shaped like a vase with full green leaves refusing to change colors. But something's wrong with the trunk, and all the branches, too, I notice, looking closer. There's a blackness running through it, like several dark veins. I've never seen anything like it on a tree before. It's like—a poison. A black poison runs through that tree, I'm certain.

The tree can't hurt us, though, right? It's not a person. I ignore it, for now, and look toward the east of our town.

Worthlapp is largely a flat community, but to our east is a long, steep hill. After a short climb, the hill gives way to a surprisingly sharp slope leading out of town into the deep woods.

"This way," I say and begin biking up a long, gradual ascent. The wind pushes forcefully against me, as if it knows what I'm doing and is trying to warn me. But I laugh at the wind.

I look behind me to make sure Teddy is following. He is, and he's laughing, too. It feels good to have the wind blow in your face.

But is the wind warning us of the evil?

Or trying to stop us from reaching the Secret beyond the Darkness?

# CHAPTER ELEVEN

Our bike route goes through several side streets to a long, winding closed-down road. It belongs to the park district, but it has been closed for as long as I can remember. Bumps and potholes adorn the road, so we keep a close eye on everything, but we never slow down. Not once. We swerve around dips, fallen tree branches, piles of dirt, and soar down the hill. On all sides, trees reach high overhead, touching one another from different sides of the roads, nearly enough to block out the sun. In some areas, it looks as if night has fallen, which makes our ride even more perilous. On other parts, the sun shoots through as if shining a spotlight on certain sections.

Even though I don't have a license yet, I hadn't been using my bike much since I started high school, at least not until this week. Did I wake up one day and think bikes are for kids? A day will come when a kid puts his or her bike away for the last time, without even knowing it. I'm glad today isn't that day for Teddy and me.

Hitting a small pothole, I almost fall off my bike. I grip my handlebars tightly and focus my attention on the beautiful and treacherous road.

We pause at the bottom. "Where to now?" Teddy asks.

I try to remember. This road is literally a path down memory lane—Elle and I used to take it. It's where it all started.

*Where what all started? What happened?*

Even then, the road was blocked off, but that didn't stop us, and it didn't stop Teddy and me today. It's a dead-end, though. The road curls into a dirt path that leads up into the woods.

"There," I say and point to the new route. "We go up there."

Teddy's eyes follow mine. The trees are full and green here, even though it's fall and they should be changing.

The dirt is dry. We haven't had any rain in weeks. We're walking our bikes uphill now, and then I hear it.

"Shh," I whisper and hold out my hand to stop Teddy. He cocks his head, and his mouth opens wide.

It's like a song, a siren that calls from deep within the woods. Or is that the sound wind makes against trees and leaves? Teddy nods. He doesn't have to say anything. I know he hears it, too.

We follow the song and push our bikes uphill over branches and a few fallen leaves eager for change. The sun fades away as the trees above us create a shelter. The snapping of branches and the rustling of wildlife hum around us, too. It's a different world here. If *Stranger Things* is an upside-down world, this one's inside-out. We're outside, but inside the outside. It's nature's hiding place, and she's whispering in our ears.

*This is beautiful,* Teddy thinks. I hear his thoughts as if he's speaking. *What is this place?*

*Teddy*, I call, but only with my mind. He turns and smiles at me.

*This is amazing*, his mind says.

*Can you hear my thoughts?* I stop for a moment to look him closely in the eye.

He nods. *How is this possible?*

*Don't think about it too much. Just follow me.*

I forget about my concussion and all our other problems. With my mind, I tell Teddy, *this is only the beginning*.

We move forward, and the woods darken. Old memories

flood my mind. It's been years since I've stepped foot on this path, but all the smells, the sights, the sounds—everything is familiar. To my left, a scattering of upside-down, heart-shaped deer tracks mark a different route. An owl flutters by a lone pine to my right, a tree that seems out of place among all the others, but I remember it. As a kid, I used to think that tree was straight out of a Dr. Seuss book. It's a full and puffy evergreen, and it leans to one side like the Tower of Pisa. Teddy grunts as he runs into a weave of spider webs, and I laugh as he vigorously wipes them off his face.

It's more than nature, though—there's an electric current here, a magnetic mist that makes this feel like a different ecosystem. We can read each other's minds, after all.

Elle and I used to share our thoughts here, too. The thing is, though, it was never a strange mystery to us. We never talked about how or why we could do it, or why we could only do it in this place. We just did it. Maybe that's a unique thing about kids—they don't question or doubt what's magical.

I feel the buzzing in Teddy's mind. We are walking, right now, in a place of magic, something that isn't supposed to happen outside of movies or books. But it surrounds us, darkening by the second.

*Darkness! Teddy—the Darkness!*

*What?* The smile vanishes from his face. *What are you talking about?*

*This place!* I gesture wildly. *We have to be careful. It will try to kill us.*

Teddy's brown eyes widen, and we both snap our heads at the sound of branches breaking to our left. His mind shouts at me. *Why?*

*Don't you hurt him!* I shout at the Darkness. *It's my fault we're here. You come for me!*

I listen as the noise gets louder. It's the sound of walking—no, stomping—in the woods. Something wicked trudges toward us.

*We don't want to meet whatever that is. C'mon! We have to get to the top of the hill before everything turns black!*

Teddy scurries ahead. I'm right behind, and the footsteps pound through the woods. They're coming faster and faster. My stomach turns, overwhelming me with nausea.

The cover of night nearly swallows the woods. My breath comes up shallow, and my chest burns as I push forward.

"Run!" I shout it out loud now. If we're even one second late, we'll fall into the Darkness. The memory of getting trapped in a pit here slaps me in the face. If we fall, then we'll have to face the thing with the loud footsteps.

We'll face Mofa.

Teddy and I run as fast as we can, pushing our bikes up the hill, swerving around trees. It's steeper the higher we go, and my lungs feel like they're on fire. My chest pounds, and sweat drips down my back. We're almost there, but the Darkness is almost upon us, too.

"Hurry!" Teddy yells. Something clomps on the earthen ground behind us, but I don't want to look. It sounds like it's about to smash right on top of us, and I scramble forward with every bit of strength I have.

The shadows of night fall like a thick curtain, and Teddy and I throw our bikes forward and tumble out of the woods.

The light blinds us, like someone opening all the curtains in the bedroom right after waking up. We're back in the sun, and I almost forgot that it's still daylight. I rub my thigh where it hit the railroad tracks when we fell.

*Railroad tracks!* I rub the steel with affection, like it's alive.

Teddy looks at me strangely, but that's okay. He'll learn soon enough that these tracks *are* alive.

"Go ahead, man," I say. "Feel them."

Teddy runs his hands over them, and goosebumps pop up over his tan arms. There's energy here all right.

"Where do we go now?" Teddy stands and walks to his bike. I

like that he doesn't ask me to explain what's going on here, not that I could anyway.

With ears perked and my head held high, my gaze follows the tracks to the right. "We follow the tracks. They will tell us where to go next."

The tracks are old. The world here is both a part of and separate from the rest of our world. Elle and I tried to get to the lake many different ways to avoid going through the woods below. One time we did find these tracks, but they weren't the same. They didn't have the energy they do now, and we were unable to locate the hidden path to the lake. Only through the Darkness can one make it here, of that I'm certain.

It's strange how memories long forgotten have suddenly become so clear.

Barren trees tower above us. The ground is blanketed with a carpet of green moss that clings to the railroad ties and runs between the roots of the trees. Teddy's gaze returns to the woods from which we came. "Will we have to go back through there?"

"I don't know," I answer honestly. "I think that's the only way in, but not the only way out."

"Okay." Teddy brushes the dirt off his shorts.

"Any regrets about not staying home and playing video games?" I ask, a grim smile on my lips.

"Do you know what that thing was?" Teddy asks, his eyes still wide and locked on the previous path. "In the woods?"

"A monster. *The* monster of the Darkness. Mister Lee calls it Mofa. It's not something you want to meet."

"Have you met it before?" His gaze turns to the dead trees that surround us now. I know what he's thinking—how can life be so full yet scary in one place and then empty yet hopeful in another?

Nature is full of contradictions.

"My memories of this place are like... like a broken puzzle." I take a deep breath, and cool air fills my lungs. They no longer burn, and my chest no longer pounds. The air here is refreshing and calm.

"Who all knows about this place?" Teddy asks after a bit.

"Elle and I went here as kids. Christina and Fiara know something about it, obviously. I think I went with other kids, too. I can't remember everyone. It's weird. And Mister Lee. There's a lot I have to tell you, but we have to get to the Secret first."

The sun warms my back, and I roll my head from side to side, stretching my neck.

Teddy stops walking. "What's the Secret really about?"

I shrug. "I don't remember. All I know is that there's a lake up here, but it's hard to find. When Elle and I first found it, other kids were swimming in it. Young kids of all ages. No parents or anything."

"What's wrong?" Teddy asks. I realize I'm frowning.

I sigh. "Elle. She should be here with me."

"Why didn't you invite her?"

I cross my arms and think. I could have messaged her, but she would have told me I was absurd and should wait for Mr. Lee's instructions. But that's not the only reason I didn't ask her. It bothers me that she wants to be with Coach Nathan, and we haven't had time to deal with that. Plus, she returned here without me, with him, before the Darkness changed him into whatever he is now.

I shake the thoughts from my head and wonder how much of that Teddy picked up telepathically. He doesn't respond to any of it, though.

"I lost all my friends when I moved," he says. We start walking again. He kicks at rocks, and I watch them fly into the distance.

"Yeah?"

"It's not the first time we've had to move for Pop's job. Each time we move it's like... like a chapter of my childhood that's completely over. You know what I mean?" He looks at me, and it's not a simple question. He really seems to want to know.

Teddy was new to Worthlapp this year. I've never had to

move, but I've lost childhood friends. Some of them moved away. And some apparently were taken by the Darkness and removed from my memory.

"Sorry, dude," I say.

His lips press together, and he breathes through his nose. "It sucks. Pop says every neighborhood you grow up in is like its own movie. Each group of friends is a different cast of characters. He says that to get me excited about new stuff. But if that's true, I think the movies feel short, and they have crappy endings."

I like the way Teddy talks, and I mutter "uh huh" while listening. He's smarter than most teenagers. Too many in my generation think they sound cool by trying to sound dumb. My gaze turns to the blue sky, empty of clouds. Power lines follow the tracks, and I wonder how far everything goes. A bird with a huge wing span—could it be an eagle?—flies overhead. It's beautiful here.

I catch Teddy's eye, and he blushes, perhaps embarrassed at sharing his feelings. He shouldn't be. His words make me feel something else, too. Guilt—for how I feel about him. He doesn't have any other friends here, and it's not like I'm bursting with popularity. I want him as a friend, and I don't want to screw this up. And even if I'm a virgin with no relationship experience, I know damn well that if anything's gonna screw up a friendship, it's hormones and emotions.

"Stop," I say, both to him and my own thoughts, and we pause in the middle of the railroad tracks. We haven't walked far. Maybe half a mile in total. "Do you feel that?"

Teddy bends his knees and puts a hand on one of the railroad tracks. I do the same.

"What does it mean?" Teddy asks.

There's such energy in the tracks. Touching it is like touching the sun. I'm warm and revitalized. There's a vibration, too, like it's trying to tell us something.

We look around, and Teddy sees it first. "There,"—he points —"look at that!"

To our left, the trees move. I don't mean they bend with the wind or something. There are two tall and thin trees, empty of leaves like the others over the tracks, but these two trees move. They travel in opposite directions, and they reveal a barely noticeable dirt path.

"How—" I almost begin to ask, but I smile. Yes, that's how it started.

That's how the tracks and the trees had alerted Elle and me all those years ago.

Teddy and I both wear smiles from ear to ear. "That's the way to the lake," I say. "That's the way to the magic."

I lose my smile with the arrival of another memory, but I don't share this one with Teddy. The Darkness and this lake, there's a reason they're so close to one another. Evil is never far from good, two sides of the same coin.

There's a force that wants to kill us, and the closer we get to the magic, its desire for us only grows.

Suddenly, I feel a monster's hot breath on my neck and hear its stomach growl.

We need to jump in that lake, quickly.

# CHAPTER TWELVE

When I wake up the next day, I grab my phone and text Elle. I want to tell her everything—but everything is a bit of blur, a refreshing but wild blur.

*Hey, need to see you today. I found it. I went back and found it!*

I push my blankets away, waking up Gracie. My skin is warm, the blood pumping through me hotter than normal. Gracie kisses me, and I try to digest everything that happened yesterday. After the trees moved and we went to find the lake... it was beautiful and magical. It was everything I had remembered and more. Once I entered, time and memory became, well, fluid. I want to go back again. With Elle and Teddy. As soon as humanly possible.

I stand and stretch. I woke up before my alarm clock on a school day—something that I'm not sure has ever happened. Most days, I hit the snooze two or three times, and even then, Mom has to yell to get me up. But not today. Today, I don't even let the thought of school depress me. I leave my bedroom, grab a clean towel from the hall closet, and walk to the bathroom. I turn on the water in the shower to a cool warm.

I'm supposed to take it easy still thanks to the concussion. No activity, no school, nothing. Today, though, I've decided I'm sneaking to school. That's right. I'm gonna wait for my parents to leave for work, pretend that I'm staying here, and then I'm sneaking off to school. I need to talk to Elle in person.

Besides, I'm fine. Whatever felt wrong after the nasty run in with Ronnie the Rattler is gone. The water in the lake, the warmth, the magic—did it feel like this when I was a child?

I step in the shower and realize that another part of me is more excited than I've ever seen it. I smile as I step under the water. It's going to be a very good start to the day.

The sounds of movement alert me that Mom and Dad are waking up and getting ready, too. They'll use the downstairs bathroom, so I have about twenty minutes before they'll come check on me.

When I touch myself, my stomach drops like I'm flying down a hill on a steep roller coaster. My heart pumps lava through my legs, my arms, even my belly. My skin tingles, like I'm in a bath of Pop Rocks. It's almost as if someone else touches me. I close my eyes and picture Teddy and me swimming in the lake. I touch myself and moan.

I grip the shower curtain when I ejaculate, and then I scream in pleasure. Gracie barks from inside my bedroom. I stumble back, catching my breath. Then I sit down in the tub, and let the shower wash away the signs of my pleasure.

"Honey, are you okay?" It's Mom calling from outside. I hope I locked the bathroom door.

"Fine!" My voice cracks. I can't help but laugh, but I cough into the crook of my elbow, trying to hide it. "Fine, I promise!" My voice deepens.

"Did you yell? I thought I heard a yell." Mom tries to turn the doorknob. She's opening the door, and nope, I didn't lock it.

"Yeah, fine! Don't come in. I'm not dressed. I... um, I... slipped and it scared me, but I'm fine."

There's silence from the outside, and I hope she believes me. At least it's not Dad. Dad would know what I had done, I'm sure of it.

"Okay, honey. Don't go hitting your head, for the love of

God. I'll take Gracie outside. C'mon, sweetie. Wanna go outside?" The puttering of Gracie's paws follow Mom's louder steps away from the bathroom. I try to stand, but my legs shake. *I'm gonna need to go to that lake every day.*

I dry off, put on a clean pair of boxers, and brush my teeth. Then I get back in bed, only to trick my parents. Like clockwork, Mom and Dad enter my room.

"How you feeling today?" Dad asks.

*Freaking fantastic*, I want to say. Hell, even these sheets feel like magic. "Really okay," I say, rolling to one side and avoiding eye contact, in case they would be able to somehow sense my plan.

"If you're still doing well tomorrow morning, then you can go back to school. One more day of rest, all right?" Dad steps forward like he's going to pat my head or something, but then he changes his mind.

Mom leans in to hug me. "I've made you lunch. It's in the fridge. You be good today. No leaving the house again, not even for homework. Do you understand?"

I nod.

"I'm serious, Lawson. It's not only about your concussion. There have been too many scary stories of missing children—"

"I'm not a child."

"Promise your mother," Dad says sternly. He speaks quickly and with fury, sending a shiver down my spine. I've forgotten to think what it must feel like as parents in Worthlapp, seeing stories of missing children on the news every single day.

"I promise." They stare at me and linger a moment longer. Mom kisses me on the forehead.

"Thank you," she says. I don't reply. It's strange that she's thanking me, and I question my plan to return to school.

When they leave my room, I listen closely to know when they've exited the house. The front door slams, and the cars start. When they've rolled out of the driveway, I leap out of bed and skip to the window. With my parents out of sight, I run back to my closet to grab some clothes. I'm only going to school, after all.

I'll be fine. And I'll be home before they can realize I was gone. It will be okay.

But something's poking out again. I look at myself in the mirror almost incredulously. I'm aroused once more, and it's seriously never looked so big. I check my cell phone. Elle hasn't responded, and by the time I bike to school, I'll have missed most of first hour. Being that I'm not supposed to even go today, I figure no one will notice or care.

So, I step out of my boxers and look at my nude self in the mirror. I certainly can't go to school with this erection. I touch myself again, and I'm glad Mom and Dad have left because it feels so good I can't help but moan. I may even miss some of second hour.

When I leave, the old couple across the street stand outside and wave. Old Man Darius rakes the yard, but there are no leaves. Toothless Tonya laughs, raises her right hand, and makes a jerking-off gesture.

What the hell?

I hop on my bike and race to school. I need to convince my parents to move. What is wrong with these neighbors?

---

BY THE TIME I make it to school, second hour classes have already started. I'm here of course to see Elle, and I need to know if she and Christina met again with Mr. Lee and what else has happened. To pass the time in my classes until I see her, I draw a map. I sketch the long, winding closed-off park district road with all its potholes. I shade in the dirt road that it leads up to, and then make little dots of all the trees that surround the hidden path into the woods. I write a little X on the spot. I start to doodle the path through the woods, and then the bell rings. I must have lost my train of thought.

Off to third hour where I get to see Teddy. I sprint to that classroom and wait for him outside. He approaches a minute later, and he wears the biggest smile. He skips to me.

"Lawson!"

"Hey."

"Dude! Oh my God. I feel... high, I guess. I've never been high, but I wonder if this is what it feels like." He looks down at his T-shirt, which has what looks like the poop emoji on it but says *Weird Science* on top.

Everything about Teddy is brighter—his teeth and even his curly hair, and the butterflies wage war in my belly again.

"Me, too." I consider telling him what made me extra late today. I almost don't, and then figure why the hell not. "I didn't think I'd be able to leave my room today. Woke up really excited. *Really* excited, if you know what I mean."

That gets him laughing. "Oh, shit, yeah. Me, too." He leans in and whispers in my ear. "I had to... you know...." He makes a gesture that makes me giggle and then continues, "Twice before I could even get out of bed. We're gonna need some serious girlfriends soon if this keeps up. Pun intended."

He laughs again, and it's contagious. I wish he didn't say that we needed girlfriends, though. "So, after school? We'll go again?"

I'm still laughing, and as much as I'd like to be alone with him, I know there's something else I have to do.

"I want to bring Elle. I'm gonna talk to her today and get her to go." I pause for a second. "We might need to see Mister Lee first. I kinda got you into something here, and I don't want you to be mad."

Teddy runs a hand through his sandy curls. "Why would I be mad? I've never felt better! See if she's got any hot friends to bring along, will ya?" He grins again, but I can't judge the guy.

"Absolutely."

That's what I tell him, even if I have no intention of doing that.

Just one more class to get through before I see Elle at lunch, but I have to get through Miss Hurst's biology lecture first.

"Do you know what would happen if all of the insects on Earth disappeared?" she asks our class.

"No more icky bugs?" a girl in the back replies, and everyone else laughs.

"Yes," Miss Hurst says, "no more icky bugs. What would happen to us?"

"We wouldn't have to buy bug spray," another student says.

"That's true," Miss Hurst says. "No more bug spray. But you know why? Because we'd all be dead." She smiles at the shocked looks on everyone's faces. "That's right. Insects, even the super *icky* ones are so vital to life that we would die off if they didn't exist. Now, let me ask you this. What would happen to all life on Earth if all human beings died off?"

A boy raises his hand. "All of them would die off, too?"

Miss Hurst shakes her head. "No. Life would flourish like never before. Think of that for a moment. If there were no humans on Earth, all other life on Earth would absolutely flourish."

I write that down next to the map I started drawing in my notebook. I think of the lake and the woods and everyone involved. Why do people create so many problems? Clearly, there's enough evil in the world, but somehow we make it worse.

---

THE BELL RINGS, and it's lunch time. Finally. I don't worry about getting food or dealing with the lunch line. I head straight to Elle's table. A few girls already sit there when I arrive.

"Have you guys seen Elle?" I ask them.

They shake their heads. I realize I never heard back from Elle after texting her this morning, either. I check my phone again to be certain, and nope, no text from her.

I stand awkwardly by her table, and Ronnie the Rattler enters the commons. I look away quickly, but it's too late. He no doubt noticed me noticing him, and now he's walking this way. My heartbeat quickens. I can't stand the thought of another fight. My hands shake and my stomach turns. Shit, my parents would get called if there's another fight. I'd get in trouble for even coming to school today. My eyes remain locked to the side like I'm studying something, but it doesn't get rid of him.

"Lawson the loser," he says and snorts at his own insult. "Heard you got hurt pretty bad. How's the little baby doing?"

"Leave me alone, Ronnie." I refuse to make eye contact with him.

"Aww, the little baby wants me to leave him alone." Ronnie's hands roll into fists and rub under his eyes, making a cry-baby gesture.

Then another voice calls out. "If he wants to be left alone, why don't you leave him the fuck alone?" My head snaps. Jesus, it's Teddy. The corners of my lips curl up, and Teddy gives me a confident, firm nod.

"Shut up, loser, or you'll be next," Ronnie says. I look around, worried about who is watching. I can't afford to get in trouble, but I don't see any teachers at all. And where the hell is Elle?

"The only loser I see is right in front of me," Teddy replies. My eyes widen. I want to laugh, but I'm also holding my breath. Ronnie towers over Teddy. He's almost twice his size. Ronnie looks down and grits his teeth, but Teddy doesn't take a single step back.

Ronnie pulls his right arm back and makes a fist. Everything appears to happen in slow motion.

He swings his arm at Teddy, who stands there as if he's willing to take it.

And he does.

Ronnie's big right fist connects with Teddy's jaw. Teddy's head turns with the punch, but then he snaps right back to face Ronnie. Teddy laughs.

A "WTF" look appears on Ronnie's face. He pulls back his fist to hit Teddy again. But a teacher has stepped into the cafeteria now, and he runs in between Teddy and Ronnie. It's Mr. Lee!

"Boys!" Mr. Lee shouts. "That's enough. Ronnie—to the dean's office. Lawson and Teddy—you come with me."

I've never been happier to get in trouble. Besides my parents, I've never had anyone stand up for me. And dammit, if I was crushing on him before, I've fallen for him completely now. What the hell am I going to do?

We follow Mr. Lee until he opens the door to the dean's office for Ronnie. "Wait here," he says to us, and they both go inside.

"Thanks, Teddy," I say, alone in the hall.

He shrugs. "No problem."

"Did it hurt? His punch?"

"It's the weirdest thing. I feel fine. Invincible."

Mr. Lee returns. "To my classroom." We follow, and I dread the lecture we're gonna get.

---

When we arrive at Mr. Lee's classroom, we're not alone. Christina is here, and Fiara, too. No sign of Elle, though.

Christina jumps up and yells, "You idiots! Lawson, when evil is after you, you don't go knocking on its door! Why did you go to the lake?"

"How did you know we went?" I ask.

She looks over at Fiara, who blushes. It makes her skin look strange, like an apple. "Fiara followed you. You can't be that stupid." She looks over at Teddy. "And now you've risked your friend's life, too."

"Why are you following us? And I thought we needed more to help us fight. Teddy's tough. Wait till he tells you what happened with Ronnie."

"What do you mean risk my life?" Teddy asks, his lips pressing together.

I gulp, and my stomach flips again. Fiara doesn't answer my question, and I choose not to answer Teddy's.

"Boys, we have a lot to discuss," Mr. Lee states, looking at us through his wide, black-framed glasses. "But first, I must pass on some troubling news."

His dark eyes fill with anguish and my arms tremble. The expression on his face—it wipes away all the pleasure and joy I felt today and replaces it with pure dread.

"There's another missing person's report that just got released. You'll get an Amber alert any second," Mr. Lee says, removing his glasses to wipe at his eyes. "I'm sorry to be the one to tell you this. It's Elle. She's gone."

# CHAPTER THIRTEEN

"No!" I leap up. "What happened?"

"We don't know for certain," Mr. Lee replies, centering the strained belt around his waistline. "It's a positive sign that we all remember her. That means she isn't... gone."

"It's my fault," I say, throwing up my hands. "We should have stuck together after everything you told us."

"That's true," Mr. Lee says, his voice harsh and unforgiving. "No one should go to Mofa or Kang Fu, no exception! Not without real training about what's going on here. You put your life and the lives of one another at risk. Do you hear me?"

I gulp, nodding. Mr. Lee's palpable anger raises the temperature in the room.

"Isn't anyone looking for Elle?" Teddy asks, lifting his eyebrows in surprise. "What's everyone doing here if she's missing?"

"Fiara's been searching," Christina says, pushing her hair behind her ears and running her hands down the front of her blue Worthlapp High cross country T-shirt. "She can move through the Darkness easier than any of us." She turns and faces her friend. "I know it's not easy for you. That's not what I mean. The memories are painful, and I'm sorry we asked you to return."

Fiara doesn't speak and looks away. One foot crosses in front of the other, and a silky black skirt rests above her ankles. She dresses more like a grandmother than a teenager.

"We need to get you all together," Mr. Lee says. The bell rings, indicating the end of lunch. "Christina has shared with me her previous experience with the Darkness. I can help, if you'll let me." He studies Teddy and me. "I need you both to meet us after school. And absolutely no more interactions with Mofa or Kang Fu."

Teddy nods, and so do I. But I have no intention of sticking around. Mofa has Elle—of course it does! I'm not even supposed to be at school today. I don't plan on waiting around to talk about a solution. I'm going after her, no matter what Mr. Lee says.

"Good," Mr. Lee says, eyeing me suspiciously. "If you don't, you'll be sorry."

We walk out of the classroom, and I consider telling Teddy my plan. He'll want to go, though, and I can't have that. I can't risk hurting him again, and I know it was stupid to involve him without talking to the others first. Waving bye, I smile at Teddy and decide to say nothing. He'll be safe in his classes. Meanwhile, I'm getting the hell out of here.

As soon as I'm out of sight, I sprint toward a school exit and grab my bike. Pedaling harder than ever, I enjoy the pain in my legs and my sides. It distracts from everything else, from the anger, the sadness, and all the worthless feelings that have been bottled up in me for as long as I can remember.

---

I BIKE THROUGH town, zooming through quiet side streets until I reach the closed-off, torn-up old park district road that leads to the Darkness and the Secret. My head feels foggy as I maneuver around the potholes, but I find the hidden entrance in the woods without falling off my bike.

*You shouldn't be here alone.* Was that my thought or someone else's? It sounded feminine. I need to find Elle. If I can find her and get both of us to the lake, maybe that can help. I leave my bike outside the path and move quickly through the woods without it. It will be faster this way, I think, and I can always retrieve my bike later. It's getting darker, faster than I remember from my walk with Teddy.

*You shouldn't be here alone!* The voice is louder this time. It's a woman's voice, but I don't recognize it. My stomach flips, filling me with nausea, an all too familiar feeling when I'm here. The trick is to not be afraid, to keep moving forward, and to never look back. My walk turns into a jog, and I search everywhere for her.

"Elle! Are you here?"

Footsteps pound behind me, and unlike last time with Teddy, I do look back. In the distance, a long, thin shadow slithers out from the dirt. "Elle, where are you?" Overhead, the trees touch, and it's as if the forest becomes one giant dome of gloom.

The shadow lunges at me, and I turn around but not quickly enough.

I fall.

I don't hit the ground beneath me. Gasping, I fall through the ground—literally right through it into some other realm. My arms flail, and I try to reach for something, anything, to grab. But there's nothing.

I scream. Saliva shoots from my mouth and slaps me back in the face. My chest burns. My eyes shut hard, but I take a deep breath. And another. Slowly, I open my eyes. I'm still surrounded by this pitch-black abyss—there's nothing to see—but I force my eyes to stay open, and I tell myself to calm down. I take several more deep breaths, and everything slows.

There's no bottom to the pit in this Darkness, at least there never used to be. I remember it clearly now. We fell in here before, Elle and me, as kids. We were trapped here for what felt like eternity until we discovered the way out. You float in the air. Well, you fall and scream and think you're going to die until you realize that this is something else altogether.

It's like a different dimension, an inexplicable physical phenomenon.

The creature in the woods tries to scare you and to get you to fall. If you fell, you fell into this pit, the Pit of Darkness we called it as kids. Mofa's pit.

*Is this where Elle is? Trapped, confused, and unable to find her way out? What about all the missing kids?*

I continue to float but can't see anything. I must calm down completely. I must stop thinking. This place can hear your thoughts. That's why Teddy and I could telepath when we walked the woods. It hears everything you think, and it feeds off those thoughts. Your thoughts are its food, and fear is by far the most delicious. Fear will keep you here forever.

I remember all this now. It was only when Elle and I had no thoughts and no fears left to give that the Darkness threw us out. So, I take more deep breaths, and I try to shut off my brain.

I breathe.

Closing my eyes, I inhale deeply, hold my breath for a few moments, and exhale. I repeat that God knows how many times, but I refuse to think or count or anything.

It takes a while, but eventually my mind becomes numb and completely free of all thought.

Then a bunch of sharp rocks slap my face. The Darkness threw me out, but it wasn't pain-free. It tossed me on these rocks on purpose. My face hurts, and my knees and ribs feel bruised. But I stand and touch my side. It's painful to the touch. Blood covers my hands. I look around, trying to figure out where I am.

I'm outside the dirt path entrance, far away from the Secret. I brush the dirt off my clothes. I walk back toward the secret path, but I remember the voice that warned me. *You shouldn't be here alone*, a feminine voice had said.

Whose voice was that? Kang Fu?

I didn't see or hear anything in the pit. Maybe Elle isn't down there. Maybe these kids are somewhere else in the woods. But where could they be? I want to go back and search for Elle, and I start to move back into the woods.

No, maybe I better not press my luck. I could have gotten trapped in there. Just because I found a way out this time doesn't mean the Darkness wouldn't try harder to keep me if I were to return. I better be extra careful. I don't want to prove Mr. Lee right or face another lecture. I walk—limp, rather, if I'm being accurate—back to my bike. Getting on it, I race toward Teddy's house instead of mine. I know what I need to tell him.

---

WHEN I GET to Teddy's block, I ride slowly by the blackened tree rooted in the front yard of the last house on the left. I can't understand why it's still standing. Surely, someone would want to cut it down? Blackness flows through a series of stringy veins that strangle the tree. The veins appear to move—like the blackness swims through the bark, making a rippling effect on the giant elm.

I make a mental reminder to ask Teddy about the tree. When I approach his house, he's sitting on the stairs of his wide-open porch with his arm around Sam, his brother. Sam's head is lowered, and Teddy rubs his shoulders. I don't call for Teddy—I sense right away that I'm seeing something private.

Sam is crying.

"We don't know anything for sure," Teddy tells his little brother.

"She's gonna die. We know that." Sam wipes drool from his mouth after he speaks, and he tugs at a red headset that hangs around his neck. He's definitely crying. Who are they talking about? Are they upset about Elle? Or one of the other missing kids?

"Maybe like fifty years ago." Teddy rubs Sam's back. His voice cracks with pain. Jealousy rises in me. I want Teddy to touch me, too. I'm also hurting, and I need my friend.

Seeing Teddy and Sam fills me with sorrow. I'm sad because I don't have anyone like that in my life. No one to put an arm around me and tell me the world is going to be okay. No one for me to put my arm around, either. Parents don't count.

I sigh, but not loud enough for them to hear.

"Fifty years ago, no one knew shit. Ya know? Today, doctors can do like anything."

I may not know Teddy that well yet, but there's something in his voice that Sam doesn't seem to catch. Teddy doesn't believe his own words.

"Yeah. I guess." Sam wipes his red-rimmed eyes. He's about eight years old, but in this moment he looks more like five. Whenever I've seen my parents cry, they always look like a decade older. But Sam—it makes him look younger. I turn around. It's best if I leave them alone, but as I do, Sam calls out, "Hey, it's Lawson."

I turn back to face them, and Teddy makes eye contact with me. He smiles gently and removes his arm from Sam's shoulders.

"Hey—shit, Law! What happened to you?" Teddy asks.

"I'm fine. I fell off my bike. I'm sure it looks worse than it is," I lie. "What's goin' on?" He shrugs at me and frowns. It's an "I'll tell you later" kind of gesture.

Sam blows his nose into a tissue and stands next to his brother. Sam's about a half foot shorter than Teddy. Putting the used tissue in his pocket, Sam tugs at the red headset again. He looks at me and asks, "Where you guys going?"

I catch a look from Teddy, and I hope I'm interpreting it right. "Actually, I was kinda feelin' like hangin' out here."

Teddy smiles when I say that, as if I read his mind. Not in the way I could in the woods, but in a way that means we're becoming the kind of friends I so very much want.

Sam cracks a small grin. "Really? Okay. That's cool." His enthusiasm makes me smile, and I walk up the stairs to their great big porch.

"Dude, you need to get cleaned up," Teddy tells me. "Here, let's get you in the bathroom before my dad sees you."

We dart to the bathroom, and Teddy turns on the light. I sit on the toilet seat, and he examines me.

"What really happened?" he asks. "And why didn't you meet us after school?"

"The Darkness. I went by myself."

"You idiot. Mister Lee's gonna be super pissed, but somehow I knew you would. Take your shirt off."

I can't help but smile at the command. I'd love to hear those words in a very different context than today, but I do as he says. He touches my shoulder, and my arm breaks out with goosebumps. "Sorry. Is my hand cold?" Teddy asks.

*It feels better than you can imagine.* "No. I dunno."

Teddy wets a washcloth and hands it to me. I wipe off the dirt, and he gets a first-aid kit from under the sink. "I think you're okay. I mean it looks like it hurts, but not too bad." He coughs a little and then asks, "Any sign of Elle?"

I shake my head. "Nothing." Silence fills the air as I take a moment to clean up. "Hey, what's with that tree across the street?"

"What tree?"

"The one that looks like it's poisoned. The super creepy one right across the street."

Teddy shrugs. "No idea, man. Guess I've never noticed it." He speaks as if he's disinterested in it, but I can't understand. There's no way anyone could not *not* notice it.

"So, what happened after school?" I ask, changing the subject. I wish I knew if he shared any of my feelings. My longing for him? My desire to tell him who I really am and how I feel? I'd let myself get beat up every day for him to touch me again.

He sits on the side of the bathtub in front of me. "Nothing. When you didn't show up, we figured you went out on your own. Christina and Fiara went looking for you. I was gonna go, too, but we got pretty bad news here today." He gulps. "I had to come straight home."

"Are you guys okay? What's going on?"

"My mom's dying," Teddy tells me. His eyes darken like storm clouds.

"Shit." It's all I can think of to say.

"Yeah. It's shit all right. Fucking cancer came back." His face twitches like he wants to punch something or scream, or maybe both. I want to tell him to go ahead, but the words don't come out of my mouth. This time it's my turn to reach for him. I rise and put an arm on his shoulder. His head is low, but then he stands and hugs me.

He puts his head against my bare chest, and I can tell he's trying to hold back tears. I want to tell him that it's okay to cry, but I don't want to move or say anything to disrupt this moment. I hug him back, and I breathe deeply. He smells like rain in the spring, and I never want to let him go.

He pulls away and looks at me. "Thanks."

His eyes darken with such sadness.

He opens the bathroom door, and I put my shirt back on. We walk into the living room, and Sam's got the VR all set up. Their parents are in the kitchen talking. "Ma, can Lawson stay for dinner?" His dad comes to us and answers instead.

His voice is quiet. "Ted, I'm not sure tonight's a good night. You should be with your family. It's nothing personal, Lawson," he says straight to me. "Today's a bad day."

I nod, but Teddy speaks up. "Dad, I... uh...." His voice softens, too. "I could really use a friend here tonight. If that's all right." Teddy's dad puts his arm on his shoulder, and for a moment it looks like he's about to cry.

But he doesn't. He swallows hard and says, "That's fine, son. That's fine."

Now I want to cry. I don't know everything that's happening, but whatever it is, I'm the friend Teddy wants by his side. I text Mom and tell her the truth. My best friend found out his mother is going to die, and I have to stay with him tonight. I promise no activity. He needs a friend to talk to.

It's an odd feeling to take any sort of pleasure in another's pain, but I kind of do. A little. I mean, it's nice that he needs me, is all. I smile at Teddy and Sam. "Let's play."

After a few hours, Teddy asks if I can spend the night. His dad doesn't argue, and neither do I.

I sleep on the floor next to his bed, and I look up and wonder what would happen if I sneaked in.

I don't, though.

---

I WAKE UP from a bad dream, almost screaming again, forgetting that I'm in Teddy's room. I sit up and let my eyes adjust. I stand and look at Teddy briefly while he sleeps. Can I put my arm around him and tell him everything is going to be okay?

But is everything going to be okay? Or am I living in a fantasy world where I think a few teens and their teacher can make a difference against the most powerful evil that has ever existed?

I leave before Teddy wakes up. I bike home, pedaling as fast as I did earlier that day to get to the lake. My bike hits a curb hard, and I fly off, my arms and face slamming against the sidewalk. My body bleeds again.

I can't even ride my fucking bike. Thoughts of worthlessness push tears out of my eyes.

Whatever. I deserve the pain. I walk home, pushing the bike, instead of riding it. Then I get the feeling someone is watching me.

"Fiara?" I ask. I stand still and listen, but I don't see or hear anything. "If you're there, I could use someone to talk to."

A car drives by quickly and out of nowhere. The driver is an old man I don't recognize, but he stares at me as he passes. It's an odd feeling. If Fiara is near, she remains silent.

When I turn on my block, I can't help but look at the neighbor's house across the street. The old couple sits on their rocking chairs. Of course they do. It's dark outside, the middle of the freaking night, and they're out in the cold, rocking away.

They stand and wave at me. The waving is overly enthusiastic, and they giggle. Old Man Darius puts his arm around Toothless Tonya. Then their eyes roll back in their heads. The eyes turn black. Their tongues roll out of their mouths.

Shaking, I race inside my house. Panicking from the sight across the street, it's hard to be quiet, but I try. Mom's in the kitchen, though, perhaps unable to sleep, and stops me. Her jaw hits the floor, and she runs over to me.

"Why is there blood all over your face? And in your hair?" she asks, approaching me with a look that's half concern, half danger. "You said you were spending the night and promised me no activity!"

I open my eyes and look at her. I want to tell her everything. *There's a terrible evil that wants me dead and some kind of magic that I don't fully understand. Elle is missing, and I have no idea how to get her back. And to make it all worse, I'm in love with someone who can never love me back the way I want. Plus, I think our neighbors may try to kill me.*

"I fell on the way home," I say, and then the tears come. I sob so hard that every inch of my body shakes. I can't tell her any of this. Who would believe me?

Mom reaches out and hugs me. "Oh, baby. It will be okay." She holds me, and I hug her longer than I have in a long time.

"You don't have to tell me everything now but talk to me. Please. I'm always here for you." I mumble a yes and pull away. "Get some sleep for now. But I want a full talk tomorrow. And a check-up with the doctor. Okay?"

"Okay," I say, grateful to not have to think about this anymore. I need to sleep.

"I love you, Lawson," Mom says.

"I love you, too."

---

A FEW DAYS pass, and missing person posters splatter around town for Elle, along with a dozen other kids. She's really gone. I kept thinking she'd show up, and everything would be okay. I haven't been back to the Darkness or talked to anyone. I know I need to see Mr. Lee and Christina to figure everything out, but right now everything hurts. The pain isn't just in my body, even though I've had throbbing, non-stop pain in my head since I came back from Teddy's.

I haven't seen Teddy since then either.

Teddy and Sam have been spending all their time with their parents.

Teddy called and told me the cancer's in his mom's breasts, lymph nodes, and bones. I guess she may not have long to live.

Everything fucking sucks, and I'm so tired of feeling like I can't do anything for anyone. I worry Elle is going to die or could already be dead, and I fear Teddy's mom is going to die. Thinking about death terrifies me. I sigh and roll to my other side in bed, pulling the covers up to my chin. I'm in bed at six in the evening. Mom will probably call up soon for dinner.

Occasionally, I gather strength to crawl out of bed and look out the window. Old Man Darius and Toothless Tonya wave at me every time I glance outside. Are they warning me? Are they infected by the Darkness or however that works?

I think I'm having a breakdown.

Suddenly, it feels like hands wrap around my throat, but I can't see anything in front of me. Choking, I reach out and swing my hands, but I hit nothing but air.

My lungs burn, and my vision blurs.

Then I pass out.

# PART THREE

## ANGELICA

"For life be, after all, only a waitin' for somethin' else than what we're doin'; and death be all that we can rightly depend on."

—Bram Stoker, *Dracula*

# CHAPTER FOURTEEN

"Angelica," Mr. Lee calls. "Angelica Cline, are you with us?"

My eyes roll under my thick, dark-framed glasses, but they don't leave my phone.

"Angelica, can you please put that away?"

I sigh and move the phone off the desk slowly, as if it weighs three hundred pounds. My social media stories are a lot more interesting than this damn class. I'll put it between my legs. No guy teacher is going to call you out then. Too much risk of sexual harassment.

"Angelica, there's only one reason a student looks down at her lap and smiles. Please put the phone completely away."

*Dammit.* Guess Mr. Lee is smarter than I've given him credit for. I smack my lips and move to put the phone in my bag when Mom texts.

*Hospice says this could be Grandpa's last night. I'm sorry, honey. Come right home after school, and keep your phone on you. I'll text if you need to come sooner.*

I throw the phone in my bag, slam my hands on the desk, and glare at Mr. Lee. *You know,* I think, *if there really is this bullshit he keeps talking about, I could use it right now. A little magic, a little escape—something, anything but reality. Is that too much to ask for?*

I gaze out the classroom windows on the right. It's fall, and the leaves on the trees show brilliant yellow, orange, and red colors. They won't last long, though. It's pretty for a week, and then everything dies. I hate this time of year. A woman passes by the classroom windows, taking a stroll on the sidewalk and kicking at the fallen leaves. Her head turns slowly toward me, her eyes catching mine. The color of her eyes changes, matching the fallen leaves she kicks. Something about the stranger sends a chill through me, and I turn away quickly.

Thinking of Mom's text again, I don't want to say goodbye. My grandfather has been the one constant rock in my life, and now this world wants to take him away? It's not fair.

I slam my face down on my desk and make a much louder noise than I had intended. Mr. Lee calls my name once more, but I groan.

"Angelica," he says, "perhaps you should stay after class so we can talk."

I lift my head and glare at him. "Whatever."

The class makes an "oooohhh" sound.

Mr. Lee blinks hard.

I brush my thick, dark hair behind my ears, and I raise my eyebrows above the frames of my glasses to let him know who he's messing with. I spread my hands wide open on my desk. I'm the only Black woman in this classroom, but I've never let that bother me. In fact, if anything, it empowers me.

I've wondered what it would be like to be surrounded by people who look like you, but I prefer being different.

The bell rings, and I stand tall. And, oh, I'm quite tall. I smile sarcastically as I approach Mr. Lee's desk, towering over him.

"Angelica," he says, looking up at me through his own glasses. "Are you okay?"

I cross my arms and shift my weight to one side. That's not

what I was expecting him to say. I had expected a lecture. Who is this guy?

I don't know how to reply to that. The first thing that comes to mind is, *Screw you. I'm fine. My grandpa is dying, and you want to lecture me about being on my phone.*

Instead, I show him my mother's text.

"Oh, Angelica. I'm so sorry," Mr. Lee tells me. He exhales deeply and in one breath looks somehow different. He's shifted from a teacher to a human.

"That's why you were on your phone," he says. I nod and he shakes his head. "Sit down for a second." He gestures at a desk in the front row.

I know he's being nice and wants to impart some kind of wisdom on me, but I want to go. It's only first hour, and it's going to be a very long day.

"I lost both my parents when I was pretty young," he starts. Tapping my fingers on the desk, I glance at the door and consider running. I don't want to listen. What is there to understand or know about death? It's unfair, it's stupid, and it sucks.

"It's hard," Mr. Lee continues. "Death is harder than anyone can explain. Those who haven't experienced it cannot even imagine. Not one bit, no matter what they tell you. It's like a secret code, Angelica. Only those who have experienced loss can speak its language."

Mr. Lee's words don't comfort me. They make me want to punch something. Someday—and someday soon—I will speak that language, too, and I don't want to be in that club.

"But let me tell you another secret," he continues. "Death isn't the end, Angelica. It's *an* end, but not *the* end." He pauses and leans in. "Do you understand?" He puts his hand on my shoulders, and an electrical shock jolts me.

Not a static shock. This is real electricity. My eyes roll back, and I see water. Deep, beautiful water, and then it hits me. I know the Secret Mr. Lee has talked about in class. I've even been there, like Lawson and Elle!

How did I forget? Why am I remembering now?

"Understand?" Mr. Lee repeats. Seriously, who the hell is this guy?

"Sure," I reply. My stomach clenches, and my desire to run the hell out of here enhances. I don't want his advice, and this is getting way too weird.

"Hmm." He looks at me closer. After a couple awkward seconds, he leans back. "It's okay that you don't. But don't give up on something just because you don't understand it. Search for it, Angelica."

Veins pulse under my skin, and I stand. "Mister Lee—I'm late for my next class."

"Yes, of course." He walks toward the door and holds it open. "I'll be thinking of you. Remember not to give up. Not on this class, no matter how weird you think it is. And definitely not on yourself. Oh, and Angelica?"

I nod slowly, hesitant about what words will come out of his mouth next.

"Let's continue this chat after school. Not today. Obviously, you need to get home. But I think you and I, um, need to talk some more. About *the* Secret," he whispers. Chills run through me, and I exit the classroom without giving him an answer.

I swallow back a noxious taste of fear and anger over the next few classes—trying not to think about Grandpa or death—but I can't get Mr. Lee's touch and words out of my head. He woke something up in me by putting his hand on my shoulder. Plus, he wants to talk to me about the Secret? I've seen Lawson and Christina meet with him, like they're some special club. I don't want to join no losers' club.

---

When it's lunch time, I march toward the cafeteria and sit with my best friend Pauline, who is already eating.

"What took you so long?" Pauline asks with a mouthful of

spaghetti. I sit down without getting food. I don't feel like eating. I feel like kicking things.

Pauline wears a sleeveless shirt even though it's cool outside. The fluorescent lighting in the cafeteria reflects off one of her many bracelets and her smooth arms. I like Pauline because she's the kind of person I want to be. She's actually nice. The more I learn about people, the more I think they all wear masks. Even my parents wear masks—they put on different ones depending on who they talk to. But Pauline has always been real, and she's never been afraid of telling me that I've got my head too far up my ass.

I look across the commons to Lawson, who sits next to Teddy. They're both so cute, and I wish I were braver. I've wanted to ask Lawson out since....

Since when? I can't even remember. We shared something as kids, didn't we? I have a foggy memory of something, and I wonder if that was awakened because of Mr. Lee, too. But I don't believe in that kind of magical or metaphysical bullshit, whatever you call it. Lawson never looks at me. Not like that anyway. My eyes move to Teddy. He's new this year, and he's absolutely adorable, too. Maybe even cuter than Lawson. He catches my eye, and I swear he blushes a little. Has he been looking at me, too? My lips curl into a smile.

"Is something wrong?" Pauline asks, interrupting my thoughts.

"Nothing." I break off a piece of her garlic bread and eat it, hoping it will calm my stomach. She doesn't seem to mind.

"How's your grandpa?"

I swallow the bit of bread and look up. My heart sinks, and salty tears force their way out of my eyes.

"Oh no," Pauline says and jumps out of her seat. She moves to my side of the table and puts an arm around me. "Did he... um, did he—"

"No," I say as the tears sting my eyes. Damn tears! The school needs punching bags in every hallway. If I could hit something, I wouldn't need to cry. "Mom texted. The doctors are saying this could be the last night."

"Oh, Ang, I'm so sorry. What can I do?"

When I look up, a few kids stare at me. "Tell them not to look at me."

Pauline stands, puts her hands on her hips, and shouts, "Mind your own damn business!"

It's so out of her character that I snort, and I enjoy the surprising laugh. "Pauline, I didn't mean for you to actually—"

"No, honey, no one disrespects a friend of mine, especially in a time of grief," she says and sits back down. She rubs my back, and I close my eyes.

"Thank you."

"*De nada.* Want me to come over tonight?"

I nod. "That would be nice. I'll text you."

The bell rings, and my phone buzzes at the same time. It's Mom, and I hold my breath reading the message. Every message could be THE ONE. Even checking my phone fills me with dread. *Remember to come right home after school.*

---

I GET THROUGH the rest of the day somehow, but I skip the bus. I don't live too far from Worthless High—too far away to want to walk to school in the morning. But the thought of taking my time getting home now sounds rather appealing. I should at least jog, I think. Get some practice in, since I'm missing again. I'm kind of happy to be missing practice. Coach has been extra weird ever since Elle went missing.

He stares at me. It's awkward and uncomfortable, and there's something about Coach's eyes that makes my skin crawl. It's almost like he's not, well, human.

The closer I get to home, the slower I walk. I know there's going to be bad news. If not today, then tomorrow.

I flash a little smile at some kids playing outside. A lump of jealousy forms in my throat. I miss those times.

Now we've got missing kids and my grandpa is dying—why can't life be tag and hide-and-seek, instead?

I clench my teeth and run. I have my bag, and I'm not dressed for practice. None of that matters, though. I run as fast as I can to get home. Once I'm there, I don't go inside, though. I enter the code to the garage, and I grab my bike. I can't remember the last time I rode it. Not at all this last summer, I don't think. Now, I crave it like ice cream on a hot summer day.

I don't have a license, either, but still I let my bike gather dust. Did I have nowhere to go? The thoughts are strange, and I don't like them. I sit on my bike, but the tires are low. I find a pump and fill up my tires hard and fast, anger pumping through my veins.

When I hop on, my mother walks out the front door.

"Angelica, what are you doing?"

I don't answer. I push away as fast as I can.

"Angelica, your grandfather—"

I pedal faster, and hot tears roll down my cheeks. He's dead. I'm sure he's dead. That's what Mom was going to say, but I refuse to hear it. It's not real if I don't know it.

I ride as fast as the wind. It feels so good, the cool air against my face.

I ride until I'm outside town, but I'm not thinking at all. I'm peddling as hurriedly as I can, pushing far away from everyone and everything. My legs are strong. I can do this for hours.

*I'm here.*

I stop riding and get off my bike. Where am I? Where and what is *here*? Somehow this place is both new and familiar.

*Here.* It's a feminine voice in my head, but it's not mine. I walk my bike through some woods, and it darkens rapidly. The sun was warm and bright, but under these trees, it feels like a different season. No, that's not right, either. It's a feeling of nothingness like something swallowed all the light and energy here. Suddenly, I get the feeling that I'm being chased. I pick up the pace, running faster than ever and gasping for breath. I don't like it here, not at all. My arms tremble with fear as I run, but I don't look back, even when hot air blows against my back.

Finally, I exit the woods at the top of a hill, and only then do I turn around. The woods are dark, but no one is there. Must have been my imagination, right?

I'm standing near railroad tracks, and I follow them.

*Don't give up on something because you don't understand it.* Mr. Lee speaks inside my head. I turn, not knowing where I'm going and knowing exactly where I'm headed all at once.

I keep walking, and before long I see it. Trees sway, bushes dance, and the branches reveal a new trail. I follow it until I come to the most beautiful sight.

It's the lake.

I spring toward it—jumping in fully clothed. For a second, I remember my phone is in my pocket, but I don't care.

I've found the magic.

I know what the Secret is. This isn't just a lake.

It's the Fountain of Youth.

# CHAPTER FIFTEEN

I swim in the cool water, and a memory washes over me.

I'm a little girl, but I'm here, in this same place. My friends and I play chicken wars, the water game where two pairs wrestle. One person from each pair sits on her partner's shoulders and tries to push the other off. I giggle, snorting on water, and when I look down, I see *him*.

The boy who went missing when I was a little girl.

I can't remember his name. He's beautiful and Black and funny, too—my first childhood friend ever. Why can't I remember his name?

In front of us, I push Elle, who sits on Lawson's shoulders. We were all here before, and I had forgotten. How would I forget this, and why can't I remember the boy's name?

Christina and Fiara swim near us and egg us on.

"C'mon, Elle!" Fiara cheers. Water glistens on her white skin. The sight of her takes my breath away. She's normal, just another little girl playing with us.

"Knock her over, Angelica!" Christina yells, water dripping from her short, brown hair. "C'mon, Asher, you gotta be stronger than that!"

*Asher?* Oh yeah, that's the boy's name! His grandmother,

Miss Charlamae, always baked us the most delicious peanut butter cookies.

The next thing I know, it's the following morning, and I wake up in my bed. The water in the lake washed over time and memory. I open my eyes, and sunlight pokes through my red curtains. I stretch out my long legs and sit up. I've never felt so rested. Every muscle in my body feels relaxed. How did I get home? And what happened after I jumped in the lake?

I remember diving in, but then my mind is blank. Somehow, obviously, I got back home. I rub my forehead and take a deep breath. The bathroom door opens and shuts, and I clutch my chest in panic.

*Grandpa. Is he okay?*

The time is near, all the doctors and nurses have been telling us. I was certain Mom was going to tell me he had passed yesterday. I swing my legs out of bed and saunter toward my window. Pulling the curtain open, I look out on the street. My window faces east, which is also the street side of the house. I like waking up early to run, so it's always worked out for me. An old couple walks down the road. Will I make it to their age? Grandpa wasn't always old. He was my age at one time. I know that, of course I know that—I'm not stupid. But I only remember him old.

The old couple on the street turn their heads. Their eyes gaze into my bedroom window. They flash a smile, but something's wrong. Their eyes turn red, and it makes my skin crawl.

I shut the curtains, rub my pulsing temples, and think of Grandpa.

My earliest memory of him fills me with warmth, erasing whatever weird vibe I got from the old couple on the street. I was four or five, and my family was over at his house. I picked my nose and had a great big booger. Boogers always made me laugh. I scraped it out, and it had to be bigger than my fingernail, which isn't all that big I suppose on a five-year-old's hand. I stared at it, awed by the big, slimy goo that formed inside my nose, and then I wiped it on Grandpa's bedroom door.

"Angelica!" Grandpa had yelled.

I giggled. He smiled and then chased me. He would have been in his sixties then, I guess, and he wasn't all that fast, but he was fast enough. He chased me out of his bedroom, through the hallway, and into his kitchen. He picked me up and playfully swatted my rear. I giggled some more, and then he turned me over so he could look me straight in the eye.

"I get that boogers are funny, honey, but we don't wipe them on walls. That's not what good girls do. Do you understand?"

I nodded. His voice was powerful and comforting all at the same time. I never wiped a booger on another wall again.

I peek through the curtains again. The old couple is out of sight, thankfully, and a boy around my age walks a dog. The dog's tail wiggles incessantly, its mouth open, its tongue soaking up the taste of the fall air.

Did I talk to my parents when I got home last night? I don't remember that, either. I choke back the fear that rises in my throat.

There's something else I notice, too. I feel... well, not angry. I can't remember the last time I didn't want to hit something or run away as fast as I could. I never used to feel that way, but ever since Grandpa got ill, I've felt mad at the world. When I wake up, I'm angry at the alarm clock. School is absolute hell and always makes me mad. People make me furious. Even Pauline—always so nice—has upset me a few times.

*Shit! Pauline!* I never texted her last night, either, at least I don't think I did.

Turning away from the window, I walk to the mirror on the back of my bedroom door. A sour taste creeps onto my tongue.

My eyes dart to the bedroom doorknob. Do I leave this moment and risk having my reality forever changed if Grandpa died?

Anger pulses throughout my body again. Rage rises in my chest the way the Chinese buffet gives me heartburn. I'm not mad at Grandpa, though.

I'm mad at myself.

I grab a pair of sweats and my running shoes. I know where I need to go, but this time I don't want to go alone. I need to make it up to Pauline for not messaging her last night.

Once I have my shoes on, I listen at the door before opening it. The shower in the bathroom turns on. It's probably Kennedy, my older brother. He always showers before anyone else. I take a deep breath and dart from my bedroom to the front door. No one is there, and no one tries to stop me.

I choose the reality where Grandpa is alive.

I run straight to Pauline's house. She's gonna freak when she sees what I want to show her.

---

"You found *what*?" Pauline asks. We're standing on her front porch. I knocked on her bedroom window, and she met me out here.

"It's better to show you," I say.

"Have you gone bat-shit, for real?" She steps close to me and sniffs at my face. "Or have you been drinkin'? Smokin'?"

I shake my head. "Just come with me. Please."

"I ain't even done my hair yet." She purses her lips.

"It's gonna get wet anyway."

"Are we skippin' school?" She relaxes a little. Pauline doesn't miss much, and the only time she does is for her own planned personal days, as she calls them.

"We could be back by lunch. We won't miss much, and no one's gonna care 'cuz we're the good kids, right?"

She flashes a smile, and I can tell she's curious. She convinces me to wait a minute while she changes clothes and gives her hair a quick fix. Pauline returns a minute later looking stunning. Maybe it's because I see her like every day, but I forget how beautiful she looks. Pauline has gorgeous light brown skin and long, curly hair that dances in the wind when she lets it. Most of the time, she pulls it back tightly and keeps it in a bun, when she doesn't want to mess with it.

"We need bikes," I tell her.

"Bikes?" Her eyes widen as if I told her we need rocket ships.

"Yes, you know those things with two wheels we rode as kids?"

"Exactly." She rolls her eyes. "As *kids*."

"I still see your sisters out riding bikes. Can't we borrow theirs?"

"How far away is this place?" She walks toward the garage.

"Not far. It's quick on bikes." I giggle at Pauline's frown, but she opens the garage. "Is that yours?" There are three in the garage. Two look dirty but used. Behind them stands a bike that's layered in spider webs and dust. Pauline groans as she wipes it clean, revealing a beautiful purple, her favorite color.

"Yeah," Pauline says. "Tires are probably flat, but I'll check." Pauline puts pressure on them, and they are. We pump up the tires, and I borrow one of the other bicycles.

"Jesus," Pauline says. "I can't remember the last time I did this."

I felt the same way yesterday, but I don't tell Pauline. Remembering what it felt like is all part of the experience.

As we pick up speed and get out of town, Pauline turns to me and says, "This feels nice." I watch her smile grow as the wind blows harder on her face. It is a fantastic feeling.

Pauline doesn't ever stop talking, so I'm also surprised that our ride is quiet. She follows me closely, and we get to the wooded area where we have to walk.

She doesn't ask me why we get off our bikes and leave them here. She follows me to the entrance to the woods.

With ears perked, I listen, and my heart slams against my chest. Something lives in here that chased me. Worse, something's here that has the power to make it dark. To consume life. I don't know how I know that, but it's true.

Should I warn Pauline? No. That would panic and distract her. If we go fast, she'll be okay.

Although the sun is high in the sky, it feels like night again the moment we step into the woods. The darkness wraps around us like a heavy coat, powerful and thick.

"What's that?" Pauline asks. Branches break from behind. "Shit, is someone else here?" she says louder. I turn around and squint. I can't see but a few feet in front of me, but footsteps approach quickly.

"Someone is here," I whisper, and my heart sinks. Have I endangered us?

"What do we do?"

I swallow hard. Do we run? Do we face it? My brain buzzes like a beehive. Thoughts swirl around, and I know some are memories and some are possibilities, but I don't know which is which. I don't know what to do.

*Come to me.*

A chill rips through my chest and goosebumps pop up all over my arms and legs.

*Come to me.*

It's a voice in the woods, a deep, dark voice.

It's the voice of a monster.

"Well shit fuck bugger, let's get the hell out of here!" Pauline spins me around and pushes me forward.

*COME TO ME!* The voice shouts at us. We run faster. Pauline breathes hard behind me. Her breath is warm and wet against my neck. I'm grateful for my cross-country legs, and I run hard up the hill.

I make it to the top, but I stumble. I roll out of the woods, scraping my knees and banging my wrist. I stand and turn around, expecting to see Pauline right behind me.

Instead, a pale face greets me in the dark woods. It looks like a man at first, but it's not exactly a man. Black eyes appear on a ghostly face, and the blackness runs down from the eyes like tears.

I cover my mouth, but a scream escapes me.

Snake-like lips form on the face, and then it laughs.

What I felt on the back of my neck wasn't Pauline—it was this thing, this monster!

*Pauline!*

She limps up the hill from behind the monster. The face turns away from me. I don't see a body, but a shadow. I can see through the face, though, like it's a ghost. Pauline screams, and the face charges at her.

It looks like a black ghost—that's all a shadow really is. It floats in front of her, and then the longest arms I've ever seen stretch out and wrap around her. Pauline's jaw drops, and she releases a piercing scream, the kind of scream you'd only ever do once.

The monster rips right through her, piercing through flesh and taking skin and bones into the ground where her two feet once stood.

# CHAPTER SIXTEEN

Fear grabs me like a chokehold. In the blink of an eye, Pauline and the monster disappear.

I clench my fists and scream. Do I run to the lake? Do I get help?

Panic floods me. I consider both possibilities. Taking a deep breath, I run back into the woods to get the hell out of here.

Help is what I need, but not the police. Yes, the logical part of my brain—there is one, even after seeing this—says to call the cops and tell Pauline's family. But this isn't normal, far from it. I need someone who might understand.

Lawson. Christina. Elle. Where *is* Elle?

They'd understand because they've been here before. Lawson and Elle said so in Mr. Lee's class, and now I remember something they apparently don't. I was here with them, too.

Why don't they remember that I was here? What about all the missing children now? And Asher and the others from before?

I sprint through the woods. I stumble, but I don't look back. Once out, I hop on my bike and pedal hard to school. When I arrive, I check my phone—somehow it survived the lake yesterday and my falls today, much to my surprise. It's near the end of first hour. Lawson and Christina would be in Mr. Lee's class, and I need to get them out of there.

Taking giant strides, I leap to the classroom. Fortunately, I don't have to make up any excuse or wait. The bell rings, and students flood the hallway. When Lawson comes out of class, I grab him.

"I need to talk to you," I say. When Christina walks out, I seize her, too, her eyebrows raising high over her hazel eyes. "And you. Come with me. Now!"

We stride down the hall toward the front of the school where I left my bike. There's no time to worry about who will see us or stop us. We need to go.

"What's going on?" Lawson asks. He rubs his neck, and raw, red scratches briefly capture my attention.

"Pauline. It took Pauline!"

Their eyes widen, and for a second, I'm surprised I don't have to explain more. They know more than me, don't they? It's like I missed a week of school and need to catch up.

"What should I do?" I ask. "Can we get her back?"

Christina's eyes are lit with fury, matching my own. It gives me hope. "As long as you can remember her, maybe there's a chance."

"Will it hurt her?" I ask, cracking my knuckles, anger pulsing throughout my body.

Christina shrugs again. "There are other monsters below the Darkness, ones that never leave the pit. The monster's monsters. I don't know." She tightens her lips.

"Don't think I'm totally weird," Lawson interjects, "but the last time I went to the lake, I dreamed about all this. But it wasn't a dream, you know? I think it was the Secret talking to me."

"The Fountain?" I ask confidently. I've been several steps behind, but that's one thing I know. "That's what the Secret is, right? The Fountain of Youth."

Lawson fixes me with surprised eyes. "How do you know that?"

"It came to me when I was there. I think it spoke to me, too. The Fountain."

Christina and Lawson nod but don't say anything. A desire to run hits me, not to run away, but rather to run back to the Darkness and fight.

"What do we do?" I ask. "Can we help her?"

"There is a way to escape from the pit if Pauline is still alive," Lawson says. "It caught me, too. Both Elle and me. When we were kids." He pauses, and I get the feeling he's leaving something else out. "There is a way out."

"How?" I ask. "What do we do?"

"We have to go to it," Lawson says. "Let it take us. Then maybe we can get to Pauline. I tried to do that to find Elle, but I messed up. I think I know what I need to do this time." Lawson's face tells me he isn't joking.

"You guys, we need to get together with Mister Lee," Christina says. "Elle is missing, Coach Nathan... well, I dunno, and Fiara won't talk to me. I think the Darkness is planning something big. Bigger than we can imagine."

"How much more does Lee know?" I ask.

"He's been fighting this or trying. Doing the best he can. He needs our help as much as we need him," Christina says.

"What the hell is the purpose of the Fountain? And the Darkness?" I ask. The more questions that come to mind, the more frustration pumps through my veins. "Screw it. Never mind that," I say, right as Lawson looks like he's about to explain more. "We need to do something, and I don't want no stupid BS right now. Do we go to the woods, or do we go get more help?" I stand tall and cross my arms. My biceps flex, and I want to rip a tree out of the ground.

"I dunno," Christina says, her voice low. "I think if it took Pauline, then maybe we can help. Or... maybe we'll just get killed." She swallows hard, then steps toward me and puts her hands on my shoulders. "There's something else you need to know," she continues. "For your own safety." She takes a deep breath, and Lawson's eyes turn down. "I killed Coach Nathan."

My jaw hits the ground. "What the—?"

"Not me exactly," she says. "The Darkness possessed me, and it forced me to do it. But he's not exactly dead. He's a monster, another evil force working for the Darkness."

"What the *actual* fuck?" I ask.

Christina lowers her head. "I don't understand everything. All I can tell you is that it doesn't have control of me now. I tell you that because I still worry it could possess me again." She rubs her temples. "When I was mean to you and Pauline at lunch, that was the Darkness. Not me. Still, I'm sorry about how I treated you. Regardless though, you can't trust me. Not completely. Or anyone really. Okay?"

"Jesus." There's a lot more I want to say. In fact, I think I should be running away now for sure—and not to the woods but far from Worthlapp, from Christina, and from everything. But I can't. There's Pauline to worry about.

And my grandfather. I still don't even know about him, and thinking about it brings a tightness to my chest.

We look at one another in silence. "Maybe we need to talk with Mister Lee, like you said," I suggest. "I want to help Pauline, but I want to be prepared."

Lawson and Christina nod. I'm ready to rip an entire forest apart if I must. With this rage that rips through me right now, I could. I will destroy that fucking monster with my bare hands. But I'll listen to what Mr. Lee has to say because I hope there's a way that won't get us all killed.

---

We run to Mr. Lee's classroom, racing and spinning through the halls. Any moment, I'm certain someone will yell at us or grab us, and maybe that someone won't be a person at all.

When we arrive at Mr. Lee's classroom, though, it's empty.

"Does he have a prep this hour?" I ask.

"No clue," Lawson says, and Christina shrugs. "You guys, look at his desk."

Papers are scattered all over his desk, and his chair is flipped upside-down.

"Shit!" Christina yells.

"You think someone came for him?" I ask.

"Someone or some *thing*," she replies. "We're on our own. It's risky, but I think we head straight to the Darkness if we want to save Pauline."

"We need a ride," Lawson says.

"Do you have a car?" I ask Christina.

"She rides the bus with me," Lawson says.

"It's a couple miles to my house," I tell them. "We can get my bike and my brother's. Two of us can share one." I'll pedal the hell out of the bike, even if I have to support another person.

Lawson nods. "Okay, yeah. I think, uh, we're supposed to bike there. You know? I know that sounds weird." He pauses for a moment and looks around.

"What is it?" Christina asks.

"Teddy," he says. "Shouldn't he be with us? He's been there with me, and he can help us fight. Strength in numbers and all, right?"

"That's a good idea," she replies. "But I saw him leave school early. The dean came into our class, whispered something to him, and they both left."

"Dammit," Lawson says. "The only chance we have is in having multiple people help fight it. If we try to do it ourselves...." He rubs the red scratches on his neck. "But also, I bet it's about his mom. She's been sick. I need to at least get ahold of him."

While Lawson's messaging Teddy, I ask Christina, "How will we even fight this thing? Do you know?"

She shrugs and gestures ambiguously. "Mister Lee had ideas he was going to share with us. I've tried to fight it, but I...." She frowns and breathes heavily. Her eyes show pain, a deep burden that makes her look ten years older than she is. "I, uh, well, I failed. If we find Mister Lee, he'll help us. He was even going to train us and show us what he's been doing. But we can't sit and do nothing, you know? I worry more of us will go missing."

I crack my knuckles. "Let's go, Lawson." I know Teddy has problems, and I'd like to be there for him, too—but I'm worried we don't have time to spare. How long can Pauline, or anyone, survive once the Darkness has it?

---

We make our way out of school and run to my house. We don't talk as we run, and I'm happy for that. I try not to think at all. I turn around a few times to make sure Lawson is keeping up. His cheeks are beet-red and he's breathing heavily, but overall he's not too bad.

When we get to my house, Lawson bends over and puts his head in between his legs. "Stand up straight. You'll pass out, and I can't carry no deadweight." Christina and I breathe hard, too. I wipe the sweat from my forehead and get on my bike.

"Hop on," I tell Lawson. "I got you." Christina takes the other bike. I flash a quick smile at her, and she returns it. Girls get shit done.

I push forward. The wind hits my face and blows my hair into Lawson. He puts his head against my back, and it makes me smile. Not in a romantic way or anything. It's hard to explain, but somehow it makes me feel stronger.

I hit a bump in the road, and he holds me tighter. His breath feels warm against my neck.

"What do you think is really going on here?" I ask. His grip loosens, and he pulls his face away from my back. "I mean with the whole Darkness and Fountain thing. What do you really make of it?"

Christina rides close and looks over to us at my question.

"You ever look up at the stars at night and wonder how big the world really is?" Lawson asks, his breathing steady once again. "Like, the stars are what? Millions of miles away or whatever?

And there are universes we haven't even discovered. I think the world has a lot of secrets, a lot of things we don't know about. I think the Darkness and the Fountain are two of its secrets, things that show us the world is bigger and more mysterious than we know."

"But why here?" I ask. "Why Worthlapp?"

"Why not?" he says. "Maybe every community has something like this. I've been thinking a lot about it, since we re-discovered it. I went to this place all the time as a kid. Did you know that?" My chest tightens. Why doesn't he remember that I was there, too? "But then I forgot about it. I bet kids have discovered a thousand secrets about the world, from every little town in every corner of the Earth. But then they grow up, and they forget."

"The Darkness made you forget," Christina says. "There are other things none of us remember. It takes kids, and not only do they go missing, but it makes the world, or most of it at least, forget about their existence."

"But not entirely. Not this time, anyway," I say. "I mean, otherwise, how do you explain the missing posters and the Amber alerts?"

Christina visibly shudders. "I don't know. I think it's saving them for something. But, yeah, at least that means they could still be alive, and that there's a chance we could save them."

"Do you know a boy named Asher?" I ask.

"Yes," Christina says. Her quick response sends a chill through me. Someone remembers! "Do you?"

"I saw a memory when I visited the Fountain. But I don't really remember him. It's a vague memory."

"Mofa made you forget," she says. My arms erupt in goosebumps. It's terrifying to think about how much I've forgotten, not just what I know.

"But why?" I ask, pushing my glasses against the bridge of my nose.

"That's the thing about secrets," Christina says. "You're not supposed to know why."

I pedal faster. The confusion enhances my anger. If Lawson is right, then the Darkness and the Fountain are some kind of secrets of the Earth or the world or whatever. But the Darkness is clearly evil—it took my best friend and Elle and who knows how many others.

And for what purpose?

All I know is that we must get them back.

"What are we gonna do when we get there?" I ask.

"I'll let it take me," Lawson says. "I know how to get out. I've done it before. When I'm in the pit, I'll look for Pauline. Okay?"

I nod, but it sounds like a sacrifice.

While we ride, I try to remember what pulled me to the Fountain of Youth when I was a kid.

Something about lines. Grandpa whispered a secret in my ear, and then I saw magic. It was a beautiful purple, a web of purple magic that led me to the Fountain, and that's when I saw Elle and Lawson. Then I saw something else... a premonition, and it terrified me.

I swallow hard and shake away the thoughts. I'm remembering more, but the more I remember, the more my arms tremble.

Suddenly, we're there—we've pulled up outside the wooded entrance, but we're not alone. Someone's bag is sitting right here, a nice leather bag.

"Is that Elle's?" I ask.

The others shrug, and we get off our bikes. We peek through the trees.

"Hello?" Lawson says. "Anyone there?"

Footsteps pound on the dirt, loud and heavy. Someone is running right toward us from inside the woods.

"Shit, Law, why you gotta talk to it?" I ask.

He clenches his fists. "I'd rather fight out here in the sunlight if we gotta fight a person. At least we can see."

"Coach Nathan, you think?" I ask. The footsteps get louder, and the three of us form a line.

I make two fists as well. My head spins, but I bend my knees and make some kind of fighting stance. I can't believe this is happening, any of it. I try to focus on the sound in the woods—the steps are maddeningly loud, and someone approaches hurriedly.

I gulp as the woods open and a man comes running out. Without thinking, I swing my right foot at him. My long leg connects with his face.

"Oof," he groans and falls immediately on the ground.

"Damn, girl," Christina says, her eyes wide with shock. "Nice kick."

I didn't know I had it in me.

"Stop, you guys," Lawson says and steps forward. He puts out his arm to the man that fell on the ground.

"Law, what are you—" I start to ask.

"You guys, that's Mister Lee," he says.

I take a closer look and throw my hands over my mouth. "Oh my God. Mister Lee? I'm so sorry."

Lawson pulls him up, and Mr. Lee brushes the dirt off his pants and places a hand on the side of his face where my foot connected.

"Quite a good kick, Angelica. That's good to know." He smiles while rubbing his jaw. Bending over, he picks up glasses that flew off his face. My hands clamp over my mouth. I hope I didn't break them. He picks them up, wipes them off with his shirt, and puts them back on. Phew. They seem okay.

"What are you doing here?" Lawson asks.

Mr. Lee steps closer to us, and I take a little pride in the fact that half his face is red from my foot.

"I've been searching for the missing kids," he says. "But I cannot fight Mofa on my own, not any longer. Not that I've been successful, anyway. There was also a fight at the high school. I just had to try one more time on my own before… well, before putting your lives at greater risk."

"Huh?" We say almost in unison.

"I had a most unfortunate visitor in my classroom. Your coach came to see me. There was a struggle. He knows I've been talking to you, and he knows I have a lot more to say." He looks at Christina. "You're right. He's a monster in human flesh, not possessed by Mofa but a part of it. He was sent to kill me, and I'm guessing he kidnapped Elle, too. I managed to defend myself against him. I think it gave me a surge of confidence to fight Mofa on my own, one last time, right in the core of its pit." He sighs and shakes his head. "I'm not strong enough on my own."

"Did you find Elle?" Lawson asks.

He bites his lip and reaches for the bag we've seen before. What's inside it and why he did leave it out here? "Unfortunately, no. I'm afraid things are about to get a lot worse. A lot more dangerous."

I stare at him incredulously.

"What do you mean?" Lawson asks.

"Mofa is stronger than ever, and it's after all of you. One of you is *Xianchi*, the Seer. I do not know which one." He looks at us the way my mother did when she told me my grandfather was dying.

"What is a Seer?" I ask.

"It's not going to stop until it kills all of you," he says. "Come with me, now. There's more to talk about, and this place isn't safe."

"But it's got Pauline," I say, also wondering why Mr. Lee isn't answering my question.

"Oh no," Mr. Lee says. He crosses his arms. "I'm afraid it may be too late for her. And if all three of you go in there, it will be too late for you. Come, now. There is much we must do. I... I almost couldn't escape. It took everything I've learned to break free from Mofa. It's time I teach you everything I know."

He holds the leather bag tightly against his chest. It moves up and down, matching his breathing. His eyes are dark and heavy, and I'm certain that he thinks some of us will not make it out of this alive.

# CHAPTER SEVENTEEN

We bike back into town and meet Mr. Lee at a park. He had driven to the woods in his Prius, and we still had to haul our bikes out of there. He arrives at the park first and waits with a milkshake for each of us.

Part of me wants to tell him that my best friend Pauline is floating in God knows what kind of shit. She could die, and here we are sipping milkshakes like a bunch of oblivious assholes. Instead, I take it. It's chocolate, and the coolness soothes my inner rage. The three of us join Mr. Lee at a picnic table.

"Mister Lee, how do you know about all this stuff?" Lawson asks. The wind whips at his chestnut hair, messy due to the ride to and from the woods, but he doesn't seem to care or notice.

Our teacher leans back on the bench. A few days ago I was kind of crushing on Lawson and Teddy. Now, my best friend has been kidnapped by... by what? I don't even know. These three are way ahead of me, and it pisses me off.

"The legend of Kang Fu and Mofa is much older than any of us." He takes a deep breath and reaches into the leather bag that was sitting outside the woods. He pulls out a journal and opens it. "I've kept notes on everything, and whenever something happens, I try to write it down right away. That's why I took this to the woods, but I left it outside. If something were to happen to me, I'd want someone to learn what I know. I figured one of you would find it."

His lips curve into an awkward grin, and my eyes linger on the journal. "There's also a copy of this in my desk drawer at school, and another copy in the top drawer of my bedroom dresser at home. I tell you that in case something happens to me."

"So how does this help us get Pauline back?" I cough into my fist and glare at him.

"To get to the point, then, we must discover the Seer and plan our attack on Mofa."

"What the... what is the Seer?" I ask and roll my eyes.

Mr. Lee blows off my tone. "The Seer has a special ability to see and harness unique energy. Without the Seer, this would be like searching for a needle in a haystack. The Seer will connect us and guide us. Show us how to fight."

"How does that work?" Lawson asks. "And do you know who it is?"

"I do not yet know," Mr. Lee says. "But I know how to figure it out. We will train, and then you will see exactly what I am talking about."

"What's this about our energy?" I ask.

"Energy, yes," he says calmly. "You each have unique energy. You just can't see it. A web of energy all your own that extends from here"—he points to his head—"and here"—he points to his heart—"and connects you to the universe. Mofa wants that energy. *Your* energy, specifically."

I think about the purple magic, the lines that my grandfather was able to make me see, the lines that first led me to the Fountain. Shit. Am I the Seer?

"I remember a little song or something about the Seer, from when I was a kid. Why would I know that?" Christina asks.

"*And one of them can see, webs but not a spider's, if only they believe, and bathe in the light*. That one?" Mr. Lee asks.

"How do you know that? How do I?" Christina asks, rubbing goosebumps on her arms.

"Kang Fu whispered to you each time you were there," Mr. Lee says.

The song comes back to me, too, a distant memory, like hearing a bedtime story you hadn't heard in a decade.

"Do you know a woman named Charlamae?" Christina asks.

Mr. Lee's lips tighten. He nods slowly. "I've been trying to find her. She's completely off the grid. No phone, no internet, and I don't know where she lives."

"She was my neighbor," Lawson says, turning ghostly pale. "She lived across the street from me."

"She's the grandmother of Asher, a missing boy from your childhood," Mr. Lee says. "She's one of the few who remembered him after he went missing. She's not the only one. But the fact that she remembers means there's something extraordinary about her, too."

"I thought about her when the Darkness possessed me," Christina says. "It doesn't want me to find her. It became furious at the memory. So, obviously, we have to find her."

"Yes, and I'm looking for her. I have notes in here that I'll share with all of you, and you can help me find her," Mr. Lee says, tapping on his journal.

I clear my throat, trying to make sense of everything. "So, we have some kind of energy that the Darkness wants. And now we have to fight it, but with the help of someone who can help us see that energy? If we lose, it gets what it wants, though. Is this the best course of action?"

Christina nods at me and addresses our teacher. "Yeah. I mean, look at Fiara. She's been through hell and back. The Darkness nearly destroyed her. You thought she was the Seer, but you were wrong then. How do you know you'll be right this time?"

Mr. Lee frowns, but I interrupt. "What happened to Fiara?"

Christina sighs and puts her hand on the table. "It just as

easily could have been me who was hurt." She pushes her milkshake away. "We tried to... to stop it, as kids. The Darkness called to us once, a long time ago. It made us do all sorts of terrible things. I worry that I don't remember them all." She massages her throat and looks up at the sky. "Fiara and I decided to fight it. Mister Lee knew of Fiara and thought she was the Seer when we were kids. That's when the Darkness went after my parents. It wanted to show me what it could do to hurt others. It did all sorts of awful things. Then it went after Fiara directly." She wipes at her red-rimmed hazel eyes. "It swallowed her whole, that shadow-thing. She was missing for days." She looks over at me.

"Like Pauline?" I ask.

Christina nods. "Eventually, though, the Darkness spit her out, but she was never the same. Her skin had changed, and her hair, and those eyes." She folds her arms and looks down. "She never told me the details, though. I don't know anything else. But Mofa ripped my family apart, and it destroyed Fiara."

"So that's what happens to the Seer?" I ask and gulp. No one answers.

We sit in silence for a bit, and I worry even more about Pauline. Even if she survives, she may not be the same.

"Do you think Elle's relationship with Coach has anything to do with this?" Lawson asks.

Mr. Lee turns a dark red. "What about her and Coach?"

Lawson freezes, and his lips tighten into a straight line. He lowers his head.

"What is it, Lawson?" Mr. Lee presses.

His feet kick at the dirt beneath the table. "They were, um, they had a relationship."

Mr. Lee scowls. "An intimate relationship?"

Lawson nods.

Mr. Lee's nostrils flare. "That's not good. Not at all."

"Of course not," I say. "It's disgusting. And illegal."

"Yes, but there's more to it than that," Mr. Lee says, rising from the table. He presses his hands against his wide waist and studies a park district employee in the distance. "Mofa possessed Christina and made her do terrible things. You've since told me that it took Coach Nathan, too. What if it was using Nathan to get to Elle?"

"I don't understand," Lawson says.

"Elle could be our Seer," he says. Mr. Lee sighs deeply, and I feel his anger. "Nathan's been trying to manipulate her the entire time they were together, and Mofa was just waiting for the right moment to take her."

My skin tingles just thinking about it. Coach had been working with me all semester, too. How often had he been controlled by the Darkness? After a moment of silence, I ask, "If Elle is the Seer and we can't get her back, what happens?"

"Then all of this is for nothing." A vein in Mr. Lee's forehead throbs, and he rubs his temples.

"What. About. *Pauline*?" I ask again. "We can't just leave her there. If there's a chance she's alive, we have to go after her."

Lawson nods. "Yes. We had a plan. I know how to escape from the pit. I can go in there and get her."

"No! Not without proper training. What happened to your throat, Lawson?"

Blushing, Lawson lowers his head. "Something I couldn't see tried to choke me. Just a regular evening in Worthlapp."

"We need to go to Kang Fu before we train. We need its strength and its magic. It may help reveal the Seer to us."

"But the only way to Kang Fu is through the woods," I say.

"That's right," Mr. Lee replies. "It will be terribly dangerous. It's a catch-22. Mofa is too strong for us to fight it right now, but we may not be able to win if we can't get to Kang Fu." A grim smile grows on his face.

"What are you thinking?" Christina asks.

He tightens his lips. "I do think we can beat Mofa. You mustn't risk going there alone, that's for sure. But together...

together, we will run faster than ever before and make it to Kang Fu. We can." He leans in. "We must."

"Mister Lee?" Lawson asks. "I took a friend to Kang Fu. Teddy. You have him in class. His mom is real sick. Can Kang Fu save her?"

"My grandpa is sick, too," I say. I worry he's already passed, but I still don't know for sure and I don't say that out loud. "If I could get him to Kang Fu, too, do you think it would help?"

"I think it could, but there's a huge risk," he says. "If they're not strong enough or fast enough to get through the woods, then... well, then they could die before even getting to the water."

I want to punch this stupid picnic table. All of this is so unfair. I picture ripping out every tree that planted roots in the Darkness.

"There are other factors that are important besides the waters of Kang Fu," Mr. Lee says. "Friendship. Family. I know you are worried about your friend, Angelica, but you have to trust me. As long as we can remember her, we have time. Time is different down there."

He puts his hands in his pockets and looks up at the sky. "So, I want each of you to do something first. Lawson, I want you to visit Teddy. Find out about his mother. Angelica, I want you to visit your family. Comfort your grandfather. Christina, I want you to go home, too. Take care of your mom." Mr. Lee pauses. "And find Fiara. Have her join us if you can. I have a feeling she understands secrets that we haven't even begun to grasp."

"Okay," Christina says, and we all agree. There's something about returning home that feels safer than running back into the Darkness.

"Oh, Christina," Mr. Lee says. "You told me about a special weapon, yes? Bring that. I believe what you have isn't some ordinary weapon. It came from Mofa, and it can hurt it."

We look at Christina inquisitively.

"A blade," she says. "A very sharp, scary blade." She shivers and rubs her arms. "The Darkness gave it to me, or led me to it, when I was a kid. I think you're right, Mister Lee. I took the knife the last time, but then... Rob...." Tears glisten in her eyes.

"It possessed you," Mr. Lee. "You must forgive yourself. With our energy combined and with the help of the Seer, we will plunge that knife right into the heart of Mofa."

Christina nods and wipes her eyes.

Mr. Lee gazes up at the sky again. "Mofa would expect us during the day, not at night. Let's meet up at sunset, by the entrance to the woods tonight. All right?" He turns away without waiting for an answer.

"I really do need to go home. My grandfather's been so sick." I pause for a moment. "I've avoided home because I don't want to face it, you know?"

Lawson and Christina nod.

"My grandfather was my everything. *Is*," I quickly correct myself. "If he's gone, well, what good is all this magic shit?"

"I'm worried about Teddy," Lawson says. "We hung out a lot when school started, but then his mom got sick. I haven't been a very good friend. I don't know how she is. Or how Teddy is."

"I'm never home," Christina says. "My mom is a constant reminder of what happened last time I tried to stand up to this evil. It scares me."

We exchange looks of understanding before we go our separate ways. My thoughts return to my grandfather. He turned ninety a couple months ago. He didn't have kids until he was much older than most who do, my parents have told me. I'm fifteen. I can't even imagine what ninety would be like.

The thing about my grandfather is that he's always been old since I've known him. Not only that but someone in my family—never in front of Grandpa, of course—always starts a discussion about when he's going to die. I can still remember his eightieth birthday. I would have been five years old. I was sitting in Grandpa's lap, he was bouncing me on his legs, and I giggled. I remember that because I got down to go play with the other kids, and my mother stopped me.

She grabbed me by my wrist and said to me, "This could be your grandfather's last birthday. You go visit with him, not these other children."

It made me cry. Thinking of the memory now, tears well in my eyes. I did go back to him, he picked me up, and I sobbed like only annoying children can.

"What's wrong, my Angel?" he had asked.

"I don't want you to die," I told him.

He laughed and wiped away my tears. "I'm not going anywhere, Angel. I will always be right here," and he touched my heart.

I hadn't thought of that day in… well, I don't know when. But it is fresh in my memory now, and tears roll down my face.

———

WHEN I RETURN home, I leave the bike out front by the porch. I walk inside, and noise comes from the kitchen.

A second later, my mother darts out and runs toward me. "Where have you been? Where the *hell* have you been?"

Her eyes are dark and puffy, and she looks like she hasn't slept. "Don't you dare ever leave without asking me first! And I know you skipped school, too! You are grounded forever as far as I'm concerned." Her face twists, and she glares at me. It scares me—it's not just anger. It looks like hate, and that terrifies me even more.

I gulp. "I'm sorry, Mom. I really am."

She stares at me like I am a stranger. Maybe it's because I am not fighting her and apologize. Or it's because I really am a stranger to her. Does she even know me? Do I know her?

The question I want to ask more than anything finally comes out. "How's Grandpa?"

She crosses her arms and nods. She nods over and over again, and her face morphs into anger.

"He passed away this morning while you were skipping

school. I called to tell you, but they couldn't find you. We knew it was coming, too. The doctors all said. I tried to tell you yesterday, and you ran away like the worthless brat you are."

I deserve that, but it still hurts.

"I'm sorry, Mom."

"Go tell that to your dead grandfather." She turns around and walks away.

# CHAPTER EIGHTEEN

Naturally, I wasn't able to meet up with everyone at dusk as we had planned. I texted Lawson to let him know, but I haven't seen anyone in a couple days. The thought of Pauline as a prisoner in the pit nags at me, and I dig my nails into my palms. There was a new missing person story on the news for both Pauline and Elle, which gave me hope. If I understand this evil correctly, no one would even remember Elle or Pauline if the Darkness had killed them.

I shake away an absolutely horrifying thought. How many people have we lost that we can't remember?

More kids have gone missing, too. My phone blows up with an Amber alert each day. I used to jump every time the loud alarm would ring. Now, it's as common as a text alert, and I barely flinch. Worthlapp instituted a curfew. Even if I weren't grounded for life, I wouldn't be able to go anywhere.

My week has been turned upside down. I want to train and fight for my friends, but I haven't been able to leave my house except to be dragged along to funeral homes and churches.

Today is the morning of my grandfather's funeral. I stare out the backseat window of my parents' car as we drive to the church, watching the trees and houses pass in a blur. I should be out there fighting!

"Ouch!" I cry.

"What is it?" Dad asks.

"Nothing." A trickle of blood pools in my palm from my nails. I take several deep breaths and try to relax.

Maybe I should be crying like my mother in the passenger seat. She's bawling into a tissue, but it looks fake to me. Grandpa was my dad's dad. Why is she so upset? And how could she be that sad when all she's been to me is a bitter bitch? I can't cry when she's crying—her tears distract me from my own grief, which pisses me off even more.

She has yet to forgive me for not being there when he passed. When she has spoken to me, it's with a mean tone, like I'm the one who killed him.

We pull up to the church, and we're greeted by other family members and friends. People that I've never talked to before hug me, and they all say sorry. I want to say, "Why?" I mean, seriously. You say sorry when a kid gets cancer, or a teenager gets in a car wreck and dies. When someone's ninety years old, you say fucking congratulations. He had a very full life.

*You should be hugging me and crying about Pauline,* I want to shout. *What if we can't get her back? What if this is it for her? She'll never see her high school graduation or fall in love.* Finally, the tears come, and they are for my grandfather. I don't know why I am so conflicted, or why I have tried to resist these feelings all week. I don't care if he made it to ninety. Death is heartbreaking.

Life sucks. It's cruel. It's unfair. Life is stupid. Any one of us can be taken at any second. That's the real tragedy.

The other day, I went with my father to the drugstore, and I browsed greeting cards while he picked up something for my mother. No doubt it was some kind of antidepressant. What does she have to be depressed about? She's alive! She should be doing something instead of sitting around moaning about how terrible life is.

Those were the thoughts that ran through my mind when I

wandered down the greeting card aisle. I used to like reading all the humorous birthday cards when I was a kid. I used to think I had an old spirit because Maxine—the old lady who always cracks jokes—was my favorite. What caught my eye this time, though, were the cards that celebrated the biggest birthday milestones. There was a section for a person's 80th birthday, 85th birthday, 90th birthday, and even 100th birthday. Each section had several cards, too.

It pisses me off. Will Pauline see any of those birthdays? Hell, will I?

The images of the birthday cards float away when some cousin whose name I can't even remember extends his hand to my family.

"I'm sorry for your loss."

I wipe away the tears as quickly as I can. Crying in front of people I don't know makes me uncomfortable.

I walk into the church and study the giant cross in the front, which makes me think of the Fountain. Perhaps no one should live forever, but no one should die young, either. It's a powerful magic, and I start to understand why something, even the Darkness, may want to keep others from it.

We take our seats in the church, and the service begins. The preacher welcomes everyone and then says, "Christopher Lewis was a great man. A loving father, husband, grandfather. Christopher is gone, but only in this world. The flesh isn't forever, but the spirit is. Christopher now is in the spirit world, sitting next to the Father in heaven, looking down on all of us now."

"Amen," several people say.

The preacher picks up a Bible. "No man suffers who believes in Me!"

"Amen," the congregation says again.

"For if you believe in Jesus, you will be rewarded with eternal life."

Everyone nods their heads and cries softly. I want to scream that they are stupid children who believe in whatever they want to make themselves feel better. Grandpa is dead, and that's all there is to it. He's not hanging out with Jesus and laughing about old times.

He no longer exists. Period.

*What if there is a consciousness that lives beyond this reality?* The question pops in my head, but I don't recognize its voice. The voice is sweet and feminine, the opposite of this preacher. The opposite of the Darkness.

It's the voice I heard when I first explored the woods, and it poses a big question. Does any part of us live on? People talk about spirits and things like that, but does any part of our memory or conscious being live on? If not, what's life for?

*There are answers, Angelica. You just need to know where to look.*

The voice in my head gives me chills, and I turn my attention back to the preacher.

"Now maybe we have some non-believers here," the preacher says. "If they were to meet their unfortunate end today, then their lives may be over. But there is still time to turn to Jesus, turn to Christ. Accept Him as the only savior, as the one true God."

The preacher walks around a table full of candles. If we had a couple dragons in here and some different clothes, it could be a *Game of Thrones* episode. Just another foolish man thinking he knows about God trying to tell everyone else what to believe.

"It's not too late to spread the word of Jesus Christ and accept His love. Be saved!" *Are we mourning for my grandfather or recruiting for your church?*

"Amen," the idiots cry.

"Now, let us pray."

*What do we have to pray for if he's already hanging out with his buddy JC?* I fold my hands and pretend to pray, but my fingernails dig into my palms again.

My eyes scan the beauty of the church. A giant cross at the

front, stained-glass windows all throughout, and tall, gorgeous pillars.

This is what people donate money to. Not people who need it, but instead to the pockets of those who promise salvation, like it's an insurance policy for an afterlife.

Everything is bullshit.

*And if it's not bullshit, well Grandpa or Jesus or someone up there, come down and tell me!*

There are no more voices in my head, and the preacher finally stops. We get back in our cars and drive to the cemetery. As if the church service wasn't enough, we have to do it again here.

I stand next to my family as Grandpa's coffin is lowered into the ground. My father spent several thousand dollars on a box that will never be seen again.

Death is a business. We all die, and these assholes know they can make money off of it.

When the coffin enters the ground, I look over my shoulder. Lawson, Teddy, Christina, and Mr. Lee stand in the back. Teddy looks the saddest among them all, and he waves at me. I nod back.

They're the only friends I have right now, and they're the only ones who might possibly understand my grief and pain.

A stranger appears about ten feet or so behind them, but my friends don't notice. Even squinting, I can't make out too many details about the person. It's a man with dark skin—almost as Black as mine—and red eyes. He winks at me, and a sharp pain hits my spine. My lungs turn cold. Who the hell is that? I turn back to the grave and pray. My eyes close tight. *Grandpa, if you're out there, wherever you are, help me. Help us all. Will you?*

Shaking my head, I think about the prayer. Are we really so weak that we have to ask for help from people who no longer exist —or from spirits or angels or whatever? We're all doomed.

I open my eyes, looking back at my friends. They smile again. The stranger is gone. Glancing around the cemetery, I can't see him.

*Thanks, Grandpa.* Despite my previous skepticism, a small smile forms on my face.

---

After a final prayer, we walk back toward our cars. My parents have organized a meal for everyone—for some reason, I've learned, you can't bury someone and not have a meal afterward. Sounds stupid to me. The last thing I want is food and to have to fucking socialize with people. But perhaps if my friends were there, it would be different.

"Dad," I say, avoiding Mom altogether. "Those are my friends. Can they join us?"

He opens his mouth, but of course it's my bitch of a mother who answers. "No. This is for your family. Not your friends."

I bite my lip. Mom always knows how to play the family card. The truth is that I couldn't give a shit about these people. Because we share some kind of genetic similarity, they're supposed to be more important than everyone else? Real family is who you choose, not who is forced upon you.

There's so much bullshit in life.

I wave at the group on our way out, keeping an eye out for any strangers with bright eyes. Thankfully, I don't see any. Then I sit in some hot, stuffy hall my family rented to have this meal. Another thing Grandpa's death made them pay for.

I eat some shitty sandwich and wait to go home. All I want is my bed. Maybe first I can grab a couple pills from Mom's prescription box. It would be nice to take something and not feel.

Worst of all, I'm helpless to do anything about Pauline.

"What's your favorite memory of your grandfather, Angelica?"

It's my Aunt Chloe. She shows up on Thanksgiving and Christmas and an occasional birthday. This is the kind of family that my mother says I should be loyal to and grateful for, while ignoring my friends. Why? No one likes her. Even my grandfather, one of the nicest people I'll ever know, said some pretty funny things about her.

That thought makes me grin, and I look Aunt Chloe right in the eye. "One of my favorite memories?" I put my hand over my mouth, trying to stifle a giggle. "I remember one Thanksgiving after you left our house. We hadn't seen you or heard from you since the year before. I was helping Grandpa put away dishes, and he said to me. 'Your Aunt Chloe is a real bitch.' Then he laughed and said, 'now don't tell anyone I said that. But, boy, I've never known such a bitch in my entire life. Thankfully, we only see her twice a year.' That's one of *my* favorite memories."

Aunt Chloe's jaw drops, and my mother grabs my arm hard.

"I don't know what you think you're doing, young lady," she snaps at me. "But you're ruining your grandfather's day."

"*His* day?" I laugh. "He's gone. This has nothing to do with him, and you know it. This day is for all of you. To make all you feel better about yourselves. It has nothing to do with him."

"That's enough," my mother says. "If you thought you were grounded before, you didn't know what punishment was. Go sit in the car until it's time to go home."

I roll my eyes at her, and the strongest impulse to run pulses through me. I could run right now and get to the Fountain and soak in its waters. If I didn't make it through the woods, the Darkness would be better than my mother. I could try to find Pauline.

I don't, though. Today I'd rather take some of Mom's pills.

Eventually, my parents come out to the car. They say goodbye to everyone, and I sit in the backseat avoiding eye contact.

When they get in the car, they don't speak to me. Not even my father. When we pull into our driveway, I hop out before the car comes to a complete stop. I run inside the house, right up to my parents' bedroom. I find the pills my father picked up for her at the pharmacy when I was browsing those stupid birthday cards. Shaking a handful out, I take several at once and swallow them dry. It takes multiple swallows, and they burn my throat, but I get them down.

I return the pill box and go to my room.

Before going to bed, I look out the window. My lungs turn cold again, like I'm breathing arctic air. The dark man stands outside my house. He winks at me. He raises his hand and waves, then his head tilts back and he chuckles. The more he laughs, the more my lungs hurt.

I stumble back, hitting my bed and falling on my mattress.

I'm asleep as soon as my body hits the bed, but nightmares plague my rest.

# CHAPTER NINETEEN

A tap on the window startles me, and I jump! The sun rises, and it's early morning. Oh, God—the dark man has come for me. I cover myself with my blankets. Taking several deep breaths, I laugh. It's an awkward, nervous chuckle. No, these blankets can't help me. I'm not a little girl who had a nightmare of a monster under the bed. These blankets can't provide the protection they once could.

I'm a young woman who has real nightmares, and I'm certain there's a monster outside my window.

I toss the blankets off me and march to the window. I won't be scared. Whatever this is—it has Pauline, and I will fight it!

Looking outside, I don't see anyone and release a comforting sigh of relief.

I grab a change of clothes and head to the shower. I spend several minutes under the hot water, letting it soak my body.

When I'm out, I dry off and wrap a towel around my body. I brush my teeth and take a good, close look at myself in the mirror. My eyes look heavy, and it's obvious I need sleep. I look older somehow. Like yesterday I was fifteen, and today I'm twenty-five. So much for the Fountain of Youth. Who knows what its powers are.

I dress and put on my favorite glasses. The frames are dark and thick. When I walk back into my room, I realize right away that something is wrong. I look up at the window from where I heard a knock. It's open now, and I hold my breath.

My lungs freeze, and sharp pain spreads throughout my chest.

Someone is in my house.

I search my room, from one corner to the other. I grab a cross country trophy off my dresser and hold it in my right hand as a weapon. I approach my closet. That's the first place a monster would hide, right? I take a deep breath and pull the door open.

No one is there.

I walk over to my bed, thinking that a hand will shoot out from under it at any minute. Surely, there's a monster under my bed. I'm living the twisted reality of childhood nightmares.

Bending down on one knee, I toss up my comforter and peek under.

Nothing.

Then my bedroom door slams shut, and I jump, releasing a high-pitched scream like one would in a haunted house.

I stand slowly, and someone enters my line of vision. My jaw drops and my heart could burst from my chest. No. No, there was no monster under my bed or in my closet.

There is no monster standing in front of me now either.

I tell myself that, but I choke back a scream when he takes another step toward me.

I brace for the monster with red eyes. But no. It's not the dark man.

"Wait. What? *You?!?*"

I grip the trophy hard.

The person standing in my room charges at me. I swing the trophy, but I miss.

The next thing I know I'm on my back, and the wind has been knocked out of me.

"What do you want?"

No answer.

And suddenly, pain!

A blade enters my side. I scream. It's the worst pain I've ever felt. Blood rushes out, and my flesh feels like it's dying. I'm dying. That's my final thought. No wise finale here.

I close my eyes and lose consciousness.

---

I WAKE UP outside the woods. My side bleeds. How deep and how bad I've been stabbed, I don't know, but it sure hurts. My head throbs, too—a terrible headache.

I'm alone now. If I have a chance to escape, now is it. I stand, but dizziness hits me, like I've been drugged.

I turn around and walk away, but that's when I hear a scream.

And it sure as hell sounded like Pauline.

I run back to the woods, and the moment I enter, it darkens. A shadow rises from the ground, and I realize that I'm an idiot. It's a trap. I was brought here for the Darkness. I turn around, but I'm too slow and dizzy from the pain.

The shadow grabs me and pulls me down. It embraces me, and we fall below the ground, underneath the Earth.

Lawson said he knew how to get out of this, didn't he? How?

I calm my mind. Believe me, all I want to do is scream and yell and cry. But I'm running on empty. Suddenly, Mom's insults deafen my ears. "You worthless brat!"

No. I'm done being worthless. I will do what I need to do to survive and save my friends, or I will die trying.

Several terribly long but calm moments pass. I meditate. I think of nothing, and when there's nothing in my mind for the Darkness to take, it kicks me out. I'm back on the ground outside the woods. It worked! I stand, and the pain in my side shoots all through me. I can't think the pain away, that's for sure. I've been stabbed. I hold my side. I could die. This is no joke. Maybe I'm dying right now.

*Grandpa, help me!*

A scream comes from the woods, high-pitched and panicked. It's Pauline. How can I help her?

*Grandpa, help us!*

Do I run back and try to help her on my own? My side throbs, nearly dropping me to my knee, as if sending a resounding *no* to my question.

I need to get help. Maybe I should go to a doctor. But wait—the Fountain is on the other side. If I can get to it, maybe it can save me? Yes, I will go to the Fountain.

As I decide to make a run through the woods to the Fountain, the asshole who broke into my room and stabbed me reappears.

"You didn't think it would be that easy?"

I snarl. "Why are you doing this?"

"You must die within the Darkness. Clearly, I didn't hurt you enough."

I grit my teeth and clench my fists.

"Bring it on," I say, and this time I charge first.

# PART FOUR

## TEDDY

"When we are children we seldom think of the future. This innocence leaves us free to enjoy ourselves as few adults can. The day we fret about the future is the day we leave our childhood behind."

—Patrick Rothfuss, *The Name of the Wind*

# CHAPTER TWENTY

I leave the funeral for Angelica's grandfather and return home even more depressed. Soon I'll be at another one, one I didn't think I'd have to worry about until I was way older. I climb my front porch steps and throw myself down on a wicker chair. Death is everywhere. I can't even escape it in my own house.

Looking down the street, I focus on the trees. How long do trees live? Certainly a lot longer than humans. Why can't people live that long?

There's a tree in front of the last house on the left that is particularly beautiful. Staring at it, my thoughts about death wash away. It's an elm, taller than the house behind it with limbs thicker than my body. A half dozen limbs spread out in all directions. Its leaves are nearly gone. A few bravely hang on, resisting fall. One of the leaves drops right as I watch, and I release a deep breath. Nothing can hang on forever.

But they'll come back. The tree will be around for a long time.

I take out my phone to distract myself with social media, trying to shake away the life and death thoughts. News stories feature one missing child after another. It started with a couple last week, a couple more yesterday, and today even more. Children are vanishing, and it feels like a plague.

Mom should be worried about us. The way parents look at

their kids right now is totally eerie. There are no smiles in the supermarket. Moms hold on to their children tightly. They study every stranger. They hurry home and lock their doors.

But Mom doesn't know all this.

*How's Mom? How is she really?*

No amount of distraction can bury the question for too long. I have to be tougher, for Mom and for Sam. I walk inside, checking on Mom in her bedroom.

"Come here, Teddy," Mom says. It's the middle of the afternoon, and she's still in bed. She reaches her hand out to me, but I don't want to hold it. It's not because I don't care. Mom's touch used to be comforting and warm. Now she's frail and cold. It's like being touched by a stranger.

"You know I love you," she says, reaching for my thick, curly hair. She always loved putting her hands through my hair. Her hand slides through it, and she tugs at my gray T-shirt that reads *Hawkins Middle School A.V. Club*. "I'm very sick. Do you know that?"

I want to tell her I'm not a little boy anymore. I'm almost sixteen, and I understand what death looks like. It's thin, with weak brown skin, and it never gets out of bed.

Instead, I say, "I know, Mama. I'm sorry."

She blinks, and even that seems slower than normal.

"Listen, Mama. I've got somewhere to take you. You have to trust me."

She takes a deep breath, several seconds in, several seconds out, and then she coughs. "I'm too weak, Teddy. Now listen, please. I want to talk to you about Sam."

Sam has been glued to my side ever since Mom revealed her cancer diagnosis. The doctors think it started in her colon, but now it's in her liver and bones. She fought cancer once before, but it was a different kind. This is new. How can one person have to fight different cancers? It's not fair. They all say she doesn't have long to live. Dad already talked to us, and Sam worries me, too. His red headset has become a permanent fixture on his body, either covering his ears or dangling on his shoulders. He plays his video games and doesn't speak to anyone unless forced. I thought we could go out with Lawson, go to the Fountain—that would make us feel better, right?

I haven't been able to hang out with anyone since Mom got diagnosed. I met up with Lawson to go to Angelica's grandfather's service, but I didn't talk much with anyone. I saw Angelica differently, though. She's always looked like a badass to me. A hot badass, I'll admit, but not someone I'd ever have the courage to talk to. At the funeral, though, I saw her anger and sadness, and I understood it. I wanted to reach out to her, but I'm not sure I'd have known what to say anyway.

When I look at Mom, the only thing I can think of is the Fountain. In my head, the idea sounds both insane and normal. I picture the conversation. *Hey, Ma. There's magical waters outside of town. Hop on my bike with me, and let's see if it can heal ya.*

She'd think the chemo was messing with her brain. I try to be subtle about it instead.

"Teddy, Sam isn't like you. You've always been—" A coughing spell makes her pause. Is the cancer in her lungs, too? It sure sounds like it. "Stronger. Older. Not just literally." She squeezes my hand. "I'm so very proud of you, Theodore. One day when you're a parent, you'll understand. I look at you and see the greatest thing that's ever happened to me. And you've got such a good heart. That's not just *Mom* talking. I know you do, sweetie."

I swallow and push back the tears.

"I wish I could explain"—Mom looks down at what's left of her body—"all this. Disease. Death. I don't want it to affect your heart. You're such a kind boy. Promise me you won't let what's happening to me ever take away your smile and kindness. Promise?"

I blink rapidly. Tears roll down my face. She pulls me close, and I release a sob.

"Mama," I say and cry on her shoulder. "You can't go. You just can't!"

"Oh, honey, I love you so much." She holds me, and I don't let go. I don't want to let go. I stand there, bent over her bed, hugging the frail body of the strongest person I've ever known.

My heart hurts so much. I've never felt pain like this. It's not sharp like how I imagine a knife would feel, but deep and dull like someone thrust a shovel into my body and digs out my gut.

"Sammy," she says. I let go and look over my shoulder, but my brother isn't there. "Take all your grief and turn it into love. Give it to Sammy. Watch over him for me."

Mom closes her eyes, and my heart slams against my chest. Has she... did she... no, I won't ask the question. I listen closely. She's only sleeping. Her chest moves up and down like a small wave about to crash on the shore.

I'm taking Mom to the lake, and I'm doing it today. I'll call Lawson, and if he can't help me, then Sam will have to help. We must try to save my mother.

---

I TEXT LAWSON, and he calls me right away.

"Hey," I say, pacing my bedroom. Old, maroon carpet lines my floors. Mom used to complain about how ugly it was and that she was going to get new carpet in my room one of these days. I don't think that day will ever come.

"Dude," Lawson says, "things are royally messed up. There's so much to tell you."

I sigh, kicking at the carpet. I don't want to be rude, but I don't want to know what else is happening. "I need your help."

"What's going on?"

"I think my mom is gonna die. I mean, I know you know a little, but I think she's gonna die like soon. Tonight. Tomorrow. She looks terrible."

"I'm so sorry, man. What can I do?"

"Help me take her to the Fountain."

Lawson doesn't reply right away. What does his silence mean?

"That's what I need to tell you about," he says after a long pause. "We didn't get a chance to talk. Before the funeral, Mister Lee told us a whole bunch of weird shit that I need to talk to you about. The Darkness is growing. It took Pauline. Probably Elle. I don't think we can get through it on our own. Mister Lee's gonna help us."

"My mom is dying. I have to risk it. I *have* to go, no matter what's there. I don't care what the risk is!"

"Your mom might not make it through."

"She may not make it through *tonight.* Don't you understand?"

"I'm sorry." He takes a long, deep breath. "Okay. When do you wanna go?"

"How soon can you get here?"

"On my way." Lawson ends the call, and I sit on my bed. I don't even know if Mom has the strength to hold on to me if I were to put her on the back of my bike. We can drive as far as the road takes us, but then we'll have to carry her. At least she'll be light, I guess.

I get Mom's car keys, and I go to Sam's room. One wall is covered with posters from his favorite *Star Wars* movies. On the opposite side, he has a *Batman vs. Superman* poster. It makes me crack a subtle smile. About the only thing we ever disagreed on is that movie. He loves it. I fall asleep during it every time, preferring the Christopher Nolan series.

I'd give anything to sit between Sam and Mom, sharing a bucket of popcorn, and watching it now.

He wears his headset on and plays VR. That should keep him distracted all night. If we're gonna face a real danger, I don't want him to come. But he should know something. I knock on his door.

He removes the headset, and his red-rimmed eyes break my heart. "Yo."

"Hey. I gotta tell you something."

"I know about Mom," he says. He frowns, and his face almost

turns inward somehow, like he's sinking in sadness. "You don't have to give me a talk."

"It's not about that." I walk over to his bed, and we sit on the edge of it. I play with his comforter, which proudly displays the Death Star. "I think I can help her."

His eyes light up.

"Lawson and I found something. I've got to take Mom to it."

"Can I come?" He jumps off the bed, and it's the most energy I've seen from him in weeks. I start to shake my head, and he says, "Oh, please, Teddy! Please let me come!"

"You don't understand. Do you believe in magic?"

"You mean, like, Harry Potter?" He lifts his eyebrows.

"No, not like that. More like…." *What was it like?*

"Like God?" Sam asks.

"Maybe. Do you believe in God?"

He shrugs. "I guess so."

"What do you mean?"

His eyes shift downward. He wipes at a glaze of tears on his face. He takes a seat again, and I put my arm around him. "I dunno. I mean, Mom and Dad told us all sorts of wild stories. Santa Claus. The Easter Bunny. The Tooth Fairy. Then you find out it's all a lie." He sniffs and wipes at his nose. "You know, all the stories with magic in them turned out to be lies. The only magical stories left are the ones about God and Jesus and all that. I…." He looks down and takes a deep breath. "I want it to be real. You know?" He rubs his eyes. "But it's all a lie, too, isn't it? There's no God, no heaven."

I shrug. "I dunno about all that. But there is magic in the world. There's magic not far from here."

He looks at me incredulously.

"Seriously. This isn't some Santa bullshit story. It's for real."

"Then I wanna go. Show me!" He stands again, as determined as ever.

"But there's danger, too. I dunno how to explain. Something

could happen to me. Or to Mom. Or both of us. That's why I'm telling you this. Here." I hand him a piece of paper.

"What's this?"

"It's a map I drew. It's how to find me. How to find the magic, if I don't come back."

"But I wanna come!"

"I know, but you gotta think about Dad. What if something happens, and you, me, and Mom go missing? Imagine what that would do to him. That's why you have to stay. If something does happen, then you tell Dad and come find us. 'Kay?"

"Okay," he says softly, pouting.

"Lawson's gonna help me. We're gonna have to carry Mom there. So I'm taking her car—"

"You don't have your license!"

"It's the only way to get Mom there. Trust me. I'll drive her there, and Lawson and I will carry her the rest of the way."

He looks at the map I gave him. "What is this place?"

"Something like the fountain of youth. Something special."

He looks up at me and doesn't blink.

"And this place?" he asks and points at the forest below the lake.

"It's called the Darkness. It will try to kill us."

Sam gulps. "Do you think you can really save Mom?"

"I dunno. But I have to try."

His eyes widen with hope. "Be careful." I reach out to hug him. He wraps his arms around me and squeezes.

"Why don't you say some prayers for us while we're gone?" I whisper in his ear.

"Okay." He moves the red headset from his shoulders back up to his ears.

---

I CARRY MOM downstairs to her car. She doesn't wake up. She

stirs a little, and I can still feel her breathing. *Oh, God, if you do exist, please help my mom!*

I do believe in God, but I also get what Sam said. I mean, even before Lawson took me to the lake, I believed. The world is too big for there not to be a God, right? I've looked up at the stars a thousand times. The world is so much bigger than I'll ever know. The universe goes on and on forever.

Someone had to create all that, right?

But then I look at my mother. If someone can create all that, couldn't that same someone heal Mom? Why did she have to get sick in the first place? I know we all die, but wouldn't it be easier if we were all given a set number of years? Like, when you're born, you get one hundred years to live. No accidents, no diseases, no surprises. Everyone gets the same amount. On the day you turn one hundred, you go to sleep and never wake up. You can prepare for it. Your family can prepare. There would be so much less sadness.

So, if there's a God who can create oceans, deserts, mountains, people, butterflies, and ten billion other things, why couldn't that God have thought of this one simple idea? Why does life have to be so painful?

These are thoughts that make me wonder if God doesn't exist. Or maybe God is stupid, as ignorant as the people *He* created. Don't people say we're made in *His* image? Well, I know a lot of dumb people.

I put Mom in the backseat of the car. Her skin is very hot to the touch, and I have no doubt she's running a terrible fever. I hope the lake helps with that, too.

Finally, Lawson approaches from down the road.

"Sorry it took me a bit. I had to sneak out. My parents are gonna kill me if they know I left the house alone," he says. "I think we're supposed to bike there, you know."

"Why?

He shrugs. "I dunno. Maybe, like, to keep adults out. Or something."

"You don't think it will take Mom?"

He doesn't answer.

"Mom won't make it on a bike," I say. "We have to try."

"Okay."

I start the car, and we drive toward the Fountain. Lawson's gaze locks on the giant elm, and he even turns his head as we pass it. "Isn't that cool? It's my favorite tree in the world."

His jaw drops and his face turns pale. "What?"

"The elm. It's awesome, don't you think?"

"It's terrifying," he says and shudders. "All that black."

"What black?"

"Huh?" He scratches the back of his neck. "Never mind." He looks out the window. I'll ask him about that later. Now I have to focus on helping Mom.

We drive in silence for a moment. "Do you believe in God?" I ask Lawson, after a bit, still thinking about my conversation with Sam.

He stirs in his seat and clears his throat. "I know there's evil. Bad things." He tightens his seatbelt and puts his hands on his lap. "Things like what's happening to your mom. Things like what I've seen in the woods. And if evil like that exists, then all we can hope for is that the opposite also exists." He shrugs and looks out the window. "Happiness. A place without pain, at least. Maybe that's what God is. Maybe more like a feeling."

I take a deep breath. There are so many things I want to believe in, but first I want to make Mom well again.

I drive as far as I can, and Lawson helps me carry Mom. We approach the entrance to the woods. He looks at me, his eyes as heavy and worried as I feel.

"This is a terrible risk," he says.

"I know."

"We really shouldn't do this, Teddy. That thing in there—it might kill all three of us."

"I'd understand if you don't wanna go with me."

Lawson frowns. "That's not what I meant. I'm here to help you. No matter what. But we all three could die."

"Can you think of any other choice? Look at her."

Lawson looks at Mom, and he does a terrible job hiding his sadness. "We're gonna have to run really fast."

I try to swallow back the fear that swells in my throat.

"Ready?" Lawson asks.

"Ready."

We step into the Darkness, and a shrill scream pierces my ears.

# CHAPTER TWENTY-ONE

"Run!" Lawson yells. We stand on opposite sides of Mom, holding her back and legs. The high-pitched scream repeats throughout the woods, raising the hairs on the back of my neck.

"What is that?" Pain rips through my chest, and my body turns cold.

"I've never heard it before, and I don't wanna find out!" We sprint through the woods.

More screams erupt, cries coming from below us. How is that even possible? Shrieks rip through the ground. Some sound like children, and my skin turns colder. How many children has the Darkness taken?

The air is much colder than I remember, and it's even darker here, too. I can't see, and I worry I'm gonna fall and hurt Mom more.

"T—Teddy?" It's a nearly inaudible whisper, but Mom is waking up.

"Shh, Mom, I'm trying to help!"

I can only imagine what she feels. My poor mother already has cancer running through her body. Then she wakes up to her son carrying her through the woods. I almost smile—it's a wild thought. Poor Mom probably thinks the cancer has gone to her brain, too.

How great it would be to laugh about this someday? I can only hope.

More cries burst from below, sending chills all through my body. Not even a horror movie could replicate these howls. They're the screams of children.

It sounds like someone is dying.

*Push the thoughts out of your mind, Teddy.*

Lawson is think-speaking to me. I forgot that we could communicate telepathically.

*Mom!*

She'll understand better this way, and she can think right back to me. We race forward, and I send her a message.

*Mom! I know this is scary and confusing, but I really am trying to help. There's magic beyond these woods. It can save you. It really can. Trust me. But first there's this—whatever this is. This Darkness. If we don't get out of here first, well... we'll all be in trouble.*

I listen for a reply. The screams have quieted, and the silence is somehow more terrifying. All I hear is our breathing and our footsteps. A breeze hits my face, and I gulp. Is it the wind or a monster? How can anyone tell?

*Theodore.* It's Mom.

*Oh, Mom, I can hear you! Push your thoughts to me!*

*Theodore,* she continues. *I love you. You are so brave. Oh, my son. I had hoped to see you get your driver's license. Go to prom. Graduate high school. Then college. Get married and have kids if you wanted. I'm so sorry I won't be around for that. It's not fair. This stupid disease. It's not fair!*

I interrupt her. *Mom, it will be okay. I'm going to save you. Trust me.*

She sighs, and it turns into a cough. *I don't have much time, Teddy.* She reaches toward me like she's going to swat a fly, but she waves them near my heart instead. *Your blue is so beautiful.*

*I don't know what she's talking about Lawson, but we have to go faster,* I think-speak to him. He doesn't reply, but I sense confusion and concern.

We pick up the pace, and it's a precarious charge through the woods. Something warm touches my neck.

*Lawson, what is—*

*Don't turn around*! The sharpness of his thoughts makes my body tremble. *It's the monster. It's chasing us. If you turn around, it will catch us for sure.*

My chest hurts, but I push ahead. The warmth on the back of my neck intensifies. It's wet now, too. Someone—or something—spits at my neck. I can't go any faster. My legs tire, and my lungs burn.

I hit my foot on a branch, and I stumble.

Mom flies from my arms.

*I got her!* Lawson grabs Mom, and they tumble forward. They hit the ground, and it sounds like a body slam.

"Are you okay? Mom? Lawson?"

"Got her," he says. "She landed on top of me. She's okay. Hurry, man. Get up!"

I stand, but something grabs me.

*Lawson!*

Its arms squeeze me, and in an instant, I can no longer breathe.

*Lawson, help!*

"Let him go!" Lawson yells.

"Come to me, child," a raspy voice says from behind, dropping me. I hit the ground hard, knocking the wind out of me.

"What do you want?" Lawson asks. The monster floats toward Lawson, its shadows flowing through me to get to him. When it moves, I can't breathe. I swing my arms, slapping and striking at the shadow. My chest tightens.

Is this what death feels like?

"I must consume your web." The voice speaks to Lawson, leaving me behind. I gasp for air, and oxygen returns now that the shadow is off me.

*Web?*

The monster laughs and its arms shoot at Lawson. Its face twists, morphing into that of a creepy old man and then a toothless woman. It morphs into a dozen faces. Its arms become trees lined with thick, black veins.

Lawson's skin turns deathly pale, but he steps in front of my mother to protect her. The monster's arms tear through him like invisible knives, and he screams.

"No!" I yell and lunge forward. "Get off him!" Although the woods are dark, the monster has its own glow—a gray and black aura that somehow shines in the night. Screaming, I dive at it.

I fly right through it, landing on Lawson, and we both tumble to the ground. It frees him from the monster's embrace. I stand, pull him up, and pick up Mom.

The monster's face floats toward me. Its body digs into the dirt like the trees in the woods, but its face stretches forward. It stares at me, and I can't breathe. I'm frozen. My body turns so cold I think my limbs could break off like icicles. The monster studies me, and I choke back a scream.

"What? What is that?" the monster roars at me. Its head floats over me and its eyes glare at me hard, like it's studying my soul. "No... are you... you can't be." Panic floods the monster's face, but then it shakes its head and its lips curl into a sinister smile. "You must die, child. You must be mine."

Its mouth opens wide, and teeth the size of my head come for me. "Run!" Lawson says. "Now!" *Is Teddy the Seer?* I hear Lawson's thought, but I can't process it.

We turn our backs on the monster, hold Mom tightly, and sprint up the final hill that will lead us to the Fountain. The monster laughs, and its hot, wet breath smacks the back of my neck again. I cringe but charge ahead. We're almost there. I can see the light at the end of the woods, and I push harder than ever.

As we approach the exit, arms wrap around my body and something stings my neck. It's the monster's teeth—it must be.

It's going to get me! I take all my thoughts of anger and frustration and scream as loud as I can.

A roar erupts from behind me, and the monster lets go.

Did that work? *Holy shit!* I'll have to figure that out later. Right now, we're moments from the top of the woods. The light shines more brightly, and Mom moans in our arms. We have to hurry.

*Almost there!* We push out, and the light of the sun has never felt so good.

"I can't believe we made it," I tell Lawson.

"For a second there—"

"Mom, are you okay?" I ask, interrupting him. She's pale, a ghostly white. She feels cool, and she doesn't respond to me. "Mom!" I look up at Lawson. "We have to hurry." We run up to the railroad tracks and race to the entrance of the Fountain.

I don't have a hand available to wipe the tears from my face, so they roll and splash right on Mom.

I can't feel or hear her breathing. *Mom, say something. THINK something. Are you... are you there?*

We hurry down the railroad tracks. Energy buzzes from them, but it worries me that I feel more life from steel in the ground than I do from Mom's body.

"Law, do you think she's—"

"Don't think it, man. We're almost there."

Up ahead is the entrance to the lake, and we race to it with every last ounce of energy we have. The air feels fresher here, and breathing it gives me hope. I think back to my conversation with Sam earlier before I left. Do I believe in God? Or magic? If anyone felt the cruel touch of the monster in the woods, then, like Lawson said, we can only hope the opposite touch exists. And that touch is here, I hope—in this water.

We finally approach the entrance to the lake, and I'm worried it may not let us in. Lawson's right—maybe not exactly about the bikes, but that the Fountain opens up only to those who deserve it, perhaps.

*If anyone deserves you, it's Mom!* I shout with my mind. Trees dance, and the bushes appear to move. The entrance opens, and the lake welcomes us.

*Thank God.*

We move forward and sit Mom down. She's unconscious and limp, and her body falls backward.

*If she has already passed away, won't it be too late?*

Lawson looks at me and shrugs.

We kick off our shoes and slide in the water. Then we each take hold of Mom and pull her in. We hold onto her, and I cry, softly at first and then louder and harder. She's not moving at all, and I still can't hear any of her thoughts. I take the palm of my hand and pour water over her head and face.

"Is this all bullshit?" I ask. "Have we been tricked?"

His eyes flash with empathy. "You felt it before? The power here? That's not our imaginations. Give it time."

We swim out farther, toward the actual fountain in the lake, where a waterfall splashes overhead. Once there, we swim to stay afloat and hold Mom so that the waterfall gently bathes her head.

But nothing happens.

Several minutes pass. We swim back toward shore. We need to take a break.

"Let's go where we can touch," I say, my lungs and legs ready to give up.

He nods, but he wears a worrisome frown.

I pray. It can't hurt.

*Dear God. Or whoever or whatever is out there. You have to help my mother. Please help her. She's a good person. She deserves better than this.*

I look over at Lawson, and he smiles gently at me. Of course, he can hear my prayer.

He puts his arm around me. We've formed a small circle, the three of us. I continue.

*Please. Whatever power is here, please help us. Help Mom. Take away this cancer. Take it all away and give back her life. Please.*

I put my head on Mom's shoulder, and I sob. Lawson holds me tighter, and I don't know what else to do but cry. I will stay in these waters all night, all tomorrow, forever if I must. I will not give up on her.

She has to be okay. *Mom, you have to be okay! Get better. Get better now! I demand that you get better! You can give me the fucking cancer if you have to! Just take it away from my Mom.*

I cry some more, and I can't stop. I weep until I have nothing left inside me. My temples throb, and cries turn into dry heaves. My mother is gone—I have nothing left inside of me but pain. Lawson rubs my back, and I hold on to Mom. I can't let go.

I'll never let go.

That means goodbye.

We stand in the water and absorb a deafening silence. Lawson doesn't speak. He stays by my side, his arm around my shoulders.

I don't know how much time passes.

And then, finally, words.

"Theodore? Theodore, where the hell are we? What's going on?"

"Oh, my God!" I choke, water and tears spitting from my mouth. Mom spoke! Not only that, she spoke as clearly as she ever had. I had almost forgotten what her healthy voice sounded like. "Mom! Are you okay?"

She looks at me then to Lawson and all around the lake. "Well, I'm awfully wet."

I laugh uncontrollably, and it's infectious. Lawson laughs, too, and Mom joins us. Her eyes fill with confusion. She doesn't know what's happening, but she's laughing. It's the most beautiful sound I've ever heard.

I thought I'd never hear Mom laugh again.

I hug her hard, laugh-sobbing, giggling through tears. She continues to chuckle—hearty, *alive* laughter—and I can't get enough of it. When was the last time I heard her laugh like this?

"Why are you crying, Theodore?"

I wipe away my tears. "What do you remember?"

She turns her head to the side. "Hmmm. My mind feels strange." She looks at Lawson again. "Oh, yeah. You had just introduced me to your new friend. You asked if he could stay for dinner. I was happy you made a new friend your first week at school. It's so important to have friends."

"What month is it, Mom?"

"That's a weird question." She laughs. "It's August, silly. You just started school." She reaches into the water. "This water is so warm. What *are* we doing here, Teddy-bear? What is this place?"

I normally hate it when Mom calls me by my childhood nickname. Today, I grin. She can call me Teddy-bear as often as she likes. Forever. Hearing her voice again is the greatest gift I could imagine.

I put my arm around Lawson. *It worked, buddy. It worked! Not only is she well, it wiped her memory of even getting sick. She doesn't even know!*

He smiles, and it turns into a laugh. I can't help but join him.

This has turned out to be the absolute best day of my life.

# CHAPTER TWENTY-TWO

"No, I want you here," I tell Lawson. We've made it back to my house, and I could tell he wasn't sure if he should stay.

We sit inside the car parked in my driveway. "I have a weird question," he starts. "Do you remember leaving the lake? Do you remember if we went through the woods, or even driving back here?"

I release a nervous laugh. "Shit! Oh my God. I have no idea." My hands let go of the steering wheel. "Come to think of it, I don't remember how I got home when you and I first went there. I just woke up in my bed the next day. What the hell, man?"

"Same. I never remember leaving. Dunno what the hell that means." He takes a deep breath and looks at my mom in the backseat. She's staring out the window like she's dreaming. "I should go home."

"Dude, you helped save her," I whisper. Mom fumbles with the door handle and gets out of the car. We're all still wet, and Mom's nightgown looks enormous on her thin body. She strides up to the front of the house, now looking fully alert. Her face glows.

"All right," he says, turning his view to the direction of the beautiful elm across the street. His eyes grow wide whenever he looks at that tree. "But anytime it gets weird, you tell me to go. I won't be offended." His voice shakes. I follow his gaze, but I don't see anything strange.

"Courtney? *Courtney!*" Dad shouts from inside the house. He runs through the screen door, literally through the screen when he sees Mom, dropping the cup of coffee he was holding. "What in heaven is going on?

"Teddy, what happened?"

Mom puts her hands on her hips and stares at us. "You all are acting awfully strange." She tilts her head to one side. "Have you been in the sun all day or something? You know the sun gets to both of you. Makes you act weird, and this might be the weirdest I've ever seen ya. Lemme tell you, that's saying something." She looks at the coffee cup on the porch, thankfully unbroken. "Are you going to clean that up?"

I grin from ear to ear, and then Sam treads uneasily outside toward us, his hands gripping his red headset that's lowered to his shoulders. His eyes are wider than a child catching Santa on Christmas Eve.

"Mom? Is that you?"

"Yes, honey," Mom says cheerfully. "I was thinking about dinner. I've got a craving for a good, greasy burger. Should we fire up the grill?"

Sam leaps toward her, stumbles, and hugs her tight. He releases high-pitched, little boy sobs, which bring back my tears, too.

"Samuel, what is it, baby? What's wrong?" She returns the hug and rubs his back at the same time. That's Mom's sympathy hug. Whenever one of us was hurt, she always rubbed our backs.

Dad's jaw falls on the floor. He shuffles over to me, embracing me tightly. "What did you do? What in the world, Teddy, what did you do?"

"I'll tell you later," I say, my cheeks burning with pride.

He looks at me as he pulls away, his eyes as big as the moon. "Whatever it is, God bless you, kid." He shakes his head incredulously and pulls me in again for another hug. With one arm still around my shoulders, we walk to Mom and Sam and embrace as a family.

A minute later, Mom says, “I’m all for a lovefest with my boys. You know this is my favorite thing in the world, but you all are starting to scare me. What happened today?”

She pulls away, and the look of disbelief on her face makes us all laugh. I put an arm around Sam. “I told you.”

“Let’s make some burgers and you tell me about your day,” Mom says. “I have a feeling you all have good stories to tell.”

“Sounds great,” I say. “Mom? Can Lawson stay for dinner?”

“Of course,” she says. “Lawson, you’ll have to excuse my strange family.”

“I’ve seen crazier things, Missus Fernandez,” Lawson says.

“Yeah, I bet you have,” she mumbles and scratches her head. “Like today.” Then she turns and looks down the street, her eyes settling on the elm tree down the road. “My mind is off or something, guys. I remember coming home, but I can’t remember where we were. That’s odd.” She turns and looks at Dad. “Don’t you think?”

“It’s the sun, Mom,” I say quickly. “We were all out, and we got a little too much sun, like you said.”

She nods, buying her own fictional rationale for now and moves inside the living room. “Maybe. All right. Let me get inside and out of these wet clothes, and we’ll get some food in our bodies.” We follow and take a seat at the dining room table. When she returns, she no longer wears a wet nightgown. Sporting a tank top and shorts, she wears something more appropriate for August than for October. “I’ve never felt so hungry,” she continues. “I feel like I haven’t eaten in days.”

It has been days, actually, since she had eaten a real meal. The last several days, Dad and I had been trying to get her to drink Ensure. I always thought Ensure was an old-person drink. Not something my mother should have needed.

I can't wait to throw out that stupid case of Ensure. I hated seeing it take up space in the kitchen.

As Mom grills the burgers, Lawson, Sam, and I set the table. Dad helps Mom at the grill. I'm guessing we're going to have burned meat because every few seconds he picks her up, swings her around like he's dancing with her, and kisses her. They laugh, and it makes me smile to see them happy. This is what life should look like—not hospital beds, prescription drugs, or the smells of vomit and diarrhea.

When they bring the meat in, it's a little over-cooked, but I don't think I've ever tasted such good food. We talk and laugh. How will Mom's memory catch up? We're a couple months into the school year, and she thought it was only the first week.

*Oh, well. Let's enjoy the moment.*

Then the monster's face—its huge teeth—enters my mind. *No... you can't be... you must die, child. You must be mine,* it had said. What did the monster see? What's wrong with me? When I open my eyes, Lawson stares at me.

*You might be the Seer*, he think-speaks to me.

"So, Lawson, what's the girl scene like at Worthlapp?" Mom asks, breaking my thoughts.

"It's okay," he answers, shuffling in his seat. He looks uncomfortable, but I don't blame him. We've got work to do, and this celebration can only last so long.

"Just okay?" she asks. "Any cute girls in your class?"

"Lawson's surrounded by hot girls," Sam says. "Christina, Angelica, Elle. I've seen who you hang out with. They're hot!"

Elle—was that her who screamed today? Or was it Pauline? And, oh, the cries of all those children!

The joy of our celebration dissipates, and my chest fills with pain. My hands turn cold. Lawson's right. We need to train.

"Ooh, tell me about these girls," Mom says.

Lawson shrugs, and I try to hear his thoughts. For a moment I sense something different about him. What is it? An attraction? He likes someone, all right. Law smiles at me, and I try to press deeper into his mind. I can't hear anything anymore. God, it'll be nice if we can ever get back to talking about girls.

"They got hot knockers," Sam says. "Especially—"

"Samuel," Dad says. "Language." But he grins, clearly interested in this conversation as well.

I wish I could think about hot chicks. A beautiful face flashes in my mind.

Angelica.

She's hot. No, she's more than hot. She's gorgeous. Even her anger is beautiful and deserved. I picture her face, that long, dark hair. Even her glasses are stylish, making her look like a smart model. At her grandfather's service, though, there was something different about her. I don't know how to explain it—a profound sadness, perhaps—but it made me like her more.

"Yeah." Sam giggles, making his headphones bounce on his shoulders. "They got watermelons. Water balloons. Hooters!"

What would Angelica look like in the Fountain? What would she wear? I picture wet clothes clinging to her athletic, beautiful body. What would she look like without—? I cough into a fist. My thoughts surprise me, and they're a pleasant distraction from all the crap I've been thinking about lately.

"Enough talk about knockers, boys. That's not very polite," Mom says, but she's smiling, too.

"That was great, honey. The entire meal," Dad tells her and reaches for her hand.

"Thank you. Well, you helped. A little. Mostly you distracted me." She giggles.

"How do you feel?" Dad asks.

"I'm fine. Why?"

"I mean—no headache, no fatigue—everything okay?" he asks.

Mom nods. "Yeah, why do you ask? Do I not look okay?"

"You are the most beautiful woman in the entire world," Dad says quickly. "More beautiful today than ever before, and that's saying something because you were always the most beautiful person I've ever seen."

Mom blushes, and Dad leans in and whispers something in her ear. Mom's cheeks redden even more. She coughs a little and stands.

"Boys, will you clean up for me, please? I actually am a little tired now that I think about it. I could use a nap."

At first, worry fills my mind, but she smiles flirtatiously at Dad.

"You know, it's been a long day," he says. "I could use a little power nap, too."

"I think, uh, can we clean up later?" I ask. "Sam, Lawson, and me wanted to do a little bike ride tonight. How about we go out and do that and clean up later?"

"You can play in the yard," Dad says. Mom heads toward their bedroom. Dad speaks to us in a whisper. "Don't leave the yard, boys, and don't leave each other's sight. There are scary things happening in town, and I don't want you on the street after dark. Okay?"

"Yeah, okay," I say. The three of us leave the table and run outside almost as fast as we ran away from the monster in the woods.

I couldn't be happier that Mom is alive and well and that my parents are happy, but there are still some things I don't need to think about too much.

"You know what they're really gonna do, right?" Lawson asks with a huge grin. "They're not taking a nap. They're gonna do it all night—"

"SHUT UP!" I shout, but we laugh as we stumble out the front door.

---

"Shit, do we have school tomorrow?" I ask Lawson. I can't even remember what day it is. We get on our bikes and ride down the block, forgetting my dad's warning. Honestly, I didn't want to risk hearing any noises from their bedroom. We'll stay close.

I ride in the middle, Lawson on my left, and Sam on my right. The wind feels cool, and it's nice to be out. It won't be long before winter strangles everything.

Lawson laughs. "I seriously don't know. Sam, what day is it?"

"You two are idiots." Sam giggles as he says it. "It's... what? I swear I just knew. But I forgot."

"Me, too," Lawson says.

"Do you think something's happening with time?" I ask. It's awfully warm for fall. The wind may be cool, but the sun has felt more powerful than usual.

"I dunno," Lawson says. We pass the yard with the beautiful elm tree. Lawson slows down. "Sam, what do you see there?"

"Mom thought it was the first week of school," Sam adds. He studies the tree to which Lawson points. Sam tilts his head to the side. "I always thought that tree would make the perfect tree house."

"You don't see anything... strange?" Lawson asks.

I take a closer look, too. Thick limbs that could be decades old spread like open arms across the yard. It's almost welcoming, but apparently Lawson sees something completely different.

"Black," he adds. "Do you see black? Like poison spreading throughout the tree?"

"Uh-uh," Sam mutters.

"Maybe you're seeing things? Does that make *you* the Seer?" I ask.

Lawson shakes his head. "I don't know. Never mind. Let's just get away from it. It creeps me out." He resumes pedaling, and we follow him out of my neighborhood.

"So, about Mom," I say. "She's either gonna have to jump ahead in memory, or we're gonna have to jump back. Maybe that's what's happening?"

Sam giggles. It's so good to hear his laugh again. "I say we forget about school," he yells. We pick up our pace and race through the neighborhoods. The pedaling feels good, even going uphill. I stand on my bike and put all my weight on the pedals, climbing up a neighboring road.

"So, there's a lot to tell you," Lawson says when we reach the top. The three of us pause, and he wipes away sweat from his forehead.

"What do you mean?" I ask.

"I don't want to be a downer after today," he says. "But I gotta catch you up. We've got a lot to do."

"Okay," I say.

"Mister Lee thinks one of us is the Seer," he says. "I thought it was Angelica, but it might be you. Or me. Mister Lee says the Seer can connect us and help us fight the Darkness." He reaches into a Velcro bag that is strapped around the front of his bike. He removes what looks like a notebook. "This is a copy of some notes Mister Lee has. I thought I could start by just reading this to you."

"Okay," I say.

Lawson shuffles through a few pages and turns on his phone's flashlight. He reads aloud from Mr. Lee's journal.

*Things to remember in the woods of the Darkness:*
*Run fast. If the shadow of the Darkness catches you, it will drag you deep down into a bottomless pit.*
*You will be able to hear other people's thoughts in the woods. When you leave the woods, some of this ability may linger.*
*The only way to reach the magic is through the Darkness.*

"How many others could be involved in all this that we don't even know about?" I rub my temples. "I know Elle's missing. Has anyone seen Fiara?"

"She hasn't been at school," Lawson says. He glances over to Sam and hesitates. Then he makes eye contact with me again. "Sam, would you give us a minute?"

"Not far," I say. "Where we can see you."

"Teddy, I wanna be a part of this, too!"

"I know. And you will. I promise. Give us a minute, 'kay?" Sam pouts but he does what we asked. He circles us while we chat. I keep my eyes on him while Lawson continues. "Christina told us that the Darkness has a direct link with Fiara. Something happened to them when they were kids. Fiara used to be, like, normal, you know? The Darkness thought she was the Seer, I guess. It wasn't about killing her. It was about using her. When it didn't work, well... you've seen her."

"That's messed up."

"Yeah." Lawson puts the copy of Mr. Lee's journal back in the Velcro bag and grips his handlebars tightly. "It's not Fiara's fault. The evil can control her or something. But not all the time. That's why it creates monsters and sometimes even possesses others, like Christina."

"Can I see the rest of that?" I ask, referring to Mr. Lee's notes.

"Yeah, there's a lot more. Scarier stuff. Deeper stuff, too. Things I don't understand."

"You should spend the night. We can read it," I tell him.

"I don't think you'll get much sleep if you do that," he warns.

"Who needs sleep after what we did today? Is there a way to get rid of the evil for Fiara? Like an exorcism?"

Lawson shakes his head. "Dunno. We have to be careful around her. Christina, too. I think she's cool. But no one can be trusted. Not fully."

"So, what do we do?"

"Mister Lee wants us to meet and do something to help us determine who the Seer is. He can explain it better. We have to get everyone together and learn how to fight it, too."

I think of my scream that somehow made the Darkness release me.

"Yeah, all right." I rub my cold hands, trying to eliminate the nervousness. "Remember what the Darkness said when we ran through there with Mom? It wanted you. Because of a web? What's that about?"

His hands shake, and he grips his handlebars tighter. "That's what we need Mister Lee for. Your mom saw something, too, remember? A blue light? Maybe because she was close to—I dunno. Anyway, Mister Lee can explain it better. And there are some notes in here that will help." He gestures at the journal in his bag. "We can read those tonight."

I watch as Sam continues to bike around us in a giant circle, and a breeze flutters against my skin. "How many kids do you think have gone missing?"

Lawson frowns and shakes his head.

"Why? What's it all for?"

"It, uh, it—" He clears his throat. "According to Mister Lee, it consumes. It needs to take life to get stronger." Lawson looks up at the night sky. "I know it's late, but we should get ahold of Mister Lee and the others ASAP."

"I'm in," Sam says. He stands right behind me, no longer riding in circles. I hope he didn't hear too much. I don't want him to be scared. "You saved Mom. I wanna help with whatever's going on. I'm not stupid, you know. Some of the kids that have gone missing are in my class."

Lawson gives him a humorless smile. "Thanks, dude. I appreciate it. But, I dunno how to explain. This isn't like fighting a bully or something. There's real evil here, and it's as powerful as the lake that saved your mom." Lawson ruffles Sam's hair and looks back at me. "Maybe we should go to Mister Lee's now. Tell him what happened with your mom."

I nod, and I try to put together all the pieces. There's a magic lake that can give people life. Mom is alive. But there's a monster, too. A monster and a place, an evil that's taking kids and wants to kill me for some reason I don't know.

Something perhaps to do with the blue light Mom saw?

The sound of a car approaches from behind—tires on pavement, a mild roar of an engine—and I look over my shoulder. The car glides, almost like it's not moving at all. But it is—inch by inch, gradually and silently, so we didn't see it before now.

Before Lawson or Sam even notice it, the car positions itself directly behind us. The person in the driver's seat sneers at me.

It's a man with wavy red hair. But, no—he doesn't look like a man at all. He smiles wide, and his white teeth contrast with the pitch-black color of the car.

It's the smile of a monster.

Before I can get one word of warning out of my mouth, the car blasts toward us at full speed.

# CHAPTER TWENTY-THREE

"Move!" I yell. The car strikes the back of Lawson's bike, as he launches himself from it.

I spin around and out of the way of the car. The car smashes into Sam's bike, and he flies straight up in the air. The car soars forward, and Sam's little body smacks into the windshield. The crack of the glass combines with Sam's cries, and I yelp.

Tossing my bike to the side, I scramble toward him. The car stops, and Sam rolls off the hood like a soda can. I charge forward and catch him before he hits the ground.

"Sam, are you okay?" I lower him gently, resisting my urge to shake him. Blood covers the top of his head, and his eyes are closed. "No! Sam, answer me!"

The car door opens.

"Lawson!"

"I'm here," he says from behind. I'm on both knees, and Lawson stands tall. We look over at the driver's side of the car, and the man—no, a monster—steps out. Fire glows in his eyes, and he sneers.

"What do you want?" I ask.

He cackles and bounces toward us. Lawson jumps out in front of me and throws his arms out. But the monster is quick.

He uses Lawson's momentum against him, easily tossing him aside. Law tumbles forward, falling face-first on the road. The monster hisses and marches toward me.

With the back of his left fist, he knocks my jaw and then kicks me in the stomach. I fall to the side, and he bends over, scooping up Sam.

"No!" I stand, jump on him, and slug at him as hard as possible.

Nothing happens.

The monster shakes me off.

I fall on the hard road but jump right back up. I can't let him take Sam!

Roaring, I kick at the monster with my right foot—aiming straight for his balls. It connects! Panic washes over me as Sam begins to fall from the monster's grip. The monster finds his balance and tosses Sam into the passenger side of the vehicle.

The monster faces us and snarls. We charge at him. Fear runs through me, but we have to save my brother! He swings his right fist at my face, but I block it and kick him in the shin. Lawson swings his left knee up in the air but jumps with his right foot and snap-kicks the monster in the face. Adrenaline races through us. I didn't know my friend could fight! Hell, I didn't know I could fight, but it's amazing what adrenaline will do when you face a monster.

But the monster grabs me, his tight grip burning my wrist. He smirks and opens his mouth. His eyes turn from white to black, and he sticks out his tongue, which morphs into a—

I gulp.

It morphs into a literal, fucking snake.

It shoots at me and bites my neck. I grab at it, but it already retracted. My neck burns, and I cry out. Lawson skids toward me, and the monster roars. His snake tongue fires at Lawson, who dive-rolls away, dodging the attack. Then the red-headed beast gets in the car and drives away with my brother.

I breathe harder and harder. I'm either having a panic attack, or I've been poisoned, or both.

"Get on," Lawson shouts, but I'm frozen. He's on my bike, the only one not damaged. "Now!"

I let go of my neck, and the pain shoots through my body. It's poison, all right. I can feel it making its way to my heart, and once it gets to my heart, I'm certain I will die.

But I do as Lawson says. I wrap my arms around him, and he races after the car.

We ride as fast as possible. The Darkness sent a monster after us, and the monster took my brother. It may have killed me, too, but I'm alive right now. If we get there in time—*if*—then maybe we can save the both of us.

I have a terrible feeling someone isn't coming out of this alive, though.

Lawson pushes fast and hard. My body feels cold, and my arms and legs have turned numb. We approach the entrance to the woods.

"Law," I murmur after a while. "How did we fight like that? Where did that come from?"

"Don't forget we just soaked in the Fountain. Maybe that helped. Made us like a lot stronger. I don't know."

"My neck burns. Bad. If I don't get back to the Fountain, I think it might kill me."

Lawson pushes harder. "We will get you back there. You and Sam. I promise."

I rest my face against his back. "Did you recognize that guy?"

Lawson nods. "Yeah. I mean, kinda. He looked familiar like I should know him. But I can't place him."

"Weird. Yeah, same here." I take a deep breath. "It really stings, Law."

"You're gonna be okay," he says, but his voice trembles.

We arrive at the path. Lawson puts his arm around me for support, and we march on.

"How you feelin'?" he asks again, breathing hard. It couldn't have been easy having to ride with me hanging on his back, but he powered through.

"It burns." I rub my neck. "Bad."

A layer of tears form in Lawson's eyes. "You'll be okay." I don't know if I believe it. I don't think he believes it, either.

"What's the plan?"

"Sam's in there. We find him, grab him, and we run to the Fountain."

Voices scream out from the woods, and my heart seizes. "All those kids. Sam's one of them now."

"We can save your brother. We'll save them all if we can."

We walk forward, Lawson still supporting me. "If I don't... if something happens, promise me you'll take Sam and run. If I can't make it, I mean. You have to keep going."

"Don't say that, Teddy." His arms shake while holding me.

"I'm being real, man. If something happens to me, you can't carry both of us. I know that. So you carry my brother. I'll be okay."

He pauses for a moment. "Teddy, I want to tell you something. But... shit, it's never the right time." He grips me tighter.

"Save my brother," I say. I can feel what he feels—it's love and heartache. It's sweet, but there's no time for that now. "We'll talk later, okay?"

He nods disappointingly, but he moves forward, leading us into the woods.

It darkens, and I blink several times to adjust my eyes. Something's changed, and I wipe my sweaty forehead with the back of my forearm. It's warmer in here than usual. No, not warmer—it's hot. It's not a fall evening. It feels like those unbearably hot summer days when the air is so thick it's hard to breathe.

"What's happening?" I ask.

"Dunno."

There's a light up ahead that I've never seen before. It's always been dark, and it's odd to see a light. It's coming from below, from deep inside the pit within the Darkness.

Moving closer, it's easy to see what it is, and it feels simultaneously impossible yet perfectly logical.

It's a fire. Flames shoot up from inside the pit, dancing dangerously close to the trees that surround it.

"Shit, man, this entire place could catch on fire," Lawson says. He removes his arm from my shoulders, and I steady myself. My neck burns, but I try to ignore the pain.

I nod. "Law? Is it... is it what I think it is?"

He runs a hand through his sweaty hair and turns to look at me. He presses his lips together.

This time I think-speak it to him. *Is that hell?*

He turns pale, whiter than I've ever seen him.

"All I know," he says, "is that we have to go in there to get Sam back." He turns and looks at the flames. *Here's what I know*, he think-speaks. *If you fall in the pit, you're surrounded by the Darkness. It's like... I dunno, what I'd picture floating in space to be like. It's scary as fuck, and it feeds off your fears. The way out is to not feed it. Be perfectly still and calm, and you can explore it, until it kicks you out.*

"But now there's fire," I say out loud, pointing out the obvious. "Um, doesn't that change things?"

Lawson sighs. "Teddy—" He reaches hesitantly for my hand. I sense that combined feeling of love and heartache again. I give him my hand. "Teddy, I need to be the one to go."

"No! I won't let you do that."

"You don't understand—"

"I do," I say. At least I think I do. He's the best friend I've ever had. He would work as hard as I would to get Sam back, but he's already fought a monster for me. If I fail, I have to be able to tell Mom and Dad that I did every single thing I could to save Sam. I couldn't face them knowing I let someone else—even Lawson—look for my brother when it's my job to protect him.

"I've been down there before," he says. "I can get out."

"Oh," I mumble, and he squeezes my hand. "No, Law. It's my brother. And—" I rub my neck with my other hand. "Something bad has happened to me. I can feel it." Tears well in my eyes at what I'm about to say. "I think I could die." *And if I am going to die, there's no need to risk your life, too.*

He embraces me. "I won't let you die," he whispers, hugging me tightly. I hug him back, and when I pull away, his eyes glisten with tears, too.

"I know you won't. But I have to do this for Sam. You know that."

He nods slowly and releases my hand.

An ear-piercing shriek sounds from inside the pit below the flames.

"That's Sam!" I say and lunge forward.

Lawson grabs me. "Remember to stay calm when you get in there. 'Kay?"

I push him off me, not thinking. That's my brother in there, and I have to get him back.

I run to the fire. A fever as hot as the flames runs through me. I jump feet first into the blaze.

*It's hotter than hell.* I've heard Mom say that a hundred times, but I doubt she or anyone has experienced heat like this. I'm dying. It's unbearable. I can't breathe. I close my eyes.

As I fall, the air turns cold, a complete one-eighty. The sudden change in temperature shocks my body even more, and my chest bursts with pain. I'm not sure my heart and lungs can take it. I'm in the pit. It's dark, cold, and I'm falling through air. Lawson was right. It's like floating through space.

I scramble for something to hold on to, but there's nothing. I'm free falling, and it's not fun like the song Dad loves to sing in the shower. It's a nightmare, and I expect Freddy Krueger to jump out any second.

*Focus, Teddy, focus. Remember what Lawson said.*

Lawson said I've got to be calm. But how can anyone be calm in this? I open my mouth and yell. "Sam! Sam are you here?"

Something approaches, a silver shadow in the darkness.

"Sam, is that you?"

It's not Sam.

It's a monster.

*The* monster.

Its arms shoot at me, but they're not arms at all. More snakes! They bite at me. I scream and struggle to get away, but they keep attacking me. My body turns hot again. I kick at the monster, but it only grins at me.

Its face is gray, but it's not a human-shaped face. It's a blob, and it morphs. It seems to be able to take on any shape it wants.

It twists into a snake's head, opening its mouth. The fangs are precariously long, and then they shift into knives. Finger-knives. It read my thoughts earlier—of course it did—and it morphs into the fingers of Freddy Krueger. I'm staring into the face of Freddy, and then he slashes at me, cutting straight through me.

I'm dying.

His face twists back into a snake, and it feeds on me. I let it, but that's not the truth. I have no energy to fight it. It feeds, draining me of blood and life. Consuming me.

I'm going to become nothing, and the world will continue as if I never existed.

I close my eyes.

An incredibly sharp pain in my heart makes me shout. My heart's exploding. I've never felt such pain. No, it's not exploding—it's coming back to life. It's beating harder than it ever has.

I open my eyes.

I can see through the darkness somehow. Everything that was black is now bright.

The monster's face fills with alarm.

What did it see in me before? It tried to kill me, but it couldn't. Is the Fountain protecting me or something else?

"Foolish boy," the monster snaps at me, laughing. "You will be a treat. A treat for Kage! Kage will consume you!"

*Kage?* I try to remember what I did in the woods. I gather all my anger, my frustration, and my energy. Then I scream louder than ever.

The monster laughs. The laughter morphs into a growl. Over its growl, I hear another scream. A terrible scream from outside this hell.

Lawson's calling for me and he's in trouble.

# CHAPTER TWENTY-FOUR

Thunder rolls in the sky, shaking the woods and the ground like an earthquake. Pain rips through my flesh from the monster's attacks, but hope and urgency push me forward. I close my eyes. I take several deep, long breaths. Picturing the joy on Dad's and Sam's faces when they saw Mom healthy, I smile.

Suddenly, in the blink of an eye, I'm back outside the pit standing next to Lawson, except Lawson isn't exactly standing.

He's floating in mid-air right above the fiery pit!

Like actually floating. What in the world? At the top of the woods—near the railroad tracks—a group of people scramble together. That's the way to the Fountain. I can't make out who they are. I listen for their thoughts, but I only hear a buzzing, the sound of energy.

What are they doing to Lawson?

I take a step forward, but the sound of stomping on the ground from behind distracts me. I turn, and familiar faces look back at me.

The first is the monster who took my brother. His name comes to me out of nowhere.

*Rob*. He's here for Christina, though. The Darkness is going to use him to hurt her.

No, his name *was* Rob. He's no longer human. His white skin looks more like paint, and his red hair like dying leaves on a tree.

Rob isn't the only one here.

From behind him, a tall, athletic girl approaches. She reaches for Rob's hand, and he takes it.

"Hi, Teddy," she says and licks her lips. "Lawson is going to taste delicious. Just like your brother." She extends her arms, as if she's controlling Lawson mentally. She looks like she's trying to bring him back down.

"Elle, stop this!" Lawson shouts.

She doesn't look how I remember her. It's as if she's aged several years. Flames flash through her eyes. Everything about her looks aged—she has longer but thinner hair and wrinkles spread across her face.

"We will consume the energy of the children, and we will take the light that we need from all of you." Elle laughs as she raises her hands. The wind catches her hair, which changes color as it moves, from blonde to a fiery red. Goosebumps pop up all over my arms.

"No!" I yell and try to understand the situation. Elle looks beyond me toward Lawson. Now he's moving away from the pit, up the wooded path toward the Fountain. Somehow it seems that the people above us are controlling Lawson, using some kind of power to keep him away from Elle, Rob, and the pit. Elle snarls. I turn my back on Rob and Elle, and I run after Lawson.

Three people stand at the top of the hill, their arms fully extended, as if performing some Jedi mind trick. Lawson floats to the top and lands on his feet. I sprint ahead, while Rob and Elle chase from behind.

When I reach the top, the three form a pyramid, and I make out who they are. Christina stands first, with Angelica and Mr. Lee behind her, each touching her with one hand. They lower their arms when I approach.

Angelica places her hand against her ribs and grimaces.

*"Teddy, help me, please! It burns! It burns so bad!"* Sam calls from the fiery pit, and tears sting my eyes.

"I have to go back! My brother!" I yell, whipping around.

*"Help us, someone! Anyone!"* It's a young girl's voice.

"We will help them," Mr. Lee says, grabbing my arm as I lunge toward the Darkness again. "First, we all need Kang Fu. It will strengthen us so we can fight. You'll be no help to your brother if one of these monsters kills you, Teddy."

"That's right," Elle snaps, bursting from the woods and jumping out at us. Rob stands tall behind her, and he opens his mouth to reveal inhumanly sharp teeth.

Elle races toward Lawson, and he steps into a fighting stance.

"Elle!" I yell, trying to distract her, but she doesn't flinch. Christina dashes at Elle, throwing her arms around Elle's head. Elle yelps, but Christina puts her in a headlock. Rob scurries ahead. I throw my leg out and trip him. He'll try to distract Christina, of course, once she sees who he is.

It dawns on me that I shouldn't know who he is. I had forgotten about Rob. His memory had been wiped from me. But my memory is back now, thanks perhaps to whatever forces are at work here.

I grab Rob and put him in a full nelson.

"Help me," I yell. Mr. Lee races to my side and helps me hold onto Rob. Lawson and Angelica assist Christina, and they get a strong grip on Elle.

"What do we do?" I ask.

"We take them to Kang Fu," Mr. Lee says. "It will strengthen us. And with any luck, it will save them."

---

WE MARCH TOWARD the lake, and Rob and Elle have stopped struggling. Is it a trick? Do they want to be saved? Or are they aware of something we're not? I hope for the best, and we push ahead.

"Rob?" Christina asks. She releases her grip on Elle, and her jaw drops. Her face turns ghostly white, and tears spill down her cheeks. Lawson and Angelica tighten their grip on Elle, as Christina takes a closer look at the boy she had loved, the boy the Darkness made her kill.

"Rob, is that you?"

Rob doesn't respond, and his face looks like a ghost.

She wipes away her tears. "I never thought I'd see him again." Slowly and very hesitantly, she reaches for him.

Mr. Lee tightens his grip on Rob. "Careful. This is not your poor boyfriend, Christina. Mofa took his light and created a monster in his image." More tears run from Christina's eyes. "We will take him to Kang Fu."

"Do you think it can save him?" Christina's hazel eyes grow wide.

Mr. Lee doesn't answer.

Christina's shoulders fall. "You don't think it can, do you?"

"We must try and hope for the best. Okay?" He smiles encouragingly at her, and she nods. She walks next to Rob, resisting the urge to touch him, but her eyes never leave his face.

The railroad tracks buzz with energy. The trees surround us, but they look different from the last time I saw them, even though that was, what, earlier today? Is that possible? Time feels strange here. The tree limbs have moved, almost as if they were gesturing to one another. Do trees talk? It wouldn't surprise me.

It's nearing dusk, but anything outside the woods seems bright in comparison. Power lines follow the railroad tracks, connected in giant Y-shaped, wooden posts. How long did it take people to connect everything? First, it was rail, then it was all these wires—a web that connected us today that is, ironically, all wireless.

The wind pushes us toward the entrance of the lake, and Rob's so calm, it feels like he's sleeping. Elle isn't struggling at all either. I listen hard to hear their thoughts, but even their minds are quiet. I don't trust them. Just minutes ago, she was determined to take Lawson and to kill me, if need be. I hope Mr. Lee knows what the hell we're doing.

We enter the pathway to the lake, and again I worry that it may reject us. It doesn't, though. We're welcomed guests, and it makes me feel special. The view is becoming as familiar as my backyard. The path is smoother than usual. How many others know about this? After all, the few of us here can't be the only ones who have visited the lake.

What other secrets exist? And how will we save my brother?

We see the lake now and slow down. Looking at it floods my mind with the images of missing children. I see Pauline and Sam. I see a dozen others, too, all the ones from the news stories and Amber alerts. There are dozens if not hundreds who have gone missing, and I don't know why I see them all, but I do.

My chest floods with panic for all these missing kids. Mr. Lee catches my eyes and nods reassuringly. Since Rob and Elle are no longer fighting us, we release them. They stand still and look lifeless.

"It's beautiful," I say, looking at the lake, hoping the magic here can help me get my brother back and save all the other missing kids.

"Indeed," says Mr. Lee. He turns to Elle and Rob. "This is what you and Mofa are trying to stop. It doesn't have to work this way. Mofa is manipulative and selfish." Elle takes a very cautious step toward the lake. "These waters have power beyond our understanding."

Even the air feels enchanted like it's some kind of magnetic force. It draws us all toward it, and we step forward together.

"Mister Lee," I say, rubbing my neck, "does, um, Kang Fu give us immortality?" It wasn't long ago, either, that I thought I would die from Rob's bite. Something's infected me, but can the Fountain save me?

"It certainly has healing properties. Does that mean it can keep you alive forever?" He scratches his chin. "I have not yet lived forever, nor do I know what forever is."

"It saved my mom," I say. I turn to Elle and Rob. "It can save you, too." Elle cracks a subtle smile, and at first, it fills me with hope. But there's something about her eyes that scares me—it's an empty stare. Rob, on the other hand, looks like he's about to collapse.

"Elle," Mr. Lee says, "are you still in there?" She drops her hands and tilts her head to the side at Mr. Lee's question. "If you can hear us, you have to help. Fight from inside, and we will fight from out here."

Her eyes brighten. Flames dance in her pupils. I pray Mr. Lee is right.

"Elle, think about the little girl that used to come here. The girl that came here with Lawson. Who played in the water with her friends. Angelica was there. So was another little boy. What was his name?"

She opens her mouth as if to speak but hesitates.

"Asher," Christina answers for her. "The other little boy's name was Asher. Say his name. Remember him. The Darkness took him, and it wants us to forget."

Elle nods, and a tear forms in one eye.

"Think about those days of innocence," Mr. Lee continues. "Remember what it felt like. Such pure laughter. Such great fun."

Christina steps toward Rob and puts a hand on his back, touching him for the first time.

"Can you remember, too?" she asks. Her lips quiver with hope and fear, and her eyes glisten with tears. "You stood by my side through all my weirdness. You never judged me, or my mom. You were my first love, Rob." She puts both arms around him, but he remains expressionless. "I'd give anything for a second chance. To take back what I was forced to do. Evil took you away from me. Can't something good and magical bring you back?"

"Just push them in," Angelica says. "Why are you trying to persuade them? Throw their damn bodies in there." Angelica puts her hands on her hips and stands unapologetically.

It's a terrible time to be attracted to someone, but I can't help it. *Damn.*

"If Mofa has control over them—" Mr. Lee doesn't finish the sentence.

Elle tilts her head back and laughs. "It's about more than Kang Fu, you fools. Haven't you figured that out, yet?" She cackles, and Angelica steps forward. Her sudden change in demeanor makes my body tremble.

"Like I said," Angelica says, "throw her in the damn water."

Ignoring her, Mr. Lee continues. "Let Kang Fu save you. Swim in these waters."

Rob takes a step toward the lake, and Christina's eyes widen with hope as Rob jumps in. I jump in the lake, too, splashing water on my neck, soothing the sting of the snake bite. The fear of death washes away with the water. I soak, hoping to absorb whatever magic it will give me.

Angelica and Lawson surround Elle, and they look like they're ready to push her in if they need to. But Elle simply grins at each of them.

Then the fire lights up her eyes, and she says, "Fools. All of you fools!" She dives in the water.

The water begins to warm. Steam rises, a little at first, but when I turn to find Elle, the steam is everywhere, a blanket floating over the water. Swirly mists engulf us. I swallow hard as fear and panic fill my chest, and I swim back toward shore, looking for the others.

"Should we get in?" Lawson asks.

"It looks like the water is about to boil," Angelica says, which panics me even more. "Teddy, are you okay?"

I open my mouth to call for help, but I'm hit in the face with a wave. Normally, the water is gentle, the most calming place I've ever been. But now it feels hot, the water slaps my face, and I can't see. I splash my way closer.

Then it hits me. Elle and Rob used us to enter the Fountain!

Lawson's right—it doesn't open its entrance for just anyone. Maybe you have to be a kid or innocent or something, but it surely wouldn't have allowed what Elle and Rob have become to enter. Not without us.

We're responsible for this! I swallow a large mouthful of water and gag. We should have known better. Mr. Lee should have known better, at least, right?

"Teddy, I'm coming!" Lawson shouts and jumps in the water. He swims toward me, grabs me, and pulls me out.

I'm breathing hard. "Something's wrong. I dunno what's happening, but something's really wrong."

Lawson and I sit on the shore, and the others surround us. Lawson's eyes turn liquid-dark with fear. The water roars, and big waves splash toward the sky and the shore.

"What's happening?" I ask.

Lawson shakes his head, and Mr. Lee crouches, putting his hand in the water. "It's heating up, all right."

"It's gonna kill them?" Christina says, more of a question than a statement.

Mr. Lee shrugs. "Actually, I think—"

Before he can finish, the ground shakes, and a scream from the center of the lake brings them all to their knees. I put my hands over my ears.

It gets suddenly quiet, an eerie silence. I open my eyes, and the steam is gone. Everything is crystal clear and calm, and I slowly stand. The ground shakes again, harder this time, and I fall. Farther back, where the Fountain pours into the lake, a fire bursts through the water.

"That's not possible," I say. "Fire in water?"

Lawson reaches out to me for balance, and we steady ourselves on our knees. The fire engulfs the Fountain, and the ground continues to rumble.

Angelica screams. The ground cracks beneath her, and she rolls toward the water. Lawson lunges for her, but he misses, and she falls into the lake. She splashes, and Christina dives in after her. Lawson and I both run to the edge and extend our arms. The water is hot, like a Jacuzzi, and we pull the girls out of the lake.

I hold on to Angelica longer than I need to, but when I look into her eyes, I can't seem to pull away.

She stands tall—taller than me—and holds onto my hands with great strength. "Thank you," she says.

I clear my throat. "No prob."

"What you did in the pit back there, I saw some of it," she says. "You were, like, super brave. It was cool."

My heart leaps into my throat.

"I think we need to leave," Mr. Lee says. "It's not safe here anymore."

"No!" Lawson snaps, shocking us. "How is this happening? They can't destroy this. It's not for them. It was meant to help them!"

Mr. Lee puts a hand on Lawson's shoulder. "I think I misunderstood," he says with fear in his eyes. I want to say *no shit*, but I keep quiet. "I don't have time to explain it all now. But I think I misunderstood Kang Fu."

"How so?" Lawson asks.

Mr. Lee looks out at the fire shooting up, fireballs bombarding the sky.

"I thought it could help them. Cure them, even. But perhaps Kang Fu enhances what's inside you. In this case—"

A roar interrupts Mr. Lee, and we grab onto one another for safety. I hold Angelica close, and maybe it's my imagination, but I swear she flashes me a smile. We look out at the water, and Elle and Rob float by the fire. Not floating, they are flying. Flying and spinning around the fire.

"It makes the Darkness darker," I mumble. "And they tricked us to get here."

Mr. Lee looks at me and nods. "I think so." His face changes and his eyes look watery, and not from the lake. "I messed up, kids. God, I put all your lives in danger." He inhales deeply and wipes at his eyes. "I will make up for it. I promise you. Forgive me, please."

"I've lost Rob again," Christina says and wipes the tears from her eyes.

"Does that mean it killed Elle? I had hoped Elle was just possessed like Christina," Lawson says. Mr. Lee doesn't respond. We stare at the shapes spinning above the water.

Surrounded by fire, flames and two bodies twirl around the Fountain like objects in a tornado.

Then we notice something else. *Someone* else.

She floats above the water with both hands extended. An energy, some kind of light, visibly stretches from her hands to Elle's and Rob's bodies.

"Fiara!" Christina shouts. Then, louder, "FIARA!" Christina looks at Mr. Lee. "What is she doing?"

"Is she helping them or hurting them?" I ask. My hand reaches for Angelica's, and she takes it.

No one answers my question, and Christina continues to call to her friend. "Fiara! What are you doing?"

Fiara extends her arms even more, and she floats across the water, an impossible sight except we know Fiara isn't, well... I don't know what she is or isn't. One arm for each body above her, as if she's using some telekinetic energy to attack them. Or to help them.

"What do we do?" I ask.

Everyone looks intently at Mr. Lee, but he doesn't answer.

I gulp, and goosebumps jump all over my skin. Rob and Elle have stopped spinning. They hang there, floating by what was the Fountain, and an orange glaze forms over them. Fiara looks as if she's holding them in place.

"They're morphing," Mr. Lee says. "They're taking the energy of Kang Fu to become stronger monsters."

"How long do we have?" Christina asks.

"I don't know," Mr. Lee tells us. "We must prepare quickly. There is more to tell you all, and we must prepare for a fight that that has never—"

"What?" Lawson asks. "A fight that what?"

Mr. Lee doesn't finish his sentence.

"Are we gonna die?" I ask.

Mr. Lee looks back up at the shapes of Elle and Rob. The orange glaze darkens, and it's clearly a cocoon.

"What emerges from those," Mr. Lee says, "will be a far darker and more powerful evil than you can possibly imagine."

"How will we stop it?" Lawson asks. Even his voice sounds defeated.

Mr. Lee doesn't answer. "We find the Seer, and we train. But I must warn you, we may not survive. The Seer, in particular—it's a responsibility I cannot ask anyone to make. The only way to win may be through the Seer's sacrifice."

Pain erupts in my chest. My body turns cold.

Mr. Lee looks grim. "This is how the Darkness consumes the light of the entire world. The only time we have to train is while those two morph into whatever Mofa wants them to be. Then we face them."

"Mister Lee, who is the Seer?" Lawson asks.

"Who can see what Fiara is doing?" Mr. Lee asks. "Can you see light? Color? Angelica, do you see it? Teddy?" We both shake their heads, as does Christina.

"Lawson? What do you see? Lawson's face turns beet-red.

"I see, um, webs. Webs full of color. Light. So much light everywhere. What does that mean?"

"That childhood song," Christina says.

We remember it, and we say it together.

And one of them can see,
Webs but not a spider's
If only they believe
And bathe in the light.

"You needed to fully believe what you see, no doubts about the power of magic or evil. And you needed the waters of Kang Fu," Mr. Lee says. "You are the Seer, Lawson. But now there's a terrible burden you must fully consider. Can you sacrifice yourself to end the Darkness?"

# PART FIVE

## THE SEER

"Things were rough all over but it was better that way. That way, you could tell the other guy was human too."

—S.E. Hinton, *The Outsiders*

# CHAPTER TWENTY-FIVE

"Lawson!"

Elle is screaming my name, but it's a dream. When I wake up the next morning in bed, my body fills with panic. Is this all happening? For a second, that moment between sleep and consciousness, everything had felt normal. But the moment I open my eyes, I remember the fires. One leg hangs outside my sheets, stretching toward the floor. Quickly, I move it back under the sheet. Gracie barks and licks my face. I pet her and wish I didn't have to leave the bed.

I'm scared I'll never return.

Elle and Rob had floated around the Fountain and became cocooned in a fiery glaze. Is Fiara still there below them, shooting some kind of energy at them? Mr. Lee was right. I didn't want to tell anyone—it was scary enough witnessing all this—but I saw Fiara's energy. A web of brilliant green came from her. What the hell does that mean?

And according to Mr. Lee, I have to sacrifice myself if we're going to win.

Taking a deep breath, I roll out of bed. Downstairs, Mom and Dad exchange brief words while getting ready for work. Should I tell them about this? What parents would believe their fifteen-year-old if he told them there are real monsters that have come out of a pit of hell? And they'd probably admit me to a hospital if I told them that I've been seeing strange webs of light around people, right?

Mr. Lee is the one adult who seems immune to adulthood, but maybe that's only because of the stories he learned growing up.

My parents almost always poke their heads in my bedroom and say good-morning, especially these past few weeks. Children keep disappearing, and all parents are concerned. Something's off, even here at home.

I sit down at my desk and turn on my computer. I'm scared to look at the local news, but I have to know what everyone else knows. Gracie crawls under my desk. I pet her with one hand and use the other to search for The Word of Worthlapp, our town's newspaper.

The first headline reads, **Police Set Curfew: No Kids Out After Sunset**

*Local police urge families to keep all children at home. All after-school activities city-wide have been cancelled. "We've never seen anything like this," Police Chief Warner stated. "We're working around the clock. We've asked the governor to send the National Guard."*

My stomach rolls, and I swallow back an urge to vomit. We were so focused on Sam, Pauline, and Elle... how many more have been affected? The National Guard? What does that even mean? As long as we can remember the kids, though, they can't be dead. That gives me a bit of hope. The Darkness has them, but it's waiting to consume them.

*Waiting for what?*

I shake the question away and scroll through more headlines.

**AN ENTIRE CLASS GOES MISSING**

*Mrs. Calore's third-grade class went on an outdoor field trip to identify plant life in the woods surrounding Worthlapp, according to Principal Teel of Worthlapp Elementary. The class, including the teacher, never returned. Investigators followed the notes Mrs. Calore had written on a field trip form. They found an abandoned school bus and several backpacks. But not a single person.*

*"Where could they have gone?" Principal Teel asked. The school and the entire community have gathered to search for the missing class.*

I stand and scream. I grab a pillow off my bed and throw it against the wall. I can't read anymore. I can sit here and read stories like this for the rest of my life and keep feeling worthless about myself. Or I can help, even it means sacrificing myself. What the Darkness is doing—it's a lot worse than any of us imagined. One more story on my computer catches my eyes.

I'm scared to read it.

I don't want to read it. But I have to.

**IS THERE A BEAST IN WORTHLAPP?**

A beast? I close my eyes. The headlines remind me about the time I spent with Elle when we were kids. We had pretended our street was a roller coaster. We called it "The Beast" after a ride at Kings Island, an amusement park that featured the fastest wooden roller coaster in the world. We had dreamed of going together.

Something about that conversation is important, and I try to recall the memory.

We were both on our bikes, riding down our street.

"The Beast!" I yelled. The decline on the road wasn't steep at all, but in our imaginations, we zoomed at lightning speed down the biggest roller coaster.

Elle and I rode side by side out of the neighborhood. We weren't supposed to stray far, but we weren't thinking at all. It was as if something was calling to us. We didn't say it out loud, but we didn't have to. I knew she heard it, too.

"Law, promise me you'll go to Kings Island with me," Elle said.

"I promise! As soon as I'm old enough to drive, we'll go. You, me, and the Beast! Gosh, can you imagine how fun it is?"

She giggled. "I bet it's faster than an airplane."

"Faster than a rocket!

"But not faster than me!" Elle peddled away quickly. I stood up on my bike, putting all my weight—a whole sixty pounds—on the pedals, and raced after her full speed ahead.

There's nothing like the wind in your face on a summer's day bike ride. Absolutely nothing beats it. Well, maybe the wind from a roller coaster like The Beast would come close.

Before I knew it, we were on the outskirts of town, nearing a forest.

"Do you ever wonder what things looked like before?" Elle asked.

"What do you mean, before?"

"Like before houses and cars. Do you think the entire world looked like this?" She pointed at the forest. A warm breeze greeted us. We got off our bikes and walked toward it. The trees appeared to invite us in.

"Oh, wow, it's so dark," I said. We walked our bikes up a hill. "Maybe we shouldn't be here."

"This is scary, Law. Should we go home?"

"I don't know. It's an adventure."

"You and your adventures," she said. "One of these days, you're gonna get me in trouble."

"We've survived so far," I said, and I heard something like a whisper. Something was waking up, and it was following us. I felt a warmth on the back of my neck, like it was breathing on me.

*I'm scared.*

*Me, too,* Elle thought back.

*Faster.* We began to run uphill. Neither of us thought it was odd that we could suddenly read each other's minds.

We made it up to the top of the hill, to the railroad tracks. We continued walking our bikes, but this time Elle reached for my hand. I didn't think about girlfriends or any of that stuff. Elle was a girl who was also a friend, and I liked holding her hand. It brought me comfort, and whatever was in that darkness was the opposite of comforting.

"What was in there?" Elle asked.

"Some kind of monster. Let's not go back there." She nodded, and neither of us questioned whether it was a monster or not. It was a given.

When we first discovered the Fountain, we screamed in joy. A swimming hole! We dropped our bikes, ran straight toward it, kicked off our shoes, and jumped in.

My phone buzzes, taking me out of my memories. It's a text from Christina.

*When are we meeting today?*

I don't immediately reply. My thoughts are still trapped in the past. There's something I'm forgetting. There's something important about our childhood adventures to the Fountain that I need to remember.

I text Christina back. *On my way. Have you seen the news?*

I return my attention to the article.

**IS THERE A BEAST IN WORTHLAPP?**

Opinion Column by Elise Zwick

*We've gone from a single missing child earlier this fall to dozens of missing children reports a week. Now, an entire class has gone missing, and the National Guard is on its way to Worthlapp. It's a scary time for us all, and I don't want to scare our readers more than necessary.*

*But we must face facts.*

*We have no reports of bodies, thank God. No blood, no torn clothing, no physical evidence whatsoever, except for empty places. Empty buses, empty bedrooms, empty spaces where children should be.*

*What does this mean? Is the National Guard expecting some act of terrorism? Perhaps they are, but anyone witnessing what's happening in Worthlapp—who still has the ability to think clearly—must come to another conclusion.*

*Once we strip away all the possibilities, what's left is an impossibility.*

*There's a beast in Worthlapp. Something beyond our understanding. Maybe it's a literal beast or maybe it's a supernatural beast, but we have to stop looking for footprints in trails. We're not finding footprints! People don't just disappear. We have to open our eyes to what could really be happening, even if it's contrary to any logic or any previous understanding we've had of the universe.*

The article continues and proposes a town hall gathering of concerned citizens. That's good. I'll tell Mr. Lee about it, and maybe he can help them out.

*Yeah. I'll leave now too. See you at Lee's,* Christina texts back.

I look in the mirror and ask out loud, "Why me?" I shake my head. *Why any of us?*

I'll die a virgin. I won't even get a real first kiss.

Before I leave, I hug Gracie tight. I kiss her several times on the top of her head. She rolls over, hoping I'll rub her belly. I do. Then she licks me several times on the face. I wipe away a fresh tear.

"I hope I see you again, girl," I tell my pup. She whines, as if she understands. She kisses me again, and a flash of blue light sparks from her. "Bye, Gracie."

My heart is heavy, and my stomach feels ill. I hope I'm wrong, but I have a terrible feeling I'll never see my parents or my beautiful Gracie ever again. And I never even got a chance to say goodbye to my parents.

After I grab my bike, I risk a glance at the old couple's house across the road. It's turned black. I don't mean that the lights are off and it's dark. Rather, the same kind of veiny blackness I saw in the tree across from Teddy's has spread out like a crippling web over Old Man Darius and Toothless Tonya's home.

I knew when I saw that tree and Teddy had no reaction that I was seeing something only meant for my eyes. That doesn't mean I want to be the Seer.

The web pulses like a heartbeat, and terror cuts through me like a knife. My breath comes up shallow. With each beat, blackness surges through the web. An insane cackle bellows from inside.

I head over to Mr. Lee's, forcing my legs to move, even as fear tries to root them to the ground. I sure hope he's not full of shit. What if that dark web entangles my house the next time I return? Or what if I never return at all?

---

I'M THE FIRST to arrive at Mr. Lee's home. I knock on the door. He opens it and flashes me a concerned smile. It feels weird entering his home. Teachers' private lives have always felt like an off-limits subject, and entering Mr. Lee's house is like getting a special behind-the-scenes tour.

"So." I don't waste any time on small talk. "Am I going to die?"

I study his energy. Ever since the last trip to the Fountain, I see the energy and light that surround each person. We have an electric force that radiates through us. Maybe that's all life is—energy. From Mr. Lee, a deep orange radiates from both his head and heart.

He doesn't answer. I sit up a little straighter in my chair. "Please tell me everything you know about who I am. Please."

Mr. Lee nods. "You can see good and evil. You see our energy. You can see who a person really is. That makes you dangerous to Mofa. It wants that power because it will enhance its own. But not only that—if you learn to use your special ability of sight, you will uncover many truths."

*Whoa.*

"What color am I?" Mr. Lee asks. His lips curl into a smile of curiosity.

"A deep orange. I've never seen anything so orange."

"And your friends?"

"Christina has a brilliant yellow. Angelica has a bright purple. Elle's energy is green, like Fiara's."

Should I tell him about Teddy? My hands shake. The first time I saw Teddy's color, it was blue. Most people have blue light, except for those of us in this group fighting the Darkness. Even though I don't understand the meaning of the colors, something starts to make sense. The Darkness wants those with unique energy. It's not just going after any kind of energy. It needs these yellows, oranges, greens... and that's why it wants our group specifically.

But then Teddy went into the pit. He had been bitten by the monster in Rob's flesh. Something changed in him.

I hope whatever I saw was only temporary. When Teddy emerged from the pit, his light had changed. I didn't tell anyone then because I thought I was going crazy.

Teddy's lights turned black.

Pitch black lights. Darkness within. The same venomous blackness that spread throughout the elm tree on his block, the same that surged through the web across from my house like a heart that pumped oil—

That's what I see on Teddy.

It can't be good. But hopefully when I see him again, his light will have returned to normal.

"So, what do those colors mean?"

"I have a lot of notes on colors. Have you read those yet?" Mr. Lee asks. I shake my head like a bad student who hasn't done his homework, but I take out my copy of his journal. "You need to read them. Think of it as a mandatory homework assignment that was due yesterday."

I take a deep breath. "How are we going to fight?"

"Mofa has survived this long by creating monsters. The legend of Kang Fu that I've researched only mentioned a cocooned creation when—" He pauses and looks nervously around the room.

"When what? And so this all has happened before?"

"Time is a strange thing. There are billions of people in the world. Each individual is the center of his or her own universe, yes? Their family and friends are their world. Time is a river that flows through many worlds."

"Can you please just tell me how to fight?"

I'm tired of lectures.

"The legends say the monsters take three days to completely morph in the cocoons. As cocoons, they are completely indestructible. Once they emerge, they will hunt us until they kill us. With your sight, we can train, and we destroy them before they destroy us."

"So how do we fight?" I ask so loudly Mr. Lee flinches. I like Mr. Lee, but I'm getting annoyed. We've been sitting around too long. Where the hell is everyone else?

"The stories describe human energy as a web or like a series of lines. Kang Fu gives strength to these so-called webs. What we have to learn to do is to connect the webs between us. Then that, I hope, will give us the energy we need to defeat Mofa."

"Did you see that they're bringing in the National Guard? And that an entire class full of kids went missing?"

The slight curve in his lips completely straightens. "It's terrible." He pauses, and for a moment, I think he's going to cry. "Lawson—do you understand how important this is? This isn't a game. This is life or death, and dozens of children may die if we don't stop it."

Nausea rises in my throat. "I understand."

"No gun will kill Mofa," he says. "Its fuel is unique human energy. But what fuels it will also destroy it."

"Are you sure?"

"Yes, I'm sure." But his gaze turns as dark as the circles under his eyes. He's worried, too. My body trembles, and I force a humorless smile.

"Are you sure the Seer must be sacrificed?" I ask.

He doesn't say it out loud, but I catch a thought. *I hope I'm wrong, dear boy. I so hope I'm wrong.*

# CHAPTER TWENTY-SIX

Christina arrives at Mr. Lee's, and with the exception of the brilliant yellow that shines from her head and heart, she looks exhausted. She clutches a purse against her chest with one hand and runs the other through her leafy-brown hair she must have forgotten to brush.

She fixes me with her hazel eyes, blinks, and says, "Hey."

"I was telling Lawson more about the legends as I know them," Mr. Lee tells her. He picks up his leather bag and looks inside. "Care for some tea?"

"Sure, thanks," she says. Mr. Lee goes to the kitchen and pours water into a kettle. He returns with tea saucers, cups, and three tea bags.

"Lawson can see our lines," Mr. Lee says. "He will help us connect them."

"You mean, the web? The Darkness said something to me about that before. Or maybe I heard it when it controlled me." Christina's voice sounds suddenly tight. "It wanted them, or something. And, well, when it possessed me, I saw flashes of light. Yellow light, mostly."

"We'll discuss more once everyone is here." I wish he'd explain how we're going to kick its ass. He looks up at a clock in the dining room, the crow's feet in the corner of his eyes crinkling, and returns to the kitchen.

"How are you?" I ask Christina.

She shrugs. "Not good. Everything we've been through. It's... it's too much." She keeps her voice low.

"Yeah. It is." My gaze wanders throughout Mr. Lee's home. We sit at a mahogany, circular table. Pictures of nature hang on the walls—woods, rivers, lakes, waterfalls. I look for pictures of family, but I don't see any.

"What did we do to deserve this?" She tugs at the bottom of a long-sleeved tight black shirt that sits just below the waist of slim dark blue jeans.

My eyes move from the wall art to Christina. Dark circles form under her eyes. "Do you believe everything happens for a reason?"

"No," she answers quickly. "That's some bullshit adults say. It's a stupid excuse that gives meaning to even stupider things. Like a parent gets in a car accident, and some asshole says, 'Everything happens for a reason.' The hell it does." Her eyes narrow, and the tone of her voice frightens me.

"Have you read through his journal?" I ask, removing my copy from my jeans and placing it on the table.

Christina rubs her temples. "Some. Right now, I can barely keep my eyes open."

Understanding, I flip through the pages to find some excerpts I want to show her. "Look at these quotes."

> *So, what is Mofa? Only a few have tried to study it. Even fewer of them survived to share their reports.*
> *The following are some theories. "It is hell. Maybe not the hell you read about in whatever Bible you were given, but it is hell nonetheless." – Giovanni Corso, 1819, Italy*
>
> *"The Universe has humans and dogs. Why shouldn't it*

*have monsters, too? The Darkness is the home of all monsters." – Sakura Takashi, 1904, Japan*

*"Portals to the Darkness exist in all corners of the world. The portals hide in the darkest of woods and lead you deep into the underbelly of the Earth. In that underbelly, monsters float through space like fish in the sea." – Dr. Audrey Burgess, 1979, England*

*"The Darkness exists to keep humans human. The world is full of magical secrets, and if humans ever discovered how to use those secrets, life would change. For better or worse, who knows? The powerful would try to harness it to become more powerful. We've seen that. So, maybe the Darkness is really good. Maybe we're not supposed to see what's beyond it." – Professor Bill Wise, 2024, USA*

"Isn't that weird?" I ask. "I mean, he's got quotes from people trying to figure out the Darkness all the way back to the 1800s. And from places like Italy and Japan! So, what does our small town have to do with this? Why us? Why all the kids here?"

She bites at her lip and looks over my shoulder to the kitchen. Mr. Lee still hasn't returned. "Let me see this," she says, taking my copy. "There was something in here I saw about kids. Here!"

*Nearly every culture in every historical period has searched for Kang Fu. It exists, and not one, but several. They aren't easy to find, mostly because they are guarded by an equally powerful mystical force.*

*Mofa*

*Not only that, but Kang Fu can only be discovered by the most innocent of humans: children. No one knows if the waters truly make one live forever. Most researchers think that Kang Fu possesses a special energy, and with proper training, the energy can be used to enhance certain abilities, such as telepathy and even telekinesis.*

*When searching for Kang Fu, one must be close to innocence. The younger, the better. And as we get older, we must find ways to remember our childlike innocence and care-free adventures. So, when searching for Kang Fu, ride a bike or walk/run/play on your way there. Do something to remember what youth feels like, and you'll have some additional luck on your side.*

*Unfortunately, adults have shown the universe that they cannot be trusted with the powers Kang Fu has, so it hides from most adults, and Mofa can also make them forget. For those who push through Mofa in search of power or immortality—especially those who have forgotten the innocence of childhood—the ultimate irony is that the price they may have to pay is death.*

"So, we could all die, of course," I say, flipping through the pages again. "And we're not the only ones in the world that have this problem. Like this isn't the only Darkness and the only Fountain, right?"

"According to his notes," she says, "it sure isn't. Plus, they're obviously connected somehow, too. Yin and yang?"

I shrug. "I remembered the first time I found the Fountain. Do you?"

She nods.

"It was like… it called to me," I said. "I was with Elle. We rode our bikes way far out of the neighborhood, much farther than we should have. And out of all the places we stumbled upon, it was the Fountain. That's an 'everything happens for a reason' story. I think there's something about that discovery I'm supposed to remember. Something important if we want to save Elle."

"Ahh, the discussion of fate," Mr. Lee interrupts. He carries a tea kettle and pours hot water into each of our cups. "Yes, because everything happens for a reason doesn't mean *every* thing happens for a reason." He looks at Christina. "What I mean is, there is a reason we were chosen. That's not random. But that doesn't mean if you win or lose a race, or if you sprain your ankle, or fail a test, that each of those things are part of fate's chapter. I picture fate like a road. You can choose to get off the road, to take a break, to go in different directions. Those are our own personal adventures. But eventually, the road calls us back, and we ride forward to what fate has planned for us."

I try not to sigh out loud. I don't want any more lessons unless they involve ass-kicking. "Are we gonna learn how to fight it?"

"Just a little more patience, Lawson." This time I do sigh out loud. He told me I will have to be sacrificed, and he thinks I have time to be patient? "Let me ask you a tougher question, then," Mr. Lee says and takes a seat at the table with us. "The things you did as a child, the first victims you brought to Mofa—do you think you had to do those things?"

Christina slams her hand on the table. "Yes! You have no idea how many terrible things I've had to do!" The yellow light around her brightens. It's intensely beautiful and powerful. No wonder the Darkness has always wanted her. "Killing Rob—that wasn't even the worst of it. You know all this, right? It made me kill my boyfriend. But it also made me... well, if there's a hell, I belong in it."

Christina doesn't fill in the blanks. What all has she done?

"Did you hear about the entire class that's gone missing?" I ask.

Tears well in her eyes. Her face twists with sadness and guilt. "It's getting stronger. God, it's going to take everyone, isn't it?"

"It's not your fault, Christina," Mr. Lee says gently.

"No, I didn't help it get these kids." Her voice softens. "But I brought it kids before."

Mr. Lee motions for us to stand. "We cannot dwell on the past. We must focus on the present, and so it's time to train. We must be prepared to fight."

"Finally," I say, and I'm grateful that Mr. Lee flashes an empathetic, soft smile.

"Have you ever knocked someone out with your mind?" His lips curve up. "If you can think-speak in the woods, you can do other things there, too. Like knock someone out with a powerful thought. In Mofa's world, thoughts have the ability to take physical form. I have a feeling you understood that, on some basic level. But we're going to do things that are absolutely wild. I think you're both going to like your training. It will certainly make you feel better."

---

We move through the kitchen, where newspapers pile on a small table and dirty dishes fill both sinks. He takes us to his backyard. A brown private fence lines the left and the right side of the yard, but the back is open, strangely. It leads into woods. Nothing like the woods of the Darkness, but there's something creepy about Mr. Lee's backyard. Near the edge of the trees, there's a picnic table, where he has lined up a series of clay pigeons. I picture old movies where the characters shoot guns at bottles. The setup looks like an old Western.

According to Mr. Lee, we're going to destroy these clay pigeons with our minds, which my inner geek is about to mindgasm over.

"Hey, where are Angelica and Teddy?" Christina asks. She adjusts the purse that's hanging across her shoulder. "Shouldn't we all be training together?"

"Yes, and we will," Mr. Lee says. "I suspect that they have a few more family matters to attend to than either of you did. Give them time. That's important, too."

Jesus. Teddy's got to tell his recently saved mother that his little brother is gone. What will he even say? And Angelica's best friend is missing, too. Plus, she lost her grandfather. Okay, yeah, everyone's got a lot to deal with.

"Now, remember how you communicated in the woods? Remember how we pulled Lawson out of the pit?" Mr. Lee begins. "Fighting with your mind is really the same as that. Picture your energy that stems from your mind and heart. Focus that energy on something like your mind is a laser."

"But that only really worked in the woods," Christina says. "How will we know if we're doing it right out here?"

"Trust me," he says. Christina and I stand near each other, and Mr. Lee walks up behind us. He puts a hand on each of our shoulders and lowers his head. Then I hear his thoughts, like we could in the woods.

*Concentrate. But don't close your eyes. Never close your eyes in the woods. Picture your energy. Move your energy with your mind, like it's an electric current and you need to expel it.*

Mr. Le, pauses. *Now, try it.*

I almost close my eyes at first, but I stop myself. As if our energy were lightning, we push it with our minds and send it to the clay pigeons Mr. Lee had lined up for us.

*Crash!* I jump back. I definitely hit something, but the pigeons stand straight up on the table. To our left, though, stretches Mr. Lee's fence. It's a tall, wooden privacy fence, and now it has a hole in the middle of it.

"Shit!" I say, and Mr. Lee laughs.

"Not bad, Lawson. Now, let's work on your aim. How about you, Christina?"

Mr. Lee's hands remain pressed on our shoulders. Her eyes flicker, and she grins. Christina's brilliant yellow energy sparkles. Her energy shoots forward, and the pigeons shatter. Not one, but all of them.

"Whoa!" I say. "Awesome!"

"That felt great." She turns to Mr. Lee. "Thank you."

"They are biodegradable, and I have plenty more for us to

destroy. There's also something both of you should know, and it's why I wanted to start before Angelica and Teddy arrive. You both have a very special web of energy. I had guessed it was a yellow power, although I don't have Lawson's ability of sight. Lawson, would you confirm the colors?"

"Yeah," I say. "We both have a yellow web. But it's not exactly the same yellow. Mine is more golden, I guess. I'm not sure what the difference is."

"Hmmm. Yes, there aren't just multiple colors. There are also a variety of degrees of each color. Lawson, your energy gives you the mental strength of sight. Christina's gives her the mental strength to fight. It's why Mofa is attracted to both of you. Harnessing others' energy makes it stronger, and naturally it's attracted to unique energies. That's why we need the Seer. If you two stay close and connected, you'll do a lot of damage to Mofa. Let's practice a hundred more times."

And we do. Over and over again until I have a terrible headache. I don't know if I've ever felt this kind of mental exhaustion before.

"Collaborative strength is what you have. Each of your energies enhances the energy of the other." Mr. Lee continues teaching us, as we destroy one group of clay pigeons after another.

"This time," Mr. Lee says now that I have improved my aim, "picture a feeling to go along with your attack. A childhood fear. Something exciting. Something you love or hate. Anything, as long as it's strong. Then throw your energy with your heart."

"Okay, Yoda," I say, and Mr. Lee laughs. This would be a lot of fun, if there wasn't this other nagging sensation in the back of my mind that soon we are going to fight real beasts.

I think about my parents. I remember the first time as a kid that I was afraid of losing them. They went out for a date night or something and left me with a sitter. I don't know why, but I sat at the window all night waiting for them to come home, the same way Gracie waits at the door for me now. What if they never had returned? Is that fear a strong enough emotion?

But then the emotion that I need comes to mind. I think of Teddy the day he helped me in his bathroom. I had my shirt off, and he touched me, ever so gently, healing the wounds that the Darkness had inflicted on me. I looked in his eyes, and I could see that he genuinely cared for me. I wanted to touch him then, but I didn't. The memory doesn't make me angry, not exactly. It fills me with a longing for something I want but may never be able to have.

I picture how beautiful Teddy looks, how I'd love to hold his hand. How I'd love to know how his lips feel against mine.

*Dammit, holy fucking shit*! Mr. Lee has his hands on us, which means he and Christina can hear my thoughts.

Screw it. I don't have time to explain or worry. Sooner or later I need to face my own truth, too. Right now, we have real demons to face.

I focus on the new pigeons Mr. Lee placed on the table. I release my energy as hard as I can.

*Kshhhhkshkshsh!*

"Excellent work, Lawson," Mr. Lee says. "Most powerful. Christina, you go."

She looks at me, and now there are tears in her eyes. Tears for me? She wipes at them and steps away so Mr. Lee's no longer touching her.

"I'm sorry for your sadness."

I reach for her hand, and she lets me take it. "I'm sorry, too. For everything the Darkness has made you do."

I hug her, and, thankfully, she hugs me back.

"Do you think we can win?" she asks Mr. Lee.

"Evil has many tricks." He pauses and looks up at the sky. "The more you practice, the better your chances will be."

Christina's fear is palpable. She's had much more experience with the Darkness than any of us. Her yellow radiates strength but also terror.

I look up, and my jaw drops. An infinite number of webs of light reach beyond the sky. It's an overwhelming sight. I've never seen light like this before. It must be coming from everyone in Worthlapp, maybe even beyond.

It gives me hope. If I can see their lights, I can use them. Maybe I can harness the energy to fight.

I gulp, and a terrible thought replaces my brief moment of hope.

That light—all of those lights—that's what the Darkness wants. If it can consume that, it can control—well, everyone, I guess.

That's what's at stake here. Not only my friends and now classes full of missing children.

There's a world of energy and light that I'm just beginning to see, and the Darkness will try to consume it all until there's no light left.

"Darkness cannot drive out darkness," Mr. Lee says. "Only light can do that." I know that quote—it's a famous one some teachers at Worthlapp have posted in their classrooms. Mr. Lee and Christina look up at the sky, and lightning flashes. But it's not an electric yellow.

It's black.

Black, like the light Teddy had after coming out of the pit. Black like the elm tree on his street and the web that has entangled the house across from me. He should be here any minute. I hope his black light is gone.

We practice until we have no energy left to give.

# CHAPTER TWENTY-SEVEN

I hold my breath and wait for Teddy to walk through the door. Maybe his energy has changed, I pray. Or black doesn't mean bad, I hope. It could mean all sorts of things, right? I'm scared to ask Mr. Lee about it, and I still choose to keep it to myself.

I've missed Teddy, too. I know there are bigger things to worry about, but I want to... to tell him my truth. And maybe just maybe he might like me back in that way? How perfect would it be to find someone who loves video games as much as you who also wants to make out with you? That sounds pretty much like a perfect life.

That is not the life for me, though. Something—fate, if you ask Mr. Lee—calls on me to sacrifice myself for the greater good. Still, Mr. Lee is only human. Humans can be wrong. I will fight the Darkness, but I will not give up hope for myself either.

Teddy greets Mr. Lee from the adjacent room. Hearing his voice excites me, but I'm scared to look at him. I saunter to the front of the house, glancing at the walls. There's a fireplace in the living room, and a black and white picture of an old couple on the mantle.

Suddenly, the picture of the old couple turns orange. A flame consumes it. The woman in the photo blinks, and the man's lips curl into a sinister grin.

My hands clamp over my mouth, and I close my eyes. When I get the courage to open them, everything's returned to normal.

I'm losing my mind.

Angelica says hello to Mr. Lee. We finally have everyone together, except for Elle and Fiara.

I will take a risk right now and tell Teddy exactly how I feel. We could die, after all. I glance at the picture on the mantle again. There's more to our world than I can see, and apparently I can see more than most. If that's the case, let me at least have a chance for a first kiss before I get killed.

Forcing a confident smile on my face, I step toward the front entryway, cautiously excited to see Teddy.

Then I'm hit in the gut, hard.

Teddy stands next to Angelica, and they're holding hands.

Angelica's hand is wrapped around Teddy's fingers. It should be a beautiful thing to see, but I hate it.

I hate them right now, both of them, more than I hate anything.

Looking up, I try to keep my smile, but it's a battle I lose.

I don't even look at his energy. I'm blinded by jealousy.

Teddy blushes, but he doesn't let go of Angelica's hand. My eyes dart to his dark brown T-shirt with the words "Overlook Hotel" printed on it. "So, what did we miss?"

I want to ask him the same thing. Why is he holding *her* hand? Why can't he be holding mine? Why does he have to wear a cool shirt that I can't even like right now, and who came on to who? I can't stand this!

Christina speaks up and smiles. Seeing her happy relaxes me a little—I have to remember that my life problems are nothing compared to what she's experienced. "Just wait till you see what training is like."

I clear my throat and turn my attention away from Teddy. It

hurts more than anything I've ever felt. I want to cry and scream and punch something.

*What about his light?*

I didn't see anything. I look back over at them, and I don't see anything around Angelica or Teddy. Christina's and Mr. Lee's lights are gone, too. What does that mean?

Christina must pick up on my emotions. "You're both going to need your full attention," she says, glancing at their hand-holding, which makes Teddy let go of Angelica's hand. Thank God. I was about to puke.

"Come, sit," Mr. Lee says. "Have some tea first. The tea will revitalize all of you. Then we train again. Lots to do."

We sit at the table. Christina takes a seat next to me, and Teddy and Angelica sit side by side across from us. Teddy smiles shyly at me like he's got a story to tell. Well, I don't want to hear it.

"How's your mother?" Mr. Lee asks Teddy.

"She looks great. Seems perfect."

"Did you tell her about your brother?"

Teddy looks away. "I couldn't. She was so happy, sir. She hasn't been happy in such a long time. I told her Sam's staying at a friend's house. We just gotta get him back."

Mr. Lee scratches his chin. "Very well. What you disclose to your mother is your own choice." He turns to Angelica. "How is your family?"

She folds her hands together on the table, lacing her fingers together. "They're okay. They're with Pauline's parents."

"Oh?"

"Pauline's parents are hysterical. I couldn't even say anything, could I? Not that they'd believe me anyway. It's all crazy. Do you really think we can get them back? Sam and Pauline? And all the missing kids?"

"But you remember them," Christina says. "If we can remember them, there's a chance. Only once they are consumed do we forget about them."

"Yes, there is hope. Angelica, you need to tell us your story," Mr. Lee says. "Catch everyone up."

I lean closer. Yes, Angelica was hurt when she saved me from the Darkness. She kept holding her side, and her eyes had flashed with terror.

"Yeah," she says and puts her hands on her lap. "I was attacked. I was stabbed in my own house and then taken to the woods. But I fought and survived."

"I think it's best if we see it," Mr. Lee says. "Everyone, hold hands. Angelica—think about what happened, and send it to all of us. Push it like any thought you would send when inside the woods."

She narrows her eyes incredulously, but she reaches out her hands. We make a circle, and I close my eyes. And then like a dream, I see what happened to Angelica.

Angelica was on her back in her bedroom, and she'd had the wind knocked out of her. Someone was standing over her.

The man's lips curled into a frightening smile. He swung a knife out from behind his back and slashed at Angelica's side. She barely had time to scream before she passed out.

The vision jumps to Angelica outside the woods. The intruder brought her here. Painfully and slowly, Angelica stood up.

"We knew you'd be tough," he said. "Clearly, I didn't hurt you enough."

Angelica clenched her fists.

"Bring it on," she said and charged right into her attacker.

Right into Ronnie the Rattler, Worthlapp High's bully, and apparently, the latest to be possessed by the Darkness.

She knocked him flat on the ground. Holding her side, she raced through the woods. There were other sounds, screams and moans, but she didn't stop. She leapt over fallen branches and reached the top of the woods. She sprinted toward the Fountain. Then she jumped in the water, letting it nurse her wound.

In the Fountain, she heard a voice. It was Mr. Lee. "Angelica.

Christina. Get to the railroad tracks. Now. Lawson and Teddy are in trouble."

The vision fades away as Angelica releases our hands.

"So, all this happened before Teddy and I got to the woods?" I ask.

"Immediately before," Mr. Lee says. "The Darkness sent a monster—in Rob's flesh—and took Sam. Ronnie, fully human but possessed as far as I can tell, tried to deliver Angelica to the Darkness."

"How did the Darkness get Ronnie?" Teddy asks.

"Remember that the Darkness has the ability to control some people. To possess them, like it did with Christina," Mr. Lee says wryly.

"It makes sense," Christina says. "I attacked him at school." We give her strange looks. "Well, you know, not me. But me when I was controlled. It made him hurt me, when the Darkness had possession of me. It's well aware of Ronnie's dark side. Probably why it chose him."

"How did you know we were in trouble?" I ask.

"I don't have your sight, Lawson, but I do see certain things," Mr. Lee says. The others stare at me inquisitively. As far as I know, they don't know what I can see, just that I am the Seer. I still don't know why I see the lights. "Like dreams, although I'm awake. It was a vision, sent to me by Kang Fu. It wants to help us. I used all my mental power to get Angelica and Christina there. We are stronger together."

Christina rubs her belly like she has a stomachache. Her brilliant yellow returns. I suppose it never left, but for some reason I couldn't see it. My anger has dissipated—did my emotions block my sight?

A bright purple light shines from Angelica's head and heart. My heart races as I turn my attention to Teddy. *Please be okay.*

I gulp. It's a dark web—a pure, terrifying black surges from him, darker than anything I've ever seen. What does it mean? I bite my lip. This secret stays with me for now.

"Drink your tea," Mr. Lee tells all of us. "And let me read to you a couple things from my journal." We follow along with our copies, our eyes scanning the words. Mr. Lee's voice becomes distant, and I lose myself within the copy of my own text.

*For select individuals, repeated exposure to Kang Fu causes them to see our webs of energy, lines that connect all living things. These individuals are called Seers.*

*Generally, each person has a web of energy that stems from their head and from their heart. Where does each line end? That may be THE greatest secret of all, and I do not know the answer.*

*Mofa has always been attracted to these webs of energy. The more one interacts with Kang Fu, the stronger his or her webs become.*

*The webs have colors, too. The most common color is blue. But some have unique colors. Yellow, for example, represents an uncommonly powerful mental strength. Individuals with green lines represent a unique ability to change or transform—either into something great or terrible. Purple energy signifies tremendous physical abilities. Then there's black energy, an incredibly uncommon color. The research on black energy is inconclusive.*

*Kang Fu enhances each person's web. That's how we rejuvenate and heal. It's been reported that when a person is near death, his or her webs shrink in length.*

*Only the Seer can visualize the webs. It is unknown how many Seers exist. A Seer can recognize the light in others, helping each person find their inner strengths.*

He stands and walks around the table, clearing his throat. We put away our copies of his journal. "Lawson is our seer," he tells us. I look away uncomfortably. "But each of you is connected in this. I imagine you all have felt something similar, pain, trauma, a feeling of worthlessness perhaps. Those dark feelings attract Mofa and make you vulnerable. But they also unite you. You're all connected to this. Now that Lawson can see your light, don't be afraid to ask him about it. And Lawson?" His volume lowers, and he looks me directly in the eye. "Don't be afraid to tell people what you see. But just remember to only report what you see. Do not interpret it. Like anything in life, interpretations vary, and we must be careful in what we assume."

He sounds like he's lecturing in his classroom, but no classroom lecture has caused my spine to tingle with fear.

"What else can you tell us about this web of energy?" Angelica asks. She looks extra curious, like she knows something she isn't telling us.

"In short, it is an energy force that connects us. It's what we will use to fight Mofa. Have any of you other than Lawson seen the light?"

No one speaks up at first, but then Teddy slowly raises his hand. "I did. For a second. When you all were pulling Lawson out of the pit. It was like, um, like lines were shooting at him, connecting you to him."

"Yes, it's just like that, Teddy," Mr. Lee says in a soothingly calm voice. "It's the power of the lines that we use in our training, and that we will use to fight these evils."

The others stare at me again, as if they're trying to see what I see. My face burns, and I shift my gaze to the hardwood floor, avoiding eye contact with everyone, especially Teddy.

"There's something else I haven't told you yet." Mr. Lee walks toward the dining room window and looks out at the street. "There is a natural creature that can consume a person's web of energy. Strangle it. Eat it. Do you know what that creature is?"

I have a terrible feeling that I do, but it's Teddy who raises his hand again, like we're in class. Mr. Lee nods at him.

"A snake," he says.

"That's right," Mr. Lee confirms. "Mofa can control snakes. I don't think snakes are inherently bad, either. Like the humans it has controlled,"—Mr. Lee glances awkwardly at Christina—"the Darkness can control other creatures, too. It makes the snakes attack your head and your heart. Why? Because that's where your energy originates." He clears his throat. "The Darkness doesn't simply want to kill you. It wants to *consume* your life force."

My skin erupts with goosebumps, and I scratch the back of my head.

"Why can't the Fountain save the missing children?" I ask.

Mr. Lee shakes his head. "Kang Fu may be able to give us strength, but we must choose to act. Good doesn't just happen. It must be deliberately chosen. So, do you understand what's at stake? Why we have to train? And why we have to fight?"

We all stand. "Pauline," Angelica says and clenches her fists.

"Sam," Teddy adds.

"That class, and all the others that have gone missing before," Christina says.

"All of us," I state. "All the kids. All our light." Angelica's purple light brightens, as does Christina's yellow. I search for something, anything else from Teddy, but a pulsating, terrifying blackness is all I see.

"Good," Mr. Lee says somberly. "It's important you know what you're fighting for. Let's train." He picks up his leather bag with his original journal inside, and we follow him out.

The moment we exit Mr. Lee's home, the earth shakes, loud and hard, like it did at the Fountain when Elle and Rob jumped in the lake. But it's not an earthquake this time.

It's an explosion.

It knocks us off our feet. When we look back, flames engulf Mr. Lee's home.

# CHAPTER TWENTY-EIGHT

The battle starts now. No more time for training. If we had stayed in there even a minute longer—

"Together, quickly!" Mr. Lee snaps, gesturing for us to join him. Angelica and Teddy exchange confused looks, but I motion for them to huddle up. We lean in as if discussing a football play, but it's sure a hell of a lot bigger than any sporting event.

Mr. Lee puts his hands on Christina's shoulders and mine. We put our arms around each other so that we are all connected, and Mr. Lee says, "Think water. Think of Kang Fu. Keep your eyes open and fill your hearts with hope. Picture it. Now!"

I bring the image of the lake to my mind—its beautiful, calming waters fill my head like a giant, blue sky.

"Now, send the water to the house."

Angelica gives us an, *is this shit for real* look, but I don't have time to confirm. My complete focus remains on the Fountain. I embrace its serenity, calm my mind, and inhale its strength.

"With your head *and* your hearts!" Mr. Lee yells.

*Hope*. Hope is the emotion I search for, and so along with the image of the lake, I recall the memory of Teddy and his mom in the moments before she found life again. We were filled with the greatest hope. I picture our web of energy, enhanced by the Fountain and our connection to each other. I see colors—brilliant purple and orange mix with a sparkling yellow. The earth shakes under my feet.

We hear a thunderous *splash*, a downpour. My mouth opens wide with shock, but my heart pumps victoriously. Water from the sky extinguishes the fire. We did it! Somehow we actually did it! Teddy flashes a smile. Angelica's eyes are wider than a deer's in headlights. My heart roars rhythmically in my ears, and breath rushes out me.

Mr. Lee lets go of us. Christina and I both fall back on the ground.

"Holy shit, that worked?" Angelica asks.

"That's your Wikipedia version of training, I'm afraid. Better learn fast," Mr. Lee says. He runs to Christina and me. "Are you okay?"

I nod, but even moving my neck hurts, like I've run several miles.

"Sit still," he advises. "It's not just my house I care about. That fire could have spread throughout the entire neighborhood if not stopped. Throughout all of Worthlapp, even."

"I thought we had more time," I say.

"Mofa has many monsters and tricks," Mr. Lee replies.

"Oh, shit," Angelica says. "Look!"

She points at something beyond the charred and crumbling roof of Mr. Lee's home. We may have put out the fire quickly, but it doesn't delete the damage. We look to the side of the house, out on the street in front, and there's a vehicle we all recognize. It's a piece of shit, old-ass Jeep Cherokee, but someone in our school is insanely proud of that car. Proud because he was the first in our class to get a license, although that pride came at a price. It was a reminder that he was held back a year, in kindergarten of all grades, because he spent too much time destroying the other kids' projects and not working on his own.

Ronnie the Rattler, who grew up to stab Angelica and tried to kill her. But as terrible as he is, I have to remember it may not really be him. He's just a pawn for evil.

"How did we do that? Make it rain with our minds?" Angelica asks. "Quick, so I can fight that asshole. I want to finish him."

"Don't overthink it," I tell her. "Your energy is crazy strong. Think of your purple light like a storm, and let it strike down evil."

Ronnie steps out of the car and runs both hands through spiked blonde hair. His muscular arms bulge through a blue track jacket. With an icy smile on his face, he sprints toward us. Panic fills me. He's a bully who is used to fighting, and I don't think we can defend ourselves in a traditional way.

He kicks the fence separating the front and back yards, and it comes tumbling down. Ronnie's face twists in shock and anger.

"How did you do that?" he asks, looking at the house, his eyes as hard as stone.

With my head held high, I face him. "You don't know who you're messing with. Go home."

A flame flickers in his eyes, which puts my stomach in knots. His aura matches the colors of fire.

"What do you want from us?" Christina asks.

Veins pulse under Ronnie's skin. He's built like a human King Kong. He brings both arms around the front of his body and squeezes his fists.

"Mister Lee!" I shout and turn around. But Mr. Lee is gone.

Ronnie charges at me, and then from the side, Angelica scrambles toward him. She's faster than I remember, and each stride is a leap. He doesn't see her coming, and when she's close enough to him, she squats, spins, and extends her leg. It's a badass sweep straight out of a kung fu movie, and it catches Ronnie perfectly. He runs right into it and flies forward.

His mouth opens wide, and the look of shock makes me laugh out loud. Even in mid-air, my laugh pisses him off, and he snarls.

He lands flat on his face, and then the four of us gather in a huddle together. Slowly, he rises and brushes the dirt off his pants. Then he turns and faces everyone.

"You'll have to go through all of us," Teddy says.

"That's fine with me." Ronnie roars, charging at us again. I grab Christina's hand and then Teddy's. I project my energy toward them, and our webs combine—Christina and I make the brightest yellow I've ever seen, and my yellow mixes with Teddy's black, forming what looks like a bumble bee of electricity.

"Hit him, with everything you got!" I shout and release our energy.

Ronnie looks like he's been shot. His mouth bursts open, and he flies backward, high up in the air, landing on the ground with a wonderful thud.

"Shit!" Teddy says. "That was awesome!"

I smile and shrug like it was nothing. Feels good to feel strong.

"That was cray," Angelica says. "Nicely done."

"You, too," I tell her. "Where did you learn that move?"

She laughs. "I took karate lessons when I was kid. Who knew I remembered anything? Didn't even think about it. Just did it." I recall the roundhouse kick she delivered to Mr. Lee's face not long ago, not realizing who it was. No wonder Teddy is attracted to her. I get it, even if I still hate it.

"It was badass," Christina says, and we all laugh.

Mr. Lee runs out of his crumbling house.

"Where did you go?" Christina asks.

"I... uh...." He sighs. "Doesn't matter now." He takes a big, noticeable swallow, and I realize something's not right. He races toward us, spins around, and extends his arms as if to shield us.

Shield us from what?

Then we see it. Someone else walks out of the house. Why did Mr. Lee go back inside?

The question vanishes when a bright metal object points directly at us.

Wearing his usual Worthlapp High baseball cap, it's impossible to not recognize him. I gulp. It's Coach Nathan, and he has a gun.

My hands tremble, and my stomach churns. I dig my feet into

the ground to keep from wobbling, and I reach for Christina and Teddy's hands again.

I stare at his clean-shaven, dark-haired face, and he has no light. Not the fiery red of Ronnie's, not a black energy like Teddy's, simply nothing.

Is he even human?

He points the gun straight at Mr. Lee, Nathan's lips stretching to his ears in a sinister grin.

Then, from behind Coach, someone else appears.

My jaw hits the ground, and I can't believe what I'm seeing.

It's Elle! She flashes me a smile, and then she taps Coach on the shoulder.

He turns around, and he lowers the gun.

"Elle? Elle, are you okay? What are you doing here?"

My eyes widen, and I try to swallow the lump in my throat. Questions flood my mind.

"I'm fine," she states. "The Darkness had control of me, but now it's just me. Only me. Are you still in there, Nathan? Is any part of you still alive?"

Coach moves toward her, and his skin reddens. He shakes his head, the bill of his baseball cap casting a shadow over his forehead and eyes.

"I can help you," Elle says. "I escaped from it. You can, too. We can be together."

I look closely for any sign of light from Coach, but I still don't see anything. My stomach flips at the only logical conclusion—he's not human at all anymore.

"Come with me," Elle says, "and leave them alone."

His face softens, and a flicker of red light sparks for an instant. He moves closer to Elle. Why is she doing this?

"What do you want from us?" I ask Coach.

"I have to take you to the pit," Coach says. His eyes radiate electricity. "Then the Darkness will reward me."

"With what?" I ask through gritted teeth. "Grade school girls next time?"

He scowls. "You've got the energy it needs." His eyes narrow, and he glares at me, his eyes lit with impatience and anger. "The Darkness has hundreds of children now." He cackles. "Hundreds! You have no idea. And it's got a simple proposition for you, Lawson. If you come with me, it will return the children. Your one, lonely pathetic life for the lives of hundreds of innocent kids. What will it be?"

Is this the sacrifice I have to make? My heart slams against my chest. How can I say no to that?

"Sam and Pauline, too?" I ask.

Nathan chuckles. "Of course. All of them. For you." He holds the gun in one hand, and he motions for me with the other.

*What do I do?* I mentally shout the question to Mr. Lee, praying he can hear me.

"It's a trick," Mr. Lee says. Did he hear my question? "Mofa wants your energy all right. *You* connect our energy. Not me."

Elle reaches for Nathan's hand and takes it. "Forget them," she says. "Take a chance with me. We can run away."

"Elle, no!" I shout. How could she return from the Darkness, from that cocoon thing, only to want to be with Coach? It doesn't make sense.

That's when she pulls his arm, knocking him off balance. Then she kicks his stomach, swings her arm around his head and puts him in a chokehold.

"Elle? Holy shit!" We lunge forward to help.

But before I get to him, he flips Elle over his shoulder, and she lands with a terrible thud on the ground in front of me.

Her skin flashes, and she exhales loudly. When I pull her up, Elle's skin flashes again.

It's not Elle at all.

It was someone who had changed her appearance to look like Elle.

Christina rushes ahead and shouts, "Fiara! Fiara, are you okay?"

Fiara groans and coughs, but she nods.

"I'm... I'm sorry. I thought I could trick him and help you."

Christina reaches for Fiara's hand. "There's nothing to be sorry about. I'm so glad you're okay. And that, you know—"

"I know," Fiara says. "I was trying to stop the others from morphing. The Fountain gave me more strength. I thought I'd be strong enough to help."

The click of a gun makes us jump, and Coach fully extends his right arm. "None of you are okay, you stupid kids."

Christina adjusts her purse, pulling it tightly against her chest.

Mr. Lee growls—a deafening roar—and lunges at Coach.

But Coach steps to the side, and Mr. Lee misses him. Coach raises the gun again, aims right at Mr. Lee, and fires.

The bullet cuts through his forehead, and I scream. Skin, blood, and bone spray out like a popped water-balloon. We all cry out, and Coach swings the gun angrily at each of us.

We run to Mr. Lee, but Coach shouts. "Stay back! I warned you." He looks from us to Mr. Lee's body, which jolts with spasms on the ground, as his head pours out what can only be chunks of brain and blood. I'm sick, and I want to scream and cry.

"Ronnie, let's go," Nathan commands. Ronnie snarls at us like a watchdog while he walks to Coach's side. Nathan looks at me again. "Come with me. Now! Or I will kill everyone else here."

I clench my fists and picture our energy. Keeping my eyes focused on Coach and Ronnie, I pray for Mr. Lee, Elle, and all the missing kids. Then I project an attack.

They fly backward and crash into the house.

But it doesn't stop them. They bounce right back up. "Not bad, kid." Ronnie whispers something into Coach's ear, and Coach nods. "All right. Here's the deal. You all meet us tonight, at the pit. If all of you don't come, I will go straight to each of your parents' houses and kill every single one. I'll kill your siblings. I'll kill all your family dogs. And I'll save their bodies so you can see what you caused! Do you understand?"

Bile rises in my throat. Should I strike again? I scared them, but what if he tries to kill another one of us? Blood pools around Mr. Lee's body, and I freeze with fear. The webs of light start to fade, and I steady my emotions.

Nathan and Ronnie exchange another look. "Come at dusk tonight, and don't be late," Nathan says. "Or everyone you have ever loved dies."

# CHAPTER TWENTY-NINE

My stomach clenches, and my pulse quickens. Ronnie and Nathan leave after making that terrible threat. What if they go to my parents' house now to kill them and Gracie? What if they were to get Teddy's mom? After everything we went through to save her, they threaten to kill all our families if we don't meet them tonight?

I look at the ground, and my heart sinks. Mr. Lee—our mentor, our teacher—is dead. Nothing but a body, and not even a full body. He's missing a chunk of his head, and I buckle over with sickness.

Angelica stands by Teddy's side, rubbing his back while he vomits. I walk over to them, and Teddy wipes his mouth.

"What do we do, Law?" His eyes are pitch black with anguish.

"We do what they say," I reply. "But we fight."

Angelica continues rubbing Teddy's back, but her jaw tightens. She puts an arm around his shoulders, and we look at Mr. Lee's body together.

"We can't just leave him here like this," Christina says.

"No," I agree. "But what happens if we call the cops?"

"Trouble," she replies. "They'll lock us up for murder and call us crazy. The National Guard is coming, after all. They'll see us as pathetic."

"He needs to come with us," Fiara states. She runs a hand through her slimy hair, and her face looks even paler than normal. I study her light—an emerald green energy encompasses her. It's beautiful, and it reminds me of Elle. Poor Elle! Is she at a point of no return? "I'm sorry I couldn't do more," Fiara continues. "I thought I could stop it."

Christina places a gentle hand on her shoulder. "What happened?"

Fiara shakes her head. Her eyes fill with a deep feeling of loss. "It's still in me, I think. The Darkness. But it's... it's distracted. It has so many children now, and it's putting its energy on the transformation." She gulps. "I think it's collecting children for...." Tears well in her eyes, and she wipes at them. "For food. Food for these new beasts. That's why we still remember all the missing kids right now. They're not dead. Yet."

I picture not one school bus full of children, but rows of school buses, each reserved for the monster's dinner. My stomach turns, and hot tears sting my eyes. If we don't do something about it, the monsters will take all the children in Worthlapp, and the Darkness will take all the light.

"I couldn't stop it," Fiara says, "so I came here instead. I wanted to help. I saw Ronnie and Nathan, and I used all my energy to shift my appearance." She takes several deep breaths. "I've never done that before."

"What about Mister Lee?" Christina asks. "Is there a chance we can save him if we get him to the Fountain?"

Fiara shrugs. "He needs to come. I've had many dreams, and Mister Lee needs to be there with us, no matter what. I don't know why. I just know he does."

"Let's get a tarp and wrap him up," Angelica says. "Then we go to the woods."

"How are we gonna get Mister Lee there?" Teddy asks.

"I guess... I guess we walk," I suggest. "Forget the bikes this time. We'll have to, no matter what we're supposed to do. By the time we get there, it will be dark. Like Coach wanted, I'm sure.

Will the cocoons have hatched? Didn't Mister Lee say it would take three days?"

"No disrespect," Teddy says, "but how did he know all this for sure?"

Christina nods. "Teddy's right. Mister Lee has, um, had experience here, but a lot of this is an educated guess. We have to be ready for those cocoons to hatch. And to face whatever comes from them."

Teddy's face turns pale, and Angelica reaches for his hand. I want to hold him, too, and I want someone to hold me. I don't feel jealous or angry, not after what's happened, but I do feel cold and alone.

Police have to show up any second and stop us, right? There was an explosion, a fire, and a shooting. We're not in the middle of nowhere. Mr. Lee has neighbors. Surely, someone saw something and called the police?

But no one comes. Maybe this is a part of our fate that Mr. Lee had discussed. This is all supposed to have happened, and we all have to fight.

Will more of us die?

Mr. Lee has a detached garage, and Angelica goes inside it. She comes out with a blue tarp, and we wrap Mr. Lee's body in it. Teddy and Christina take his legs, Angelica has his middle, and Fiara and I try to roll his shoulders and what's left of his head into the tarp without getting sick. It's bloody and messy, and it smells. I hold my breath when I touch him, and we quickly cover him with the tarp. I wipe my hands on my pants over and over again afterward, trying to wipe away the feel of it all.

"Should we say a prayer?" Teddy asks.

"If you want to."

He nods. The five of us hold hands and stay on our knees with Mr. Lee's body wrapped up in the blue tarp.

"God," he begins. "Or whatever power is out there. I don't know what this is all about. But please help Mister Lee, wherever he is now. And please help all of us. Let there be a purpose to this madness." He looks at us for approval, and I nod.

"Amen," Fiara says. She blinks, and I've never seen such a pure, clear blue in someone's eyes before.

"Okay, let's go," I say. Angelica brings out a wheelbarrow from the garage, and we place Mr. Lee's body in it. Teddy goes in the garage and brings out a lawnmower.

"What's that for?" I ask.

"Maybe we won't look so weird walking down the street if we're pushing this, too," he says.

"Yeah, okay. Good idea." A group of teens walking down the road with a body in a wheelbarrow covered by a tarp should catch someone's attention. But then again, I look out the front of the house and wonder why no one has come to see what an explosion, fire, and gunshot were all about.

Christina holds her purse tightly as she walks. It's been strapped around her body during all of training, and I nearly forgot why she had it until she presses it hard against her chest.

There's a blade in there, a special blade from her past. I don't know its origin or the entire story, but I know that blade is important. Christina's muscles tense as she grips the bag.

It's a long, quiet walk to the woods. I try not to think. The moment I take a break or try to process what's going on is the moment I'll have a complete nervous breakdown, I'm sure. So, it's one foot in front of the other, until the sun begins to fall and night consumes the sky.

Not a single person stops to talk to us or even looks at us during our entire journey. Occasionally, Angelica hits a bump with the wheelbarrow, and we all gasp thinking that Mr. Lee is going to spill right out on the road, but nothing happens.

---

WE ARRIVE AT the entrance to the woods. This is our one and only chance to save Elle, Sam, and Pauline, and of course the hundreds of children being saved to feed the new beasts. Who knows how many people are at stake? Some names are like dusty memories—like Asher and his grandmother, Charlamae. How do they fit into this? Didn't Christina say she needed to find Charlamae?

"I'm scared," Teddy says, the first to break the silence of our walk. Teddy takes the wheelbarrow from Angelica, who puts a hand on the back of his shoulders.

Christina reaches for Fiara's hand, and they walk behind Angelica, Teddy, and the wheelbarrow. Behind them, I push the lawnmower and study their lights. Christina's brilliant yellow and Fiara's shiny green spark when they touch. Angelica's radiant purple looks magnificent, but Teddy's black energy still bothers me.

I'm scared, too, but I don't want to say it out loud.

"Hold on," Angelica says when we make it to the woods. "What do we do with Mister Lee? I don't think we'll be able to push the wheelbarrow through those woods very well."

"Leave his body inside. Right here," Fiara says. We look at her with uncertainty. "Please trust me. I don't know how I know. It's all part of a dream, I think."

We set down the wheelbarrow right inside the entrance to the woods. I leave the lawn mower outside. I put my hand on the tarp. *Please watch over us, Mister Lee. If you can. I hope you can.*

We walk farther into the woods. It's no longer dark like it had been. It's full of fire now. Flames shoot up from all directions, and I'm reminded of the lava game we all played as kids.

"Careful where you step," I say.

"Do we have to—"

"Go all the way in?" I finish the question for her. "All the way into the pit. Down into its hell."

I reach for Teddy's hand, not caring what anyone thinks. He doesn't judge me either. He takes it and squeezes it. I keep waiting for something to jump out at us. Where are Ronnie and Nathan? And what about Elle and Rob? Have they morphed?

We approach the edge of the pit.

"Don't let go of each other," I say. "Down there—that's where Sam and Pauline are. And all the children, no doubt." I pause, but not too long. Now's not the best time to have second thoughts. "Are you ready?"

"Will we make it back out?" Teddy asks.

I don't know, but I say, "Yes."

"I trust you, Law," he says.

"Me, too," Angelica adds.

"Can you do this?" Christina asks Fiara. Out of all of us, she's had the most traumatic experiences in the pit.

"To conquer fear, you must face it," Fiara replies. She forces a half-smile, and her blue eyes sparkle. "I'm ready to defeat my fears."

"Let's go," Christina says. We step forward, each of us taking the hand of another, and we jump into hell.

Inside, a pitch-dark abyss swallows us. It's still like floating through space, and I think-speak to anyone else who may be here. *Sam? Pauline? Is anyone here?*

It sounds like being underwater. My ears feel clogged, but my mind is clear.

We hear a scream.

*HELP!*

It's a child's voice, but I don't recognize it. The one word, though, triggers the voices of many others.

"Help me!" It's a young girl's voice.

"Over here!" This time, it's the sound of a young boy.

"Please! I'm scared! Mommy! Daddy! Someone! Anyone! HELP US!"

Hundreds of screams, hundreds of different voices all echo throughout the pit. Panic floods me. Where do we go? How will we save them all?

"HELP ME!"

*That's Pauline!* Angelica tells us. *Holy shit! Pauline, we're coming, girl!*

We push forward to where the screams sound the loudest, and we arrange our bodies like we're skydiving. We try to find a rhythm, a motion that will give us control. Forming a circle and falling face-first down into the pit's hell, we hold onto to one another's hands. Angelica's on my left now, and Teddy's on my right. Fiara and Christina detach from us but they hold each other tightly.

A face emerges from the Darkness. It's Pauline! She pushes toward us, and her arms flail like she's swimming through the open air of the pit.

*Are you okay?* Angelica asks.

Pauline shakes her head. *I'm so afraid! I don't know what's happening or what to do!*

Something long, slender, and gray approaches from below Pauline. It's a... no! It's the shadow of the Darkness—its hand approaches, each finger long and thin like a tree root. It's bigger than it ever was above ground. Each finger is as long as our entire bodies. The hand could grab all of us and squeeze us.

And kill us.

It races toward Pauline.

*Grab my hand!* Angelica lets go of me and reaches for Pauline. Pauline kicks forward, grabs Angelica, who swings her up to join our circle. I grab Pauline's other hand, and we are four strong now. Fiara and Christina reach for us. Make that six. We will defeat this thing!

The fingers race toward us, and we scurry away. The children continue to scream. "Sam has to be with them!" Teddy cries. "We have to find him!"

"We will," I say.

I close my eyes.

*Never close your eyes in the woods*, Mr. Lee had told us during training. But we're in the pit. This is different, and I'm trusting my gut.

When I close my eyes, I no longer see my friends or the

shadow of the Darkness. I see our webs of light, and I smile. This is what I'm meant to do.

*Down to the left*, I think-speak.

*How do you know?* Christina asks.

*Trust me. I can see their lights. So many lights! There are hundreds of them!* My heart races, and we push ahead. The shadow monster approaches rapidly from behind, and my body trembles. We can't worry about that. We have to get to those kids!

*Use your thoughts to push us that way,* I think-speak to everyone. *Picture our movement. And make it fast!*

When everyone brings their thoughts together, it feels like we're flying. We soar deeper into the pit toward the light of all the children.

*Sam!* Teddy yells his brother's name over and over as we fly through this infinitely deep hell. *Sam! Can you hear me?*

It's hard to hear anything over the hundreds of screams, but one voice projects louder than the others.

*TEDDY! IS THAT YOU? HELP ME, TEDDY!*

That's Sam's voice all right! He's here! The lights of the children brighten, and I know we're close. But so is the shadow monster.

"Owww!" Fiara cries. I open my eyes, and the fingers tighten around Fiara's body.

"No!" Christina yells, and she pulls at Fiara. We all turn, soaring sharply to the right to escape the shadow's clutch.

We run into its face.

It snarls at us. Its face is the size of a mountain, and it has fangs. It chomps at us.

We scream and swing in the other direction. *Faster!* I shout and close my eyes again. We fly toward the children.

*To Sam!* Teddy yells.

*TEDDY!* Sam cries. We're there! He's right in front of us, floating, and full of fear. But he's not the only one. At least a hundred kids float below us, imprisoned in something. It's not literal bars, but—no!

Those fingers again! Another shadow monster? No—not one shadow monster. Dozens of them, with hands locked around the children like the ultimate prison of hell.

*Careful! They could kill them all!* I shout. All they would have to do is curl those giant fingers into fists.

*What do we do?* Teddy asks.

My eyes remain closed, and I study the energy of the kids.

*KIDS!* I scream. I take a quick risk, open my eyes, and look behind me. The shadow monster is right behind us! I don't have a second to waste. *KIDS! Listen carefully, and do exactly as I say. Close your eyes. NOW! Picture an explosion. A giant bomb! On the count of three, I want you all to picture a giant bomb exploding on the fingers that surround you. Same for us, guys,* I say to my friends. *We all have to work together, and we've got just one shot at this. No time to waste. Think of the biggest nuclear explosion you can imagine. Right now! READY? ONE! TWO! THREE!*

Something bursts in the air, an eruption that surges right at us, but it does the trick! The fingers release the children, and they soar toward us.

*Close your eyes, and follow my light!* Now, I picture my own energy and make it brilliant—a bright yellow sun in this pit of hell.

Sam flies right toward us, and Teddy and I grab him. We pull him into our circle, and the other children follow from below.

*OUT!* We have to get out of here and swiftly.

But the shadow monsters aren't dead. They're angry and flying right at us. *FAST AS YOU POSSIBLY CAN!* I yell. The monster that was chasing us charges right for Sam. I open my eyes, and Teddy jumps in front of him, ready to sacrifice himself for his brother. Angelica yells and reaches for Teddy, and she throws herself in front of him.

The giant fingers wrap around Teddy and Sam, and Angelica swings her legs and kicks at it.

Pauline lets go of our hands and dives at her best friend. "Angelica, no!" she cries, and the monster grabs Pauline.

It squeezes Pauline's body, and she screams the most piercing sound I've ever heard. In the blink of an eye, her full body flattens like a pancake. It tosses her into the dark air, as if she's nothing.

"Pauline!" Angelica's face twists with horror, and tears pour from her eyes.

I close my eyes. *EVERYONE, FASTER! FOLLOW ME!* We race ahead. We must. There's no time to mourn. We have to worry about the children and all our lives. It's going to get all of us if we don't get out of here.

The secret is not to engage. *CALM MINDS! CALM HEARTS! BUT DO IT FAST!*

The monsters still chase us, and there must be dozens of them. How can I get a hundred kids to be calm? It's impossible! We'll never save them all.

Is this where I sacrifice myself, then?

If I must, then I must.

I take a deep breath and try to swallow my fears. I will give myself to the Darkness if it will release these children. I'm ready, I think.

But is anyone truly ready to die?

# CHAPTER THIRTY

Light breaks into this abyss—it's my energy! A golden energy radiates powerfully from me, and it keeps the shadow monsters away. For now. How? I don't know. I'm not questioning the one bit of good luck we have right now.

We rise through the light. Hand-in-hand, we emerge with Sam. His red headphones bounce on his neck as we soar out of the pit, a sight that forces me to smile. How he still has those damn headphones I have no idea. I want to celebrate for Teddy and Sam, but I look at Angelica and know that we didn't come out of this unscathed. And this certainly isn't over.

We stand at the top of the pit, and we extend our hands down, lifting one child out at a time. Children arise with wide, wet eyes, scared but hopeful. It's a glorious sight. I sure hope we got every kid. How would we know? Within minutes, over a hundred children stand in the quiet woods. Mumbles and soft cries reverberate among the trees. The shuffling of footsteps and the cracking of branches bring life back to a place that has been void of hope.

Where is the Darkness? Why don't the monsters come after us now?

I shudder at my own question because I think I know the answer. The energy of the Darkness is focusing on something else.

Elle and Rob. The cocoons.

"Are you okay?" Teddy asks Sam, putting a hand through the tiny curls of his brother's hair. Sam flashes an exhausted smile and puts his hands around his headphones.

"Yeah. I think so," he says. "Are you?"

"I guess so," Teddy says, looking down at his Overlook Hotel T-shirt. Black energy radiates from him, and he rubs his hands right through it. Can he see it now, I wonder?

We turn and face the children. "Is anyone hurt?" I ask. They wipe tears from their faces, and they look exhausted and in complete shock. But they're all in one piece.

"We have to get the children out of here," I say. "Far away from this pit. The Darkness has moved on, I think, but anywhere is safer than here."

How did we get out of there? I am either stronger than I realize, or the Darkness is truly focusing on Elle and Rob. Both, I suppose, could be true. I question my sanity and turn to the children. "You kids have to go where it's safe. Just right outside these woods, and you'll be all right. We're gonna get help. Okay?" A few kids sniffle a little affirmation, while others all out cry. I don't want to leave them, but they can't follow us, that's for sure.

"Follow me," I tell my friends, and we head out of the woods. I look back one more time before we leave. "Go! We have to finish this, or we'd stay with you," I tell the kids again. "Get out. Hold hands until we get back."

"Let me come with you," Sam says. "Let me help."

Teddy looks at me for advice.

"I feel safer with you," Sam states.

"Okay," Teddy says hesitantly. I nod. "Don't you leave my side. Not by an inch."

"Angelica, are you gonna be okay?" I ask.

"What choice do I have?" she says, pulling at her thick, sweaty hair. "We destroy this evil tonight. Destroy it so it can't hurt anyone else ever again!"

"To the Fountain," I say. I glance several times over my

shoulder as we march up the hill toward the railroad tracks, hoping the kids will be okay.

We step up the hill and push the branches out of our way to get to the next path. This path has changed, too. I have no idea what time it is, but the sky is dark. Wait, is that even the sky? It looks rather like something has engulfed this trail from overhead. It's metallic, and I don't see stars. There are pieces of this new sky-ceiling that glimmer. It looks more like an amusement park attraction than anything from nature. What the hell is it, and how did it get here?

A terrible noise up near the entrance of the Fountain distracts us. We turn, and a thousand fires burst forth along both rails of tracks. I remember being able to feel the energy in those tracks, thinking that they were alive, and now that energy has exploded. The flames dance, and more lights flash from above. They look like lasers, and they rain down through the metallic roof.

"What's going on?" Teddy asks.

"Get ready to fight," I say.

Christina and I hold hands. Out of all of us here, we share the most similar lights, and I think it's important that we work together. I study the others' energy again. Blue lines shoot from Sam. Angelica glows with a radiant purple. Fiara's energy is green, and not like the green of grass. It's the green of the sea, absolutely magical. I grip Christina's hand tighter before looking at Teddy's.

Still black.

"Holy shit! Lawson!" Teddy screams.

The railroad tracks rise from the ground, slowly elevating as high as our heads.

The tracks slither and hiss, buzz and twist. I gasp, my stomach churning at the sight. The tracks are turning into snakes, and they fly toward us. We duck, and they go over our heads.

"Fight the snakes! The tracks!" I yell. "Hold hands and let your energy loose! Don't stop!"

More snakes pop out of the ground from all directions—behind us, in front, and even over the top of us. Looking up, I realize the lights may not have been lasers, after all. They are the glowing eyes of more serpents of evil, and they drop down on each of us. It's literally raining fucking snakes.

I bend down on one knee and place my palms on the ground. With the other, I grip Christina's hand, and the two of us mentally attack as many of the snakes falling from the sky as we can. I risk a glance at the others, who are fighting, too, although Sam crouches and hides behind his brother.

I attack with one mental strike after another, and it feels like nothing can stop me. Then, *bam!* Something hits me from behind, I roll forward losing my grip on Christina, and fall into a ditch. I scramble, quickly trying to recover.

It's Ronnie the Rattler and Coach Nathan.

Nathan grabs Angelica, and I prepare to send the hardest punch I can right at his face.

Fiara runs in front of Angelica and howls. She spins in a circle and lands with her right knee on the ground. She glares at Coach and Ronnie, her bright blue eyes sparkling and her slimy hair blowing in the wind. With another scream, she sends energy through the ground. The ground rips with tremors, knocking Coach and Ronnie off their feet.

I pick myself up and run out of the ditch. Teddy races toward Angelica, and shades of orange spark in Coach Nathan's eyes.

His body smacks hard on the ground, but it bounces right back up. He adjusts his Worthlapp High cap and flashes an icy smile. Facing Fiara, he laughs, and his eyes turn a brighter red.

"I've found creatures more powerful and far more loyal than you, bitch," Coach says to Fiara. It's not Coach's voice, though. It's dark and raspy, and Fiara snarls right back.

Coach cackles and grabs Angelica's arm with lightning speed. Fiara sends another wave of energy through the ground. This time, Coach jumps and floats mid-air, and he cackles even more.

Coach pulls Angelica closer, turns his Worthlapp High cap backward, and leans in and licks her face. My stomach flips. Coach picks up Angelica and holds her up in the air, about three feet off the ground. Fiara's attacks have failed, and I search for Christina. If we combine our powers again, maybe we will have enough to stop this. We have to send all of our energy at this monster.

But then more snakes drop on us from above. They wrap around my neck and my arms. Some bite at my ankles, and I yelp as fangs pierce my skin.

"Christina!" I yell. She crawls out of a ditch from the other side of the path and races toward me. I grab her hand as more snakes drop, nearly burying us in the ground.

We lock hands, and together we visualize our mental energy and throw everything we can to blast the creatures away. They fly in the air, and it looks like a nuclear mushroom cloud. Then we shift our focus to Coach. Teddy and Fiara whip their energy at him. We hit him twice, and then a third time, and we don't stop there. We hit him so hard that both he and Angelica fly through the air.

Shit! Angelica! The last thing we want to do is hurt her. I run toward them, as they spring into the air. Sprinting now, I try not to lose sight of them, and they begin to fall. Oh, no! They're easily twenty feet off the ground. No one is going to survive a fall like that.

But she drops right above the ground, not hitting it, just floating there.

Fiara grabs her. Fiara stopped her from crashing. She's far more powerful than I ever realized.

Fiara lets Coach Nathan fall, though. He crashes hard on the ground, his body and his head turning in impossible directions.

I'm both thrilled and disgusted. Coach's body pulses with spasms on the ground, and adrenaline surges through my body.

Christina reaches for my hand, and the others follow. Each holds the hand of another.

There's still one monster left on these tracks, and we've faced him before. We each take a fighting stance. Christina and I squeeze each other's hand, and my lips twitch with anticipation. I want to see this asshole's head hit the sky.

Ronnie tugs at his blue track jacket. He runs one hand through his spiked blonde hair, and he grips a knife with his other. He charges toward us, raising the knife high over his head like a slasher in a horror movie.

"No!" I yell. I quickly picture my energy to shoot at Ronnie, but he's faster than my thoughts.

"Remember, he's possessed," Christina shouts. "There's still a boy in there."

I don't care if he's human. I only care about protecting my friends.

Ronnie reaches Angelica first.

She whips her legs around, bends her knees, and takes a fighting stance.

"You stabbed me once, asshole," she snaps at him. "You won't hurt me again."

"Angelica!" Teddy yells. Christina squeezes my hand, and I release an attack at Ronnie. But it misses him, and he pounces on Angelica.

Ronnie swings the knife down, and it catches Angelica right in the side of the neck.

Blood shoots from Angelica, and we all scream. She holds her neck with one hand and kicks Ronnie right in the groin. He bends his knees together to protect his groin and laughs. Then he stabs her again.

We scream and race for her. "Angelica!" Teddy cries.

Ronnie's eyes turn bright red. The Darkness in him is powerful, and he swings the knife again at Angelica. Yelping and racing like I've never seen before, Teddy jumps on Ronnie's back.

Christina grabs me. "Quick, we have to help!" We hold hands and shoot all of our energy at Ronnie. Teddy drops his elbow on the top of Ronnie's skull, hops off, and then kicks him in the back. With Ronnie's focus on Teddy and Angelica, he doesn't see our energy coming, and we hit him hard. Ronnie flies backward.

Fiara spins on the ground and takes her low stance, down on her right knee. She sends her energy toward Ronnie, and flames burst from underneath him.

Right before our eyes, Ronnie's body explodes.

Literally explodes. Chunks of him spray at us. We'd be vomiting and crying in any other reality. Instead, we wipe the chunks of Ronnie from our faces and check on our friends.

"Angelica!" Teddy yells, running to her. "Are you okay?"

Angelica's bleeding. Blood covers the side of her neck. Angelica's purple light still shines, giving me hope. No, wait—the line is shrinking. Didn't I read in Lee's journal that a person's lines shrink before they die? Tears spill from my eyes. I grab Christina's hand with my right, and with my left, I place my hand on her neck.

I close my eyes, and I try to hold the tears back. We've lost Pauline. We lost Mr. Lee. We can't lose Angelica, too.

I don't know how much time passes, but soon a yellow burst of energy comes from the wound on Angelica's neck.

*Thank you*, Angelica think-speaks to us. *I think I'm okay, but I don't know if I can fight anymore.*

"I think I'm going to need a complete psychiatric evaluation when this is over," I say, rubbing my head after I remove my hand from Angelica's neck. Did I heal her with my energy?

*To the Fountain.* It's Christina's voice this time. *We destroy those beasts and bury the Darkness once and for all.*

I take a deep breath, and we enter the Fountain. My stomach turns, thinking about what we will have to face next.

Mofa's biggest monsters yet await us. Monsters that need one-hundred children just for dinner.

Beasts strong enough to consume all our light, killing everyone.

# CHAPTER THIRTY-ONE

The cocoons where Elle and Rob had morphed are gone. There's an orange glow everywhere throughout the Fountain, like the fires left an ugly ooze behind.

"Help!" It's a girl's voice coming from the lake, and I recognize it right away. It's Elle!

I jump right in the water. "Elle, are you okay?" She puts her arms around me. The edges of her thick, blonde hair touch the water, her head and shoulders not wet.

"Oh, thank you, Lawson," she says, her voice faint. "Thank you for helping me."

"Of course."

"I found the secret, Lawson." She searches my eyes for a reaction and runs a hand through my wet hair. "*The* secret. You know—the one even bigger than this Fountain. The place where our light goes."

"What is it?" I ask, my eyebrows lift in surprise.

She kisses me. It takes me by surprise at first, and she grips me hard. Her tongue enters my mouth. I don't enjoy it. Why is she doing this?

"I love you, Elle," I say when she pulls away. I do love her. Not in a romantic way, but in a best friend way. I've missed her so much, and I miss the times we used to come here as kids. Those were the best days of my life.

A grim smile hangs at the edge of her lips. She's not the little girl I was best friends with. She wrinkles her tiny nose, and I wonder if this is the real Elle. "Wanna know the secret?" she asks, interrupting my thoughts. "The waters here—it's all a lie. The Fountain won't make anyone live forever. It reminds them of what life was like when they were young. True immortality is only found in the Darkness. And that's where the light ends, of course. Light ends in darkness."

A chill runs through me, and it's not because of the water. My pulse quickens, and cool wind whistles past my ears. "I don't understand."

She moves her arms along the calm, blue water. The sky, like a mirror, stretches above us in a cloudless, endless stream. The vast open blueness of it all is dizzying, until the sight of orange globs spackled throughout the Fountain remind me what's at stake here. My feet shuffle in the shallow water. Suddenly, I have a deep urge to run back to shore. When I turn my head around, Elle grabs me, her grip unbelievably strong. She turns my head around and kisses me again, but I start to choke. Her tongue is inside my mouth, but it's not a tongue.

I pull away, and Elle laughs. Her tongue slaps against the water and dances in the air. She laughs again and tells me, "Join me, and we will live forever."

"Get away from him!" Teddy jumps in the water, and Elle hisses. He ignores her and grabs me instead. He pushes me out of the water, and Sam helps pull us out. When I'm back on the shore, I search for Elle, but she's gone.

"We can still save her," I say, but Teddy looks incredulous. "The Darkness tricked her!"

We don't have time for discussion, though. Looking up, I no longer see the infinite blue sky. Dark clouds rush in at a dizzying speed. Thunder rolls and lightning shoots through the sky, and two giant, dark shapes drop from above.

They are two incredibly huge beasts. Four-legged creatures with jaws the size of a fucking car. Jesus, they could fit our entire bodies in their mouths.

They roar at us, and fire shoots from their mouths. This must be the metamorphosis of the cocoons, but then where is Elle? I just saw her in the flesh.

Christina reads my mind and grabs my hand. "We can't trust anything here. Are you ready to fight them?" She runs her hands down her tight, long-sleeved black shirt and clenches her fists.

After cracking her knuckles, she opens her purse and removes the blade. She swallows hard, and she grips the dark handle tightly. She moves the blade in the air, and it reflects all of our colors.

The ground shakes, and I lose balance. The creatures step forward like Godzilla coming out of the ocean, and more than chills run through my body, like I have the world's worst fever.

One beast is larger than the other, and there's something special about the paws on the bigger beast. Each toe is—I take a closer look, and my stomach drops—each toe is a snake. Every single toe. They're alive and hissing.

Fiara moves closer to the water.

"Wait!" Christina shouts. "What are you going to do?"

"It's okay," Fiara says. "Part of what's in the Seer is also inside me. Don't you see? Mofa thought I had Lawson's gift. I didn't, and it turned me into this in its rage. But bad news for it—I have an energy that I think can kill it. Let me try."

"You don't have to do this," Christina says.

Fiara shakes her head. "But I do. My existence is a portal for evil. The longer I live, the greater chance I have to become something like that." We look up at these huge beasts, and they snarl.

"What do we do?" Sam asks. Teddy pats his little brother on the back, and Sam's red headphones bounce. Teddy brushes his big, beautiful curls out his eyes and grabs Sam's hand. He squeezes it tightly.

The beasts step forward. Giant drool drops from their

mouths. They're hungry, and my knees weaken. Part of me screams that I should be running the other way. *Sprint as fast as you can out of here, man!* But then I look around for Elle. Where did she go? Was that purely an illusion, or is she physically part of one of these creatures?

Teddy and Sam stand behind me, and I turn around. I could die, we could all die in seconds, but there's something I've always wanted to tell Teddy. I reach for his free hand, and he takes it.

"Look, I—I dunno what to say," I tell him quickly. "There's something I want to tell you. But—" I choke on the words, and my hand quivers.

He steps closer to me. "Lawson, I *know*. You're my best friend in the entire world. You helped me save my mom and Sam. And I know, well—you *dumbass*, you know I can hear your thoughts when we're in here!" He lets go of Sam's hand. His eyes flicker, and he cracks a subtle smile. Then he leans in and kisses me on the cheek. "I hope we have a chance to really talk about it. I'll always be here for you, no matter what."

Drawing back, his eyes fill with affection and empathy, and he grabs Sam's hand again. I swallow hard and wipe tears from my eyes. Teddy knows how I feel. He knows who I am. He may not be like me, and I guess that's a pain I'll have to live with. If I'm lucky enough to live, that is. But he's my friend, and he accepts me. Maybe that's all I needed. Maybe it's all anyone needs.

Now, it's time to fight. We have to make sure these beasts don't get those kids. It would eat them all, and all of this would have been for nothing.

"Ready?" Fiara yells at the lead.

I see all of their energies, and I keep my eyes open.

I sprint, and we keep up with them because our energy connects us all. This is our chance—connected forces, different kinds of energy. This is my fate. To guide the energies and attack these monsters.

The beasts swoop down and strike at us.

We spin away from the attacks. We become something bigger

than ourselves, our lines converging. Christina, Teddy, Sam, Fiara, me, and even Angelica. She's weaker—I see it—but she's giving everything she's got to help us.

Our unique webs of energy coalesce into one powerful line. The lights combine into the brightest orange I've ever seen. It's the sunrise over the ocean, the brightest light reflecting off pristine waters.

Flames pour down on us like rain in a typhoon, but together we dodge them easily. A few even hit us, but I don't feel anything. No pain whatsoever, like our energy and the Fountain have a shield over us.

Behind me, Teddy and Sam still hold hands. With their opposite hands, they reach out as if pushing all their energy into the ungodly beasts ahead of us.

Stomping and flying, the beasts shoot more fire mixed with drool and snot. They've taken the power of the Fountain as well to enhance their evil.

*Elle, are you still in there?* My old best friend is now the size of a semi and has snakes for toes. She's gone from the beauty to the beast.

It barks and snaps at us, and we dodge to the side. Our lines brighten even more, and we move together without thinking. We have become one.

Flames fly from both beasts' mouths, and we avoid the attack this time by diving into the water. Fiara plunges first, taking the driver's seat as to who controls us. We follow and swim underneath. I hold my breath. Swimming faster than I ever thought possible, we rip through the water to where the Fountain pours in the lake.

Under Kang Fu, our strength grows.

We emerge from the Fountain and wash up on the shore. We are wrapped in our own cocoon now, a giant ball of yellow light. The beasts throw flames at us, but they bounce off our combined energy.

*We're going to win! Everything will be all right!*

Elle splashes in the lake below the monsters. She looks younger, as young as when I first met her. She's a little child, and she swims out of the water.

"Lawson, don't you want to play with me?" she asks.

I gulp. It's a trick, and I am determined to remain strong.

A beast approaches Elle, and it roars at her. Elle screams and throws up her hands. "Help me, Law! Help!" The beast bites the little girl. It snaps at her, and Christina's grip on my hands strengthens.

*Be strong.*

Elle swims under water, and Rob appears. "Christina. You can save me. Now's your chance. You didn't have to kill me." He shakes his head, and water drips off his red hair. Then his eyes widen, and tears pour out. "I thought you loved me."

I grip her hand tighter. I hear her pain. She knows it's not real, but it doesn't make it any less agonizing.

The little girl Elle bounces out of the water again. The beast wraps its jaw around little Elle's arm. Her arm looks like a toothpick in its mouth, and I swear the beast smiles at us. Then, in a rapid motion, the beast bites Elle's arm off. She screams, and blood rushes out of her shoulder like water from a hose.

"No!" I break away from Christina, and the yellow light that had engulfed us disappears.

*Lawson!* It's Angelica's voice. *You know it's a trick!*

I do know, but I also can't watch a little girl get eaten by a beast. Elle reaches out with the one arm she has left, and I grab it.

"The Fountain will help," I tell her. "Swim away from these things." I try to pull her away. The child Elle vanishes and teen Elle returns.

"Thank you, Law," she says, and she rests her head on my shoulder.

"Is it really you?" I ask. I turn so I can look directly in her eyes. "How do I know if it's really you?"

"I remember why we forgot," she says.

"Huh?"

"About this place. It was them, Law!" Elle points at my friends, and they scream. The beasts throw balls of fire, and without our webs connected, each of them is vulnerable. What am I doing? I have to help them!

Elle cries, distracting me. "Fiara and Christina! They took our friend Asher when we were just kids! They fed him to the Darkness. Then we forgot all about him and all about this place. They're the real monsters!"

My body trembles. I have to save Elle and help my friends. I pull at her arm and try to make her move, but I can't look away from the monster. Its eyes are monstrously wide, the size of a bus and just as orange. Both monsters roar again and strike at my friends.

"You lie!" I tell Elle. "They were forced to do those things. It's not their fault."

"You've been duped, and now they will die," Elle snaps back.

"Come with me! We can help them!" I tell her and pull at her again. But her arm feels awfully slimy, and it's not from the water. The arm morphs into an eel. Elle hisses at me, and her arm slaps me.

That's when I remember! When Elle and I discovered the Fountain as children, we weren't alone. Christina, Fiara, Angelica, and a boy named Asher were all here.

The Darkness didn't simply take Asher. We were in terrible trouble, and Asher sacrificed himself.

Asher's sacrifice saved us. I know what I need to do now.

It is fate, after all. To save my friends and to save the missing children, I too must sacrifice myself.

"Lawson! We need you!" Teddy screams as one of the beasts raises a leg and slams it down near Fiara, trying to crush her.

Its snakes-for-toes kick Christina in the face, and she tumbles to the side. It grabs Sam. With one large hand, it lifts Sam up to its mouth, much like I'd picture King Kong picking up a rabbit to eat.

Sam screams, and I swim for shore.

I roll toward Christina. She's still in shock from getting kicked, but I lift her to her feet. "C'mon," I say, and we rise.

It slowly brings Sam to its mouth. We clasp hands and strike it with our bright yellow light.

It turns its face toward us and cackles. We barely made it flinch.

"We need everyone!" Teddy says. "All! Quick!" We make a circle, lock hands, and strike the beasts again. Sam screams as he enters the monster's mouth, but our strike sends it flying backward.

It drops Sam, and he shrieks, falling toward the lake.

"Shit! Sam!" Teddy yells, and he races to the water. Sam hits the lake hard and falls below. Teddy swims after him.

"Stay together," Christina snaps at us. "Strike again!"

We send shot after shot of energy at the monsters, knocking them back one step at a time.

The other smaller beast charges at us. Fiara spins, taking a knee like she did over the railroad tracks. Instead of sending an earthquake shock at the beast, she lifts both hands up toward the sky. It looks like the pose she took when she tried to stop these beasts from cocooning over the Fountain. Her hair rises, and the slimy braids twist and turn into what I always thought they resembled but never wanted to say.

More snakes.

Her hair points to the sky, and a tremendous flow of energy shoots from her hands.

The smaller of the beasts explodes.

Fire and flesh burst out into the open air and across the lake.

The last remaining monster howls, and it swings a giant fist at us. We roll to the right, scarcely dodging the strike.

Fiara spins again, setting up another attack. The snakes hiss in her hair, and somehow she summons an even greater force of energy. Christina and I will all our mental energy with theirs, and a giant beam strikes the monster's heart.

It shrieks and pulls us toward it. It's absorbing the energy.

Unlike the other beast, this attack doesn't seem to affect it. Instead, it's soaking it in like a sponge. Its chest grows bigger. We push harder, all of us yelling and striking with everything we've got.

And then my jaw drops open. Fiara floats through the light right toward it. We hold a beam of light, the convergence of all our webs of energy, fiercely on the giant beast. As the monster absorbs the energy and pulls us closer, it takes Fiara with it.

Is Fiara letting it take her? Fiara!

She hears my thoughts. *When I'm inside the beast, I will strike again.*

*What if it doesn't work?* Christina shouts.

*I must try*, Fiara says, floating toward it. *Thank you for always accepting me for who I was, Christina. You are and will always be my best friend.*

From our right, Teddy and Sam wash up on the shore. Thank God for that! They both kneel, clasp hands, and extend their outside arms, preparing to hit the beast. Sam's blue mixes with Teddy's black lights.

I keep my eyes open and attack, too. I think of all the kids waiting for us outside the woods. If we don't stop this, the monster will not only destroy us, but it will feast on a buffet of children.

And it won't stop there. Those kids will give it even more energy, and then what? Then it will destroy our entire town. It will easily consume the National Guard and rip through our state, and every state and the entire world!

This isn't enough. We have to do more.

I let go of Christina's hand, and I fly through the beam toward Fiara. The beam is so powerful, I don't even have to do anything. It takes me.

*What are you doing?* Christina shouts.

*What I'm supposed to do*, I reply. *If I add my yellow to Fiara's green energy, we'll have a brilliant orange to shoot from the inside. We fight fire with fire! This is what I am meant to do.*

I fly through the beam of light.

My gaze follows each of my friends' lines as far as I can humanly see. Perhaps it's fate, or what Mr. Lee had tried to teach us before. Part of each of their futures appears in my mind, or at least a possible future. Each is a flash of light, and it happens quickly.

I want to cry for what the visions show me in Teddy and Sam's future. If they survive this, they will face new tragedy. Christina's future shocks me even more—oh, God. It's absolute terror! It's something none of us had ever thought about, and my heart completely breaks for what she will experience.

Are these only possible futures?

What about my future? My lines shrink before my own eyes.

I think I am going to die. Minutes ago, I thought I could sacrifice myself, but in this moment, fear and doubt rip through me. What's one life, though? What's my one life worth in comparison to the hundreds of children and my friends?

I soar toward the monster.

Rising high above the ground and over the lake, I crash into Fiara. Her beautiful blue eyes blink tears.

*Together!* I grab her hand. The beast opens its mouth. Fiara and I extend our arms and strike it. We dig deep for energy, and we shoot it straight into its mouth.

It shrieks, an absolutely ear-piercing cacophony.

The beast opens its mouth. I hear one sound followed by another. "Mo," the beast cries, its mouth opening wide. "Faaaa." That last sound comes out of its mouth as it swallows us. It was pure fire and beast on the outside, but on the inside, it's completely dark.

It is the Darkness. It is Mofa.

We let it consume us.

I close my eyes. Fiara and I summon our energy again. I can feel the others blasting the beast from the outside, so there's just one thing left to do.

Lifting our arms, we strike it with everything we have.

It's almost enough, but not quite. It yelps, and Christina flies toward it from outside. She grips the special blade by its ominously dark handle. While Fiara and I strike the creature from inside, Christina thrusts the knife into its heart from the outside.

She crashes into the water below.

The creature screams. It shoots Fiara and me right out of its body.

We fly through the sky and hit the water hard. The wind is completely knocked out of me, and I can't even find the strength to swim. The water fills my lungs, and I can no longer breathe. Fiara falls in the water, too, and she sinks deep into the Fountain. I try to find any extra energy to paddle or call for help, but I have no strength left. I close my eyes and let the water wash over me.

I sink deep into the lake, deeper than I've ever gone before. The world is completely dark. My mind fades to blackness, too.

Kang Fu takes me away. This is my sacrifice.

# EPILOGUE—ASHER

"It was like a great bee come home from some field where the honey is full of poison wildness, of insanity and nightmare, its body crammed with that over-rich nectar and now it was sleeping the evil out of itself."

—Ray Bradbury

# CHAPTER THIRTY-TWO

"Happy Halloween," Christina greets me at the door, less than enthusiastically. Dark shadows form under her hazel eyes. "Nice costume, Ash."

"Thanks," I say. I'm a ghostbuster, simple but fun. The ghostbuster outfit and proton pack wear me more than I wear it. They're big, and I'm still praying every day for a growth spurt. I always loved the *Ghostbusters* movies, though, and I refused to buy a child's sized costume. I made Mom shop with me in the adult section.

We ride our bikes over to their house. Christina isn't in costume yet. She says she's dressing at Teddy's party and that it's a surprise. I hope she's a sexy vampire or something. She's extraordinarily hot, and I plan on finding the courage to ask her out tonight.

I ride next to Christina and enjoy the looks of neighbors as a kid in a complete ghostbuster costume rides his bike.

We come to a complete stop at the end of a hilly road. Small houses line the road on both sides of the streets. Old trees reach out from each side, as if they're trying to touch the ones on the opposite. They hang on to their fall colors, red mixing with yellow, orange, and brown. I look down, briefly reminiscing about all the times I'd race my bike to the bottom, pretending I was on a roller coaster.

"What is it?" I ask, as Christina looks around pensively.

"What do you remember about... the last few months?" Christina asks.

I rub my forehead and wonder why she's asking me. But the strange thing is... I can't remember. "I dunno," I say, my skin erupting in goosebumps.

"What about last year? Or any year. What's the last happy memory you have?"

"Easy," I say. "Playing in the hidden lake. With you and Angelica." I rub the goosebumps on my arms. That wasn't last year, though. That was a long time ago.

"What do you remember in between that time we played in the lake and today?"

I don't like all the questions. They frustrate me. I don't know why I don't remember!

"It's okay," she says softly. "That's one of the secrets we need to talk about. Something happened, but it's hard to explain. You don't remember because you weren't there."

"Where was I?"

Christina shrugs. "We're still trying to figure that out."

"We?"

"Angelica, Teddy, and me. Yeah." She pauses and bites her lower lip. "Look, let's have a little fun tonight. We could all use that. But tomorrow, after Halloween, we all need to fill you in on something. Something big."

"What? What's going on here?"

She flashes a subtle smile, staring at my hair. "I've always loved your dark hair. Dark as a raven, even darker than your skin. You have such tight hair, with just the cutest curl to it." Her lips straighten. "And your face. Such a sweet, baby face."

My cheeks burn. I hate feeling and looking so young around my friends. Everyone looks older than me. It's not fair, and I don't take it as a compliment.

Christina clears her throat. "Look, if I tell you something else, will you promise not to tell Angelica or any of the others?"

"Of course," I say.

"There's something else I desperately want to tell someone, but... I'm scared," she says. She blinks slowly, and she's even more beautiful in her sadness.

"What is it?"

She takes a deep breath. "I'm pregnant."

"What?" My eyes and jaw widen. "But... but you don't even have a boyfriend." I pause for a second. Or am I forgetting that, too?

"Yeah, well, that's why this is even more complicated." She grabs her handlebars. "Now, you keep my secret, and I'll tell you everything else tomorrow. Okay?"

"Um, I dunno. I mean, no, that doesn't make sense. How can you be pregnant?" I mumble, confused. That sure throws off my plan to ask her out.

She doesn't answer. She doesn't seem to know. But how is that possible?

I shake my head. Questions fill my mind, but I keep quiet. For now. We ride to Teddy and Sam's house in silence. The houses and trees blur together, until we turn on Teddy and Sam's street. A strange elm tree captures my attention. It's lost all its leaves, the only one on the street to do so. The tree's bark is darker, too, like it's dying. It's both beautiful and creepy. We bike past it, arriving at their house, and Sam runs out right away. He wears a green suit. Sam is Slimer from the movie, and I pretend to shoot him with my Proton Pack.

Teddy comes out next, and he's the Stay-Puft Marshmallow Man. He wears one of those costumes with a fan inside, and he wobbles outside to greet us.

"All right, let me get dressed, boys," Christina says. "Be out in a sec."

Teddy turns to me. "What is she going to be?"

I shrug. I don't want to ruin the night, but I can't stop

thinking about what Christina told me. She hasn't even had sex, at least I don't think she has. And why can't I remember anything? I shiver. Something's not right.

"Where's your girl?" I ask Teddy.

"Angelica will be here soon," he says. "She got in another argument with her mom. Her mom's pretty mean."

"That sucks."

"She's been super nasty ever since Angelica's grandfather died," Teddy says. "She takes out all her anger on her daughter. Pretty lame."

"Hey, there she is now!" I point out front.

We quickly quiet as Angelica rides her bike up to Teddy's porch. She gets off, and all our jaws drop open.

She's dressed as a warrior, an unbelievably gorgeous fighter.

"You look amazing," Teddy says.

"Thanks," Angelica replies. "I thought I'd try to be like one of those fighters you're always talking about, like in those fantasy books."

Then the front door opens, and Christina walks out.

Once again, our jaws hit the ground.

"Wow." It's all I can say. She's beautiful but scary.

"What is it supposed to be?" Teddy asks.

"Do you like it?" Christina smiles and walks down the steps. "I don't know. I've been thinking a lot. Thinking that the way to overcome the things that scare you is to embrace them." She laughs awkwardly. "Maybe that's weird, but I don't want to be afraid anymore."

Teddy and Angelica both nod and put an arm around her. I don't know what she's talking about, but her costume is kick ass.

Around her middle is a long snake. It curls around her stomach and her chest. It shows off her chest and her belly, but the snake's head strikes at her neck. It makes her look sexy but frightening as all hell. On her arms, she has a black cloth cut into long spikes. It looks like slim, pointy fingers.

"It's amazing," Angelica says. "Did you make that yourself?"

"My mom helped," Christina replies. "She was feeling pretty good these last couple weeks."

"She let you get that tattoo to remember Elle. That was pretty cool of her," Angelica says, touching a pair of green running shoes tattooed on her forearm. "I still can't believe Elle is gone, too. Pauline. Elle. Rob. I even feel slightly bad for Nathan and Ronnie. Just a little."

"Yeah." Christina rubs the fake snake and then her stomach. I think about the life growing inside her.

Angelica and Christina smile at me. "But we found someone, too. Come here, Asher." They both open up their arms, and who am I to deny a hug from two beautiful women?

The moment I touch them, something flashes. It's a series of bright lights. It flashes around all of us, and we gasp. I'm not the only one to see it.

"What the hell was that?" Angelica asks.

"It happened when we all touched," I say.

We look at one another, and everyone reaches out a hand. We form a big circle, and I'm the last to take their hands.

The moment I do, it happens again! A blast of yellow comes from Christina and purple from Angelica.

"Guys," I whisper. "I heard a name. When the lights sprung from us, there was a strange voice in my head, and it told me... well, something weird."

I gulp, and my arms tremble. What voice is in my head? Why am I hearing things, and why does this light from everyone scare me?

They look at me with concern.

"It told me to find my grandmother, Miss Charlamae. It says she'll know how to find Lawson and Fiara." I clear my throat. "But, um, who are Lawson and Fiara?"

# ACKNOWLEDGEMENTS

This is my chance to thank all the people who helped me shape this story into what it has become.

It was the winter of 2017 when I had my reading group critique the first draft of this story. We had an all-night conversation about the book. That's what makes writing so much fun. Thank you especially to Brian McWilliams and Brandy Kennington for your absolutely wonderful feedback. Seven years later, you won't even recognize this story, which is a good thing. Revision is where the magic happens.

After that night, I rewrote it. Then I took it to more test readers. I reached out to some *Rabbit in Red* fans and other readers, and for the first time, let a small group of people I really only know online read parts of the book. Thanks go to Jennifer Flaig, Kristen Kelly, Spencer Mullikin, Valerie Robert, and Katie Jackson. Your time is valuable, and I appreciate the time you gave reading and providing your insight. It motivated me to keep working!

I also need to thank the first agent who rejected me. I won't mention her by name because she only wanted to represent me if I agreed to write a fourth *Rabbit in Red* book. She provided some feedback early on, and we ultimately didn't work together. Still, that feedback helped me understand the literary world a bit more.

After all of that work, I took the manuscript to my Rabbit in Red editor, Kathy Calore Teel in spring 2018. We worked on it for months, and it continued to evolve into a much better story. With writing in particular, a first draft from the perspective of the author may look like a diamond. But it's really just a dirty piece of coal. Kathy's editing skills found the diamonds in the rough. She's exceptionally talented, and I can't thank her enough.

Once I felt comfortable with the story, it was time to proofread. Line by line, two wonderful readers went above and beyond to not only catch my typos but help improve my writing style. Special thanks to Elise Zwicky and Tracy Walper for your time and critical eyes.

Still not quite done, the book went back out to a few agents that I had always wanted to work with. Right away, three wonderful folks requested the full, and two gave me great feedback, with revise and resubmit requests. I went back to my friend and colleague, Tracy Walper, who read the manuscript a second time. She's got a great eye for style, and I can't thank you enough, Tracy.

Of course, I must thank my agents, Patty Carothers and Amy Brewer. Patty has provided essential feedback on this novel. I signed with her—and got a team— because she had the critical eye I was seeking, someone who saw the story's potential and who believed in it, but who also could provide great feedback to improve the story. Thank you, Patty. Having someone believe in you is one of the greatest gifts anyone can give, and I will always appreciate you for giving me that.

Ultimately, Amy Brewer sold this manuscript to Roan and Weatherford, the publisher of this book. The best part was my experience working with a new editor, George "Clay" Mitchell. He went through it, labeling every scene in the book and discussing what worked and what didn't. His first comment to me after finishing it was that I had a "FUCKING BANGER" of a book. Yes, all caps. I'm writing these acknowledgments in the summer of 2024, seven years after my first reading group critiqued the story. From there, Amy Cowan did a round of line edits to check for my numerous typos, and Casey Cowan created a beautiful cover. Thank you to all at Roan and Weatherford for your help.

Good things take time. Sure, I could have self-published this years ago. But it wouldn't be the story it is if that had happened. I hope you all also thought this was a fucking banger, and I can't wait to tell you what happens next. Sign up for my newsletter at www.joechianakas.com or follow me on your favorite socials to be the first to know when the second book releases. The good news is that I've already written it!

JOE CHIANAKAS is an author and a college professor. He's won multiple teacher-of-the-year awards and inspiring students in his greatest passion. He loves long walks with his furbaby Bailey, a mini-Australian Shepherd. He lives in Peoria, IL with the love of his life, Brian.

Joe's known for his horror series *Rabbit in Red*—a three book trilogy that became a huge hit after multiple subscription boxes bought and mailed thousands of copies to horror fans around the world.

Chianakas is currently represented by Amy Brewer of Metamorphosis Literary Agency and has multiple publishing contracts with Roan & Weatherford Publishing Associates. Learn more about Joe and send him a message at **www.joechianakas.weebly.com** or follow him online at www.facebook.com/chianakas or search for him on your favorite socials.

www.ingramcontent.com/pod-product-compliance
Lightning Source LLC
Chambersburg PA
CBHW020840060726
PP18531500001B/4
*9781633739536*